CHAPTER 1

Flynn

"I can't fucking believe she left me." I pace the length of Marlowe's deck in Malibu, the million-dollar view of the Pacific completely lost on me today. I feel like my heart has been ripped from my chest and run over by a Hummer. Natalie is gone, and the pain is excruciating. "She actually *left* me. She promised she never would. She made *promises* to me, Mo."

"Flynn… You need to calm down."

"*Calm down?* How do I *calm down* when my wife has *left me*?"

"I'm afraid you're going to have a heart attack or something. Your face is all red, and you're sweating."

I rub my chest, feeling as if I might actually be having a heart attack. "What am I going to do, Mo? Tell me what to do." I've told Marlowe only that Natalie caught me in a lie and left.

She looks at me for a long moment before she breaks eye contact and gazes out at the endless ocean. "I don't know. This is a tough one."

I flop into the chair next to hers, only because I'm exhausted and despondent and can't pace anymore. I can't imagine an hour without Natalie, let alone a week or more. That's how long she said she needed to "think" before she'll call me. A *week*. It feels like a lifetime.

"I broke a window at my house."

"When?"

"This morning after she left."

"Did you tell someone so it can be fixed?"

I shake my head. The window has been the least of my concerns, what with the fucking FBI showing up about five minutes after Natalie left for the airport.

Marlowe picks up her phone and places a call. "Addie, it's Marlowe. Flynn is here, and there's some stuff going on. He asked me to tell you he broke a window at his house earlier. One of the big ones in the back of the house. Could you call someone to come by to fix that for him?" She pauses. "Let me ask him." She holds the phone out to me. "She'd like to talk to you."

I'm tempted to say no. The only person I want to talk to is Natalie, but that's not possible. I extend my hand for Marlowe's phone. "Hey."

"What's wrong?" As my faithful assistant for the last five years, Addie can tell with one word that something is very wrong. "I got a call from the pilot that Natalie took the plane you were supposed to take to Mexico to Colorado—by herself—and she's not answering her phone."

So she went to see her sister Candace. I'm not surprised. I'm also reminded that the FBI has my phone, and until I get it back, Natalie has no way to call me. I will fix that first thing in the morning. "I, um…" I don't want to say the words out loud. If I keep saying it, that makes it real. "Our plans changed."

"Okay… So what's wrong?"

"Natalie and I… She… We… She's gone back to New York by way of Colorado to see her sister."

"Why? For how long?"

"It's a long story, and I don't know."

After a pause, Addie says, "What can I do for you?"

"See about getting the window fixed?"

"Already done. I sent a text from my computer while we've been on the phone. I'll go over there to meet the workers."

"Thank you."

"What else?"

"I don't know yet."

"I'll be here when you figure it out."

"Thanks."

"Flynn… Don't let her get away. No matter what, do *not* let her get away."

"I won't." But as I say the words, I'm petrified that she's already left me for good.

"So what did the FBI want with you this morning?" Addie asks.

"How do you know about that?"

"They came to the office first."

"Apparently, Rogers's wife told the officers investigating his murder that I was threatening him, and he feared for his safety."

"You threatened him with legal action, not physical harm."

"Which is what I told Vickers."

"Was he satisfied by that?"

"I guess. He went away. For now. I gotta say, Addie, I have a bad feeling they're trying to pin his murder on me."

"Let them try. We all know you didn't do it. You'll bury them."

"I didn't do it, but I wanted to."

"Wanting to is a long way from actually committing murder. Did he say when you'll have your phone back?"

"He said it would be sent to the office sometime today."

"I'll get it to you as soon as it arrives."

"Thanks."

"Don't give up, Flynn. Whatever happened between you and Natalie, you can fix it. You guys are the real deal. You can't give up."

I cling to her assurances that it can be fixed, but I'm not at all certain that's the case. "I fucked up bad, Addie."

"She's crazy about you. Whatever happened, you have to remember that."

"I'm trying."

"I'll be over to let in the workers to fix the window, and I'll get you the phone as soon as we have it."

"I'm at Mo's now, but I'll be home later."

"I'll see you then. Hang in there, okay?"

"Okay." What choice do I have? Natalie hasn't left me with any alternative but to wait until she's had time to wrap her head around what happened this morning. I end the call with Addie and hand the phone back to Marlowe.

"She found out about the BDSM, didn't she?" Marlowe asks. I consider Marlowe my "fourth sister," but she's the only "sister" who knows about the BDSM.

"Yeah. Fucking Valerie told her. Can you believe it?" I want to find my vindictive bitch of an ex-wife and kill her every way I can think of.

"Ouch."

"And then I made it worse by lying to her about it when Valerie had already told her where she could find the room in my house. So she knew I was lying." I'm up again, pacing the deck. "I did it for all the right reasons, Mo. You'll never convince me otherwise. There's no way she could handle that side of me after what she's been through in the past, so I tucked it away and chose her over the lifestyle."

"What was your plan for when you couldn't hide it from her anymore?"

I start to reply, but she holds up her hand to stop me. "It's not a *choice*, Flynn. It's *who you are*. It's who you've always been, and you've already ruined one marriage by trying to be someone other than who you are."

"This was different. Natalie isn't Valerie."

"No, she isn't. She's made of much better stuff. Valerie could only dream of being a fraction of the person Natalie is."

"So what're you saying?"

"If you can't be yourself with her, Flynn, truly and completely yourself, she's not the one for you. We've all tried to have relationships outside the lifestyle, and they've ended in disaster because none of us can deny who and what we are. You know this."

"I love her, Mo. I love her like I've never loved anyone. I love her more than I love myself, which is why I left the lifestyle for her. I still believe it's the right thing for her."

"But is it the right thing for *you*? *You* matter in this relationship, too."

"She matters more."

"Flynn… Come on."

"I gotta go." Suddenly, I can't stay here and pace anymore. I feel like a pent-up tiger who needs to bust loose and roar from the rage and fear that have overtaken him.

Marlowe follows me inside. "Don't go. You shouldn't be alone right now."

"I can't sit still. I gotta do something."

"Please don't do anything you'll regret."

"What could be worse than lying to my wife and driving her away?"

"A lot of things." She gestures to the Ducati that's parked in front of her house. "Like wrapping yourself around a telephone pole or driving off the Pacific Coast Highway."

I kiss her forehead. "I won't do either of those things. I promise. Thanks for listening."

"Call me later and let me know how you are."

"I will." I drive off, determined to keep my promise to be careful, but I'm half-tempted to aim for one of the steep cliffs that line the PCH. If I've lost Natalie for good, I'd rather be dead than be forced to live without her.

Natalie

After crying all the way to LAX, I get on the plane that was supposed to take Flynn and me to Mexico for our honeymoon. The security guys with me won't hear of me flying commercially, which is just as well since my credit card is nearly maxed out anyway.

Two of Flynn's security personnel, Josh and Seth, have insisted on accompanying me, even though I told them it's not necessary. They tell me they're under orders, and it's not up to me.

Great. Since I'm apparently stuck with them, I decide to ignore their hulking presence as we prepare for takeoff. I try to stay focused on the fact that I'm going to see my sister Candace for the first time in eight years. If I think about Candace—and only Candace—I can breathe. If I allow myself to think about Flynn and the scene at his house this morning, my chest begins to ache, and all I want to do is cry.

I've been away from him only a few hours, and I already miss him like I haven't seen him in a year. Still, I did the right thing. I refuse to be in a marriage that's based on lies. He's lied to me for weeks. He married me without telling me he's a sexual dominant. The hard part is, I understand and even appreciate why he did it.

He was thinking of my painful past as a sexual assault survivor. He was deeply affected by the episode on our wedding night when he pinned down my hands while we were making love, triggering a flashback from the assault. I screamed and cried, and he was right there with me through it all. I love him. I love every minute I've gotten to spend with him, even the difficult ones.

But I can't bear that he looked me in the eyes this morning and lied to me after I'd already uncovered the truth about his sexual desires, thanks to a heads-up from his spiteful ex-wife. I'm more confused than I've ever been. My heart is crying out for him, but my better judgment tells me I need this break to figure out how to deal with what I've learned about my husband without his overwhelming presence influencing my every thought.

Tears roll down my cheeks, and I immediately wipe them away. Though I trust the security personnel Flynn has hired, I'm wary now of what even the most consummate professionals will do for a buck. I can't afford to be seen crying such a short time after I married Flynn. I can't do that to him, so I struggle to maintain my composure.

I try not to think about the last time I was on an airplane with Flynn and how we made love in the private plane's bedroom. This time, I'm sitting alone with only Fluff on my lap to keep me company.

The flight to Colorado is turbulent, and the flight attendant isn't allowed to get up to tend to us. I can't help but think about holding hands with Flynn on bumpy approaches into Teterboro and LAX, his nearness calming my anxiety. I have no such comfort now, so in addition to being heartbroken, I'm also petrified.

By the time we land at Fort Collins-Loveland Airport two and a half hours later, I'm a certified disaster area and in absolutely no condition to see my sister for the first time in eight years. But nothing will keep me from her now that we are finally in the same place at the same time.

Josh and Seth position themselves in front and in back of me, which makes me feel ridiculous. No one will recognize me in the airport, because they aren't expecting to see me here. Why would they? My life with Flynn has taken place in New York and LA, not Colorado.

I'm nauseated from the rocky flight and the fact that I haven't eaten anything since last night, not that I could have eaten even if I tried. The thought of food makes me feel worse.

Fluff is losing her mind with excitement as we get off the plane, and she pees right on the tarmac.

We walk up a flight of stairs and into the quiet airport, my heart beating faster with every step. Any moment now, I'll see Candace, who promised to be waiting for me at the airport when I arrive. This whole thing was thrown together via a series of texts while I sobbed my way to LAX after leaving Flynn's.

I plan to return to New York tomorrow to rejoin my life already in progress, but I can't wait any longer to see my sister, thus the stop in Colorado. An escalator delivers us to baggage claim, and there she is. My baby sister is all grown up and gorgeous at nineteen. I forget about my heartbreak and the mess my new marriage has become and run for my sister.

She throws her arms around me, and we hold each other for a long time, both of us sobbing. My very first thought is she still wears the same perfume she favored at eleven, and the familiar scent only enriches this long-overdue moment. By the time we pull apart, her face is blotchy and red. I can only imagine what mine must look like after weeping for hours. She's got hazel eyes and long auburn hair, the same color mine used to be before I changed my appearance. The chubby cheeks she had the last time I saw her are long gone, replaced by the well-defined cheekbones of a grown woman. She's stunning, and I've never been so happy to see anyone in my life.

Fluff is spazzing out, demanding my attention. I pick her up so she can see her Aunt Candace, whom she seems to remember. "I hope your place allows dogs."

"It doesn't, but we'll sneak her in."

"Um." The rumble of a deep voice reminds me I'm not alone. "You're not going to her place," Seth says. "We've got reservations at a Marriott in town."

"I'll be staying with my sister."

"No, you won't."

I want to snap back at him that he can't tell me what to do, but he's only doing his job. My anger needs to stay focused on Flynn and not on his messenger. To Candace, I say, "How do you feel about a night at the Marriott?"

"Sounds good to me! Let's go."

Candace doesn't own a car and has taken a cab to meet me, so she comes with me as the security guys lead us to a pair of black SUVs. They must order them in bulk, as they seem to be everywhere I am lately.

"What's up with all this?" Candace whispers, gesturing to the security guys and the SUVs.

"My husband. He's paranoid about security."

"I sort of hoped he might be with you," she says with a silly grin that lets me know she's a fan of his work. Who isn't?

"He couldn't make it this time." I have no intention of ruining my reunion with Candace by airing out my marital troubles.

"Bummer. I can't wait to meet him."

Because I'm not sure now that'll ever happen, I don't say anything. The thought of never seeing him again makes my whole body ache.

"What's wrong, April?" Candace asks when we're settled in the back of an SUV and heading for the hotel.

I force a smile for her benefit. "Nothing's wrong. I'm thrilled to see you."

"Even though we haven't seen each other in a long time, you're still my sister. I took one look at you and knew something is very wrong." She takes hold of my hand. "Let me help."

"My baby sister isn't a baby anymore, is she?" I'm saddened to have missed so many years with her and Livvy.

"I haven't been since a monster attacked my big sister and ruined all our lives."

It has never once, in all the years since I last saw them, occurred to me that what happened to me ruined their lives, too. "I pictured you guys going on like nothing happened."

"That's not how it was. We were heartbroken. Nothing was ever the same without you." She covers our joined hands with her other hand. "I'd like nothing more than to be close to you again."

"I'd like that, too. More than you could ever know."

"Talk to me, Ap— I mean, Natalie. Talk to me, Natalie."

"You can call me April. It's okay."

"You've made a whole new life as Natalie. That's who you are now, and I want to respect that. Livvy does, too."

"She's so grown up, too. I can't believe how amazing her grades are and that she has her pick of colleges."

"Natalie..."

I sigh, realizing I can't hide my torment from my sister. "Flynn and I are taking a break." I keep my voice down so only she can hear me.

"You just got married!"

"Believe me, I know."

"What could've gone so wrong so fast?"

"He kept something from me. Something important. And then when I found out about it and confronted him, he lied to me."

"Oh damn. Wow. You guys looked so happy on TV. I watched every second of the SAG Awards. I couldn't believe that was *my sister* on national TV!"

"It was a very exciting night." Recalling Flynn winning two Actor awards, making love in the limo on the way home and then eating In-N-Out burgers and fries in Hayden's living room brings me to tears again. The weeks I spent with Flynn had been the sweetest time of my life, and I have no idea what I'm supposed to do without him.

"So is it over, then?" Candace asks tentatively.

"I don't know." I don't know anything other than he lied to me, and I had to get away from him to get some perspective.

"Well," she says after a long pause, "if he's making you stay at a hotel, I assume he's paying, so we might as well take *full* advantage. I have to work tomorrow, but I don't care. We can stay up all night watching movies, sleep in and order room service."

Candace's cheerfulness and upbeat personality are a balm on my wounded soul. Her plan sounds heavenly, and it's just what I need.

Chapter 2

Flynn

I'm losing my mind. There's no other way to describe the desperation that has overtaken me. I can't eat, sleep, breathe or think about anything other than Natalie and what I can do to fix things between us. I can't live without her—not for a minute, a day or a week. I'll go mad if I don't see her for a week.

She told me to leave her alone, but she didn't tell me I had to stay in LA and leave her alone.

True to her word, Addie brings my cell phone to me around five that afternoon.

"I need you to get me on a flight to New York. Tonight."

"I'm not sure I can get you a private plane with so little notice."

"Then I'll fly commercial."

She hesitates, and I know she's thinking that I've been asked not to fly commercial because of the uproar my presence causes in the airports. At times like this, I fucking hate the fame that comes with my chosen profession.

"How long is Natalie planning to be in Colorado?" Addie asks.

"I don't know." I don't tell her I didn't know she was going there. "She's got security with her, right?"

"Two guys, and they're staying at a Marriott rather than at her sister's place. I took the liberty of overnighting the credit and debit cards you asked me to get for her to the hotel. I hope that was the right thing to do."

"Yeah. I want her to have money, even if she doesn't want me anymore."

"She still wants you. I've seen the way she looks at you. Whatever this is, you'll never convince me it can't be fixed." She withdraws her phone from her pocket. "You still want to go to New York?"

I think about that for a moment. "You said when you talked to Candace about coming here, she had a really busy schedule at school, right?"

"Yes and a part-time job, too."

"So it'll probably be a short visit. I'll go to New York. Natalie will end up there sooner rather than later."

"I'll see what I can do." Addie gives my arm a squeeze before she heads off to make arrangements. A team of workers is finishing up replacing the window I smashed with a crystal vase this morning after Natalie left. I need to get a grip on my rage. That's not going to help anything in this situation.

I scroll through the calls and texts I've missed since the FBI took my phone and see two calls from my mother. Since she usually texts, I decide I'd better call her back, even though I don't want to talk to anyone—except Natalie. "Hey, Mom, what's up?"

"There you are. I was starting to wonder if you two would ever come up for air."

The reminder that I'm supposed to be on my honeymoon hits me like an arrow to the chest. "Crazy few days."

"I'm sure," she says with a low chuckle. She and my dad are thrilled with my choice of a wife. What would they think if they knew that my need for dominant sex and the fact that I lied to my wife about it has sent their new daughter-in-law running from me? "I wanted to talk to you about the wedding reception we'd like to have for you and Natalie."

Tears fill my eyes, and I take a seat on the sofa, pressing my thumb and forefinger to my eyes. It becomes very clear to me right then and there that if I've permanently lost her, I'll never get over it.

"Flynn?"

"Yeah, Mom, I'm here. Let me talk to Natalie and see what works. I'll let you know, okay?"

"Of course. Whatever you guys want. We're beyond excited to celebrate with both of you and to welcome Natalie into our family."

My parents have been so wonderful to her, so amazingly welcoming and supportive during the firestorm that followed her painful past being made public. I can't bear to disappoint them by confessing to how badly I've fucked things up with her. I hope I never have to tell them that. "It's really nice of you to want to do this. Thank you."

"Are you kidding? It's purely selfish. I'm so happy to see you in love with a sweet, caring woman who loves you for all the right reasons. You have no idea how long I've waited for this moment. You bet your ass we're going to celebrate."

It's all I can do not to break down into sobs, to beg my mom to come over and tell me everything is going to be okay. But I don't do that. I can't do that. "We're looking forward to it. I'll get back to you."

"I'll talk to you soon. Love you, sweetheart."

Sweetheart. That's what I call Natalie. "Love you, too, Mom."

For a long time after we end the call, I stare at the pool in the backyard, trying to imagine life without Natalie. There is no life without her. And I've spent enough time dicking around today feeling sorry for myself. It's time to fucking fix this.

Natalie

My sister and I pick up right where we left off, and by the end of our afternoon together, it's like no time has passed since we last saw each other. We talk about everything and everyone we ever knew back home in Nebraska. She catches me up on all the gossip from Lincoln and what has become of the girls I was friends with before my life imploded.

"They asked about you for years," Candace says. "We never knew what to tell them. Dad warned us not to talk about you to anyone. It was so bizarre. It was like you were dead, only we knew you weren't. Dad was like a madman. He couldn't believe it. He couldn't believe one of *his kids* did this, like you were the one to blame rather than Oren. He got rid of the Wi-Fi at home and tried to make it so we wouldn't see the trial coverage, but we read the papers in the library at school so we'd know what was going on. And then, when Oren was convicted... Dad was worse than ever."

"I'll never understand how a parent picks a lifelong friend over his own child in a situation like this."

"You wanna know our theory? Mine and Livvy's?"

"Um, *yeah*?"

She laughs at my blatant curiosity. "We think they were in love with each other and pretending to live a hetero life because back then, Oren never would've had a chance in politics if he was living as a gay man."

I'm stunned speechless. "That sure would explain a lot."

"Think about it—did you ever once see Dad act affectionately toward Mom? Did you ever see them hug or kiss or hold hands or anything?"

"No. Never. I just figured they kept that stuff private. This is such a bombshell, but suddenly it all makes sense."

"No, it doesn't make sense, because he still should've protected you. No matter what he felt for Oren, you are his *daughter*. You deserved so much better than what you got from them." She glances at me, seeming hesitant. "After they saw you at the hospital, they had the biggest fight ever. Mom was crazy over him forcing her to leave you there alone after Oren raped you."

"If you really think Oren and Dad were gay and in love, how could Oren rape me the way he did?"

"Livvy and I think Dad was resisting him on something, and attacking you was Oren's way of making a statement. We also think he was a freaking pervert."

"But, you know, they both had kids and how could he like… have assaulted me that way… if he wasn't into women?"

"Pills," she says bluntly. "We think they both were bisexual, but they would've chosen each other over their wives in a second if they'd had that option. But they didn't back then, not if Oren wanted the career in politics his family had always groomed him for. I'd actually think it was kind of sad, except for the fact that they were a couple of lawless monsters who hurt so many people. When Oren died in jail? Dad was inconsolable for weeks. He was never the same after that."

"God…"

"Of course, all of this is speculation on our part."

"No, it makes all kinds of sense. The pills would also explain how he was able to be so... relentless... during the assault." I look up to see Candace blinking rapidly.

"That's the one thing we were never able to bring ourselves to read about. We couldn't bear it."

"I'm glad you didn't. It's bad enough those images are in my mind. You don't need them in yours, too."

"I wondered... If you were able, with Flynn..."

"Yes, and it was amazing. At least for me." The question is a reminder of why I left him, and the pain sears through me, hot and sharp.

"You don't think it was for him, too?"

I get up from the bed where we've been relaxing to walk over to the window. "He said it was." But how am I to know if he was only saying what he thought I wanted to hear or if he was telling the truth? Everything is in question now.

"You don't believe him?"

As much as I want to share the details of what happened between Flynn and me with my sister, I can't. I have to protect his privacy—and mine. I trust my sister, but I also have to acknowledge I don't know her very well anymore. I hope that will change, in time, but if she told even one person about Flynn's sexual preferences... No, I can't tell her or anyone, as much as I'd love Candace's take on the situation. I realize she's waiting for me to reply. "It's kind of complicated."

"And personal, I'm sure. I don't mean to pry."

"It's okay. It's just tough because of who he is to the rest of the world. I can't spill my guts as much as I'd like to."

"I understand. Don't worry." She sends me a cheeky grin. "As long as I get to meet him someday."

"I hope you'll get to meet him." I hope *I'll* get to see him again...

Candace's phone rings, and she lets out a squeal that wakes Fluff, who has been lounging on the other bed. "It's Livvy on FaceTime." She accepts the call. "You won't believe who's here with me."

"Who?"

"Natalie." She turns the phone toward me, and I wave at her. Even though I've FaceTimed with both of them in the last few weeks, I still want to weep at the sight of my youngest sister, who is also all grown up and gorgeous at seventeen. She has the dark hair and eyes that come from our father's side of the family and actually resembles me now that I've darkened my hair.

"What're you doing there?"

"I came to see Candace, and I hope I'll see you sometime soon, too."

"Flynn's assistant called about us coming to LA in the next couple of weeks."

My stomach hurts at the mention of him. "I hope we can make that happen."

"Is he there?" She looks around, hoping for a glimpse of her famous brother-in-law.

"No, he couldn't come, and I couldn't wait any longer to see Candace. Or you. I hope we can do it soon."

"We will. I have a long weekend in February, if not before. Get this, you guys…" With those four words, it feels like old times. "Mom is dating someone, and he's actually rather normal. She's out with him now."

"Mom is *dating*? Like, a *man*?" Candace asks.

"No, an alien," Livvy says dryly. "Yes, a man! A guy she works with. She's talked about him for months, and now they're going out and stuff."

"This is huge," Candace says for my benefit. "She hasn't dated at all since she and Dad split up."

What's even more important to me is how, after only a few minutes back in the presence of my sisters, I feel like I belong with them again.

A knock on the door early in the morning sends Fluff into convulsions, reminding me I need to take her outside at some point. The thought of going out into the freezing tundra does not appeal to me. "I'll get it," I say to Candace, who hasn't moved. She was always a heavy sleeper, and we were up half the night talking.

Josh is outside the door with a large envelope he hands to me. "This came for you."

I start to ask who knows I'm here, but of course Flynn knows. He's paying for the security, the hotel, the airplane.

"Would you like me to take Fluff out for you?" Josh asks.

"Are you sure you don't mind? That's not in your job description."

"I don't mind. I'm going to get coffee anyway."

"How do you feel about getting two extra coffees?"

"Happy to do that, too."

I clip Fluff's leash on to her collar and hand it to him. "Thank you so much."

"No problem. Be back soon."

I bring the envelope to my bed to open it. Using the light from my phone, I find a note from Addie along with an ATM card and an American Express card with "Natalie Godfrey" embossed on it. The note from Addie says, "Flynn wanted you to have these and to use them for anything you need. The ATM code is 0119." It isn't lost on me that our wedding date is the PIN code.

And then I'm crying in loud sobs that wake my sister.

She comes across to my bed and takes me into her arms, holding me while I get it all out. I miss my love, my husband, the best friend I've ever had. I hate that he lied to me, but I'm no longer sure it matters, not if it hurts like this to be without him.

"You should call him," Candace says as she strokes my hair, making me feel loved and cared for.

"I can't. Not yet." Not until I figure out what I'm going to say to him.

Candace has to work today and has class tonight, so after a room-service breakfast, we prepare to go our separate ways for now. I'm so thankful for this time with her, even if I was a heartbroken mess for most of it.

"Whatever happened with Flynn, I hope you guys can work it out," she says when we're in an SUV heading for her place. "You looked so happy on TV. It looked real. Livvy and I both said that."

"It was real." It was the most "real" thing I've ever experienced. "Please don't tell anyone about me being upset with him. Please, Candace… It would cause so much trouble for him if that ever got out."

"I won't say a word. I promise."

I hug her again. "I love you, and I'm so glad I got to see you."

"Love you, too. We'll get together again soon."

"Yes, we will. Call me. Text me. FaceTime me. Any time. All the time."

"I will. You do the same."

When we arrive at her apartment building, we hug again, clinging to each other like we're both afraid to let go.

"You're not going to disappear again, are you?" She sounds like the little girl I left behind eight long years ago.

"Never. I promise."

"Okay, then I'll let you go. For now."

I'm happy to see where she lives, but she's running late for work, so I don't go inside, which is just as well. I have no desire to go in there, dragging security behind me. She hugs me one more time before she gets out of the car and runs off with a wave.

Once she's inside the building, the SUV takes off like a shot for the airport, and I'm forced to confront the pain I've mostly managed to put on hold while I enjoyed the reunion with my sister. It comes down on me all over again, and when we arrive at the airport, it's all I can do not to ask them to take me to LA rather than New York.

I have to get back to work before I need to use the money Flynn has made available to me. I don't feel right taking money from him after having left him.

The flight to New York on the private plane is better than yesterday's flight, but the pilots tell us it's snowing and sleeting in New York. The weather only adds to my morose mood. I console myself by thinking about the cozy apartment I share with my good friend—and colleague—Leah. Decisions have to be made, and Leah will help me figure out my next steps.

When we get the word that Teterboro is closed to arrivals due to the weather, we are forced to land at LaGuardia and to navigate the terminal, which is mobbed. A woman in the concourse screams my name when she sees me, which attracts the attention of everyone in a half-mile radius. So much for my certainty that no one will recognize me unless Flynn is with me. Fluff starts barking and snarling at the screamers, so I pick her up to carry her.

Josh and Seth leap into action, escorting me through the crowd that surrounds us so quickly, I have no time to do anything other than put my head down and keep moving. I'm deeply grateful for their presence and to Flynn for caring enough to provide for my safety. I wouldn't have the first clue how to deal with this by myself.

Fluff is going crazy in my arms, barking, snapping and trying to get free.

After my cover is blown, Josh and Seth move quickly to get me out of there, bypassing baggage claim to deliver me directly to an SUV that waits at the curb. How they arrange these things the way they do is a source of constant amazement to me.

When he's settled in the driver's seat, Seth turns to me. "Did you know your school announced that they've offered you your job back?"

"N-no. They didn't tell me they were doing that."

"The paparazzi have your building, Mr. Godfrey's place and the school surrounded. We can't take you home. There's no way we can get you in there."

I'm temporarily petrified by the idea that I have nowhere to go. Ending up homeless was once my greatest fear, when I was struggling through college on a shoestring budget, always one step ahead of disaster.

"Where… Where will we go?"

"We can get you into Mr. Godfrey's apartment through the garage."

Before I can tell him I don't want to go to Mr. Godfrey's apartment, Josh is getting into the passenger seat and we're leaving the airport. If I tell them I don't want to go to Flynn's, how can I be sure they won't tell someone I said that? I'm very concerned about doing something to draw more attention to my relationship with Flynn. We've already had more than enough.

So I say nothing. It's not like his place isn't lovely. It'll hardly be a hardship to spend time there. And he has that amazing tub that he never uses, a memory that has tears stinging my eyes. I can't imagine what it'll be like to be there without him.

I snuggle Fluff closer to me. "We have each other, right, Fluff?"

She licks my face, and I'm immensely grateful for the one "person" I can always count on no matter what. We've been through everything together.

At Flynn's building, the photographers are set up out front, so we drive around the building to the garage entrance in back. The mere sight of the building and the door to the garage is enough to resurrect some of the sweetest memories of my life, and I'm again on the verge of tears.

Seth punches in the code to open the big metal door. He has the SUV inside and the door closing before the photographers can mobilize.

I stare at Flynn's priceless Bugatti, remembering him picking me up for our first date in the gorgeous car and teasing him later about loving that car more than he loves me. My gloved hand over my mouth is the only thing that keeps my sob from escaping.

"We'll get your bag, Mrs. Godfrey. You can go ahead up."

I'm left staggered from being called Mrs. Godfrey for the first time by someone other than my husband. I clear my throat. "I, um, I don't have a key. With me." I add that last part because I don't want them to know I've never had a key. Well, that's not exactly true. Flynn gave me one the night we met so I could use his awesome tub any time I wanted. I'd left it on his dresser because I didn't feel right about taking it.

"We'll be close by if you need us," Seth said. "Just send a text." Bringing my bag to me, he uses his keycard to send me to the top-floor apartment. I let Fluff off the leash in the elevator. The doors open into Flynn's foyer, and Fluff trots into the apartment like she owns the place. And then she starts barking, snarling and growling.

I pull my bag off the elevator and follow her into the living room, where I see that she's barking, snarling and growling at Flynn.

"Natalie…" He looks awful. His gorgeous face is ravaged by despair. I can tell with one quick look that he hasn't slept since I saw him last.

I'm still angry that he lied to me. I still don't know how I feel about discovering he's a sexual dominant with desires I can't begin to understand. I have no idea where we can possibly go from here.

But none of that matters when compared to how much I love him. All I see when I look at him is the man who came running to me at my darkest hour, who went to war on my behalf, who donated half a million dollars to my sick friend and gave me the sun, the moon and the stars. I see my best friend and my love.

I run to him.

He meets me halfway and lets out a low moan as he hugs me fiercely, lifting me off my feet into his embrace.

I cling to him, breathing in his familiar scent, relief coursing through me. The turbulence inside me settles and quiets. I'm back where I belong, and that's the only thing I know for certain right now.

"I'm so sorry, sweetheart," he whispers. "This was all my fault. I should've told you everything." His face brushes against mine, leaving dampness behind. His tears shatter me all over again. "I'll do anything… Anything it takes to fix this. I can't live without you, Nat. I love you so much. Tell me you still love me."

"I do, Flynn. I still love you."

And then he's kissing me, fiercely, intently, and it's like the first time all over again, that day on the street outside of Aileen's when he kissed me like he would die if he couldn't kiss me right in that moment. I wrap my arms around his neck and kiss him back, every bit as desperate for him.

He pushes my coat off my shoulders, and it lands on the floor behind me. Then he's lifting me and carrying me into the bedroom. We come down on the bed in a tangled mass of limbs, all without missing a beat in the kiss. His hands are everywhere, as if he's taking inventory and making sure I've returned to him whole and intact.

I can't get close enough to him, even with my fingers fisted into his hair, my legs intertwined with his and his tongue in my mouth. It's not enough. It's nowhere near enough. "Flynn…" I break the kiss, gasping for badly needed air.

"Tell me, sweetheart. Tell me what you want."

"You. I want you." I tug at his T-shirt, which quickly disappears over his head. Nuzzling his muscular chest and taking comfort in the soft brush of his chest hair against my face, I am home.

He drags my sweater up and over my head, releases my bra and unbuttons my jeans. I fumble with the button to his jeans, so he helps me.

The second we are both naked, he rolls me under him and pushes into me in one smooth stroke that stretches me to the point of pain. It's the most exquisite pain I've ever experienced. His eyes close and his forehead comes down on mine. The relief I see on his face is so profound it brings me to tears.

For the longest time, neither of us moves. We simply exist, together, breathing the same air, our bodies joined, our hearts beating as one again.

"Natalie..." He kisses my face, my lips, my neck, and then returns to my lips.

I wrap my legs around his hips, hoping to encourage him to move, but he remains maddeningly still.

"I love you so much," he whispers against my lips. "I almost lost my mind without you. I fucked this up so bad, and I'm going to fix it. I'll do anything it takes, but please don't leave me again. Please."

"I'm not going anywhere." For better or worse, he's my husband, and I love him. Every beat of my heart is for him.

His tortured moan seems ripped straight from his soul, his tears dampen my face and neck as he begins to move in me, thrusting deep, withdrawing and slamming into me, over and over again. He hooks his arms under my legs, pulling them up higher and driving farther into me.

He keeps watch over me in that sharp, knowing way of his, looking for signs of trouble. But there's no trouble. There's only piercing pleasure as his forceful strokes trigger a powerful orgasm that makes me scream from the sheer magic we create together. At least it's magic to me. I'm not sure now if he feels the same.

Thrusting deeply, he throws his head back, his eyes closed and his jaw tense as he comes. I've never seen anything more magnificent than the sight of my husband lost in passion, lost in me.

As amazing as it was, however, I'm again left to wonder if he's as satisfied as I am.

He releases my legs, which are quivering in the aftermath. I hold him close to me, his face nuzzled into the nook between my neck and shoulder. His heavy breathing sets off goose bumps that make my nipples tighten.

He groans. "Do that again."

"What did I do?"

"Tighten your pussy around my cock."

His earthy language, which would be off-putting from anyone else, is a huge turn-on coming from him. I give him what he wants.

"*Fuck*. Christ, I'm already hard again."

I'm surprised when he withdraws from me and flops onto his back, his big, hard penis extending above his navel. I surprise myself—and him—when I rise to my knees and bend to take that beautiful part of him into my mouth.

His gasp of surprise makes me smile. He's taught me how to do this, how to give it to him the way he likes it—deep and tight and wet. I begin by wrapping my lips around the wide head and sucking—hard.

He arches his hips, his hands full of my hair. "Nat, God… *Natalie*… I don't deserve this or you."

I moan, letting my lips vibrate under the sensitive head. He's taught me so much in the last few weeks, things I never would've considered doing before I loved him.

He pulls himself free of my mouth. "No, Nat."

"Did I do it wrong?" Will I always wonder now if I'm pleasing him? How will I know?

"Come up here." He holds out his arms to me.

I settle on top of him, his erection pressed tightly to my belly, my breasts flat against his chest.

With his hands on my face, he stares at me. "I was grossly unfair to you. I knew it while it was happening, and I struggled with it. I need you to know that."

"I do know. I even understand why you didn't tell me."

"I'm so sorry I lied the other day. I'm looking you in the eyes right now and promising you, swearing on my life, that it'll never happen again—ever. I need you to believe me when I tell you—"

I lay my finger over his lips. "I do. I believe you."

"It killed me to know that I'd hurt you so badly, that I'd done the same thing to you—"

"No, Flynn, *no*. It was nothing even close to that. It hurt me, yes, but you lied to me because you love me, and you thought you were protecting me."

"*Yes*," he says, sounding relieved that I understand.

"That's not the same thing as what happened to me before. You… You're…"

"What, sweetheart? What am I?"

"*Everything*."

He closes his eyes as his cheek pulses. "The day we met," he says softly without opening his eyes, "when Hayden told me there was no place in my life for a sweet girl like you…" He opens his eyes, and I see the agony he has endured. It's plainly obvious now. Has it been there all along, but I missed it because I didn't know to look for it? "He was absolutely right. I knew it then, and part of me knows it now. But my heart recognized you that day in the park. I knew you as mine. That's why I went after you. It's why I've done everything else since then. That moment of recognition has governed every choice I've made where you're concerned."

I'm deeply touched by his heartfelt words. "After our first date, when you didn't call me… You said it was because of you, not me. This is what you meant?"

"Yes." He keeps one hand on my face and raises the other to run his fingers through his hair. "There's so much to it. I don't even know where to begin."

"Start at the beginning. I want to know you, Flynn. I want to know *all* of you, even the parts you think will scare or unsettle me. I want everything with you."

Caressing my cheek, he says, "You've already had more of me—more of the parts that truly matter—than anyone else ever has."

"Then give me the rest, too."

His deep sigh lets me know this isn't easy for him. He turns us so we're on our sides, facing each other, sharing the same pillow. Then he tugs the comforter up and over us.

Fluff jumps up on the bed and settles in a huff behind me, her back pressed against mine. The relief at having our little family back together almost makes me forget we are far from out of the woods, despite our passionate reunion.

"I want to tell you everything. I want to tell you because you deserve to know, and you have to believe I trust you with my life. But what I'm going to tell you involves other people, too, and it's imperative that you never speak of it to anyone. Ever."

"You have my word, Flynn. You can trust me to keep your secrets the same way I trust you to keep mine."

His face lifts into a small half smile, but his eyes are still troubled. "The summer we were twenty-one, Hayden went with his dad to make a movie in Amsterdam. They were there the whole summer, and Hayden became friends with the lead actor on the film, a hotshot young star whose name you'd recognize.

He introduced Hayden to a whole new world neither of us knew existed. I got cryptic texts from him that I wouldn't believe the shit he was doing. When he finally got home to LA, he was a different person. Like any young guy who's had the ultimate sexual experiences, he wanted to talk about it. And like any young guy whose friend has done crazy shit, I wanted to hear about it. Rather than tell me, though, he showed me. He took me to some clubs in LA where I got an eyeful, to say the least. It wasn't just the sex, even though that was incredible—both to watch and to participate in. I was equally fascinated by the exchange of power, the emotion, the connection.

"I was brought up to respect women, and I always have. I was raised by a mother who blazed her own successful path in show business, and I was heavily influenced by three strong-willed older sisters. So to discover there were women who were willingly submissive was eye-opening to say the least. But it was more than that… I felt like a part of myself that had lain dormant my entire life was awaking to discover who I was really meant to be. I'm not sure if that makes any sense at all."

"It makes a lot of sense. I've felt that way since I met you."

"I've felt the same way, Nat. Even though there were things I kept from you, I've felt more alive and more settled since I met you than ever before."

"How is that possible if you were also denying this huge part of yourself to be with me?"

CHAPTER 3

Flynn

This is excruciating. I can't bear to see her doubting our connection or thinking I've been finding fault in her when that couldn't be further from the truth.

"It's possible because I love you so much."

"I believe you when you say that, I honestly do. But I still don't understand how you can love me so much if that means you can't be yourself with me."

I stare at the wall behind her for a long time, trying to find a way to explain something I've had a hard time understanding myself. "After we first met, and you told me how you felt about sex, I sensed pretty early on that something awful had happened to you. I had to resist the overwhelming temptation to have someone find out what. I decided I wanted to let you tell me when you were ready. After what happened on our wedding night and then when I heard the whole story... I just knew I could never let you see the dominant side of me because it would scare the hell out of you."

"So you were prepared to live without that for the rest of your life?"

"If that's what it took to make you happy."

"But what about *you* and what *you* need?"

"I was willing to live without it if it meant I got to have you."

"Flynn... You shouldn't have to do that."

I reach over to run my finger over her kiss-swollen bottom lip. "I spent one day without you and felt like I was going to die. Trust me, if the alternative is to lose you, I can live without anything—except for you."

She looks up at me with eyes gone liquid with emotions she doesn't try to hide. "While I was gone, I relived every minute we've spent together, every second, every touch, every kiss, every time we made love. I thought about all the things you did for me when my story went public, how you helped Aileen and brought my kids to see me before we left New York... You made me feel so safe and loved, even when my life was falling apart."

"There's nothing I wouldn't do for you, Natalie. Nothing at all."

"Then you'll show me what you want from me? You'll let me see your darkest desires?"

"No."

"That's it? Just no?"

I curl a strand of her long hair around my finger. "You've given me a priceless gift by trusting me enough, after what you endured at such a young age, to let me make love to you, to take me into your body and allow me to be with you this way. It would kill me, and I mean literally *kill* me, if I did anything to ruin that trust or to scare you so badly you wouldn't be able to stand my touch."

"How will we know if I can stand it if we never try?"

"You have no idea what you're asking."

"Then tell me! Show me. Educate me. But don't leave me in the dark wondering what you really want and making me wonder, every time we make love, if you're unsatisfied."

I stare at her, incredulous. "I'm not unsatisfied."

"But you want more."

"Yes, I want more! I'll always want more with you. But I'm satisfied with what I have, and that's enough."

"How long will it be enough? How long will it be before you're having fantasies about doing things with me that you've done with other women?"

I divert my gaze because that's already happened, but in dreams over which I have no control.

"Flynn?"

I've promised to be honest with her, and I intend to keep that promise. "I've already had those fantasies. I've had dreams about being at the club and in the dungeon with you."

"That day in LA… When I asked you what was wrong and I thought I'd said something in my sleep that had upset you…"

"I'd had a dream that left me out of sorts, but I worked it out."

She is quiet for a very long, unsettling moment.

"What are you thinking?"

"I don't know if I can do this."

Her words strike fear in my heart that ricochets through my entire body. "What can't you do?"

"This. Us. Any of it."

"Natalie, come on. This is only one part of our relationship. The rest of it is fucking perfect. You'd really throw all that away because of this?"

"I can't possibly answer that question without knowing what *this* entails."

"So, what? You want details?"

"That would be a good place to start."

I can almost feel my blood pressure inching into the danger zone at the thought of detailing my kink to her. My sweet, beautiful Natalie hasn't the first clue what she's asking for. She'll never look at me the same way again if I tell her, and I can't risk that.

I get out of bed and pull on a pair of sweats.

"Where're you going?"

"I need a drink." I leave the bedroom and go into the kitchen, where I pour myself a couple of shots of Bowmore, my favorite Scottish single malt. It burns all the way through me, reminding me I haven't eaten much of anything in the last twenty-four miserable hours.

Natalie appears, wearing my robe, which is huge on her. She's like my conscience, putting me on notice that she's not going to let this go.

I feel cornered, trapped, unable to escape from the mess I've created for myself. I've promised her the truth. But how do I give her that and still preserve our precious bond, which has been made fragile by my lies?

After pouring another half glass of whisky, I bring it with me into the living room, brushing past her as I leave the kitchen.

She follows me.

"What do you want me to say?" I ask her in defeat. There's nowhere to run from her or this conversation she's insisting we have, even if I'm certain it will ruin everything between us.

"Tell me about your dreams, the ones you had about me."

I shudder as a chill runs through me, and the whisky threatens to come back up. Turning away from her, I focus on breathing my way through the nausea. "I don't know if I can tell you."

"Why not? They were about me, weren't they? Don't I have the right to know?"

I want to argue with her. No, she doesn't have the right to my every private thought, just as I don't have the right to all of hers. But I'm on a slippery slope here, well aware that despite our passionate reunion and her words of love, I still have a long way to go to fully repair the damage I've done.

"When I was married before," I say reluctantly, as the thought of Valerie still infuriates me, "it took me two years to tell her what I really wanted. In bed… She… She said I was depraved and disgusting and sick. Then she cheated on me and made sure I caught them in the act so I'd know just how disgusting she found me. I had to threaten her with lawsuits up the ass to keep her from going public with what she'd found out about me. I've actually been afraid ever since that she would give in to temptation and tell the real story behind our split, and my career would be irreparably harmed by her version of the truth."

Natalie comes to me and lays her hands on my chest, the heat of her hands warming the part of me that's gone cold. "I would never, could never, *will* never tell anyone what goes on between us. *Ever.*"

"You say that now when you're wildly in love with me. What happens if that changes? If you're so turned off by me that you don't love me anymore?"

"Flynn… I'm not Valerie. Even if everything were to go bad, and I can't see that happening, I will never speak of our private life to anyone."

"What about when I scare you so badly you feel like you don't know me at all?"

"Even then." She tips her head adorably. "You want me to sign something to that effect?"

"No."

"Then how can I make you believe you can trust me with *everything*? Every single part of you?"

The same sweetness that has slayed me from the beginning brings me to my knees once again. I'm helpless to resist her, even when she's asking me for things I never intended to give her. I recognize defeat when I'm staring into its sweet face.

"In my dream," I begin haltingly, wishing for more liquid courage, "you're not a rape survivor."

"In my dreams, I'm not either."

"Nat..."

"It's okay," she says with a wry smile. She takes me by the hand and brings me to sit next to her on the sofa, wrapping a cashmere throw around us.

I'd prefer to stand and pace the room for this conversation, but she's craving the closeness, so I give her what she needs.

"We're at Club Quantum in New York."

"There's a club?"

"Yeah," I say with a sigh, "here and in LA. In the basement of our office buildings."

"So... all of you..."

"Yes, and that's the part you can never talk about."

"I swear to God, on the lives of my sisters, I never would."

Because I know there's no greater assurance she could give me, I force myself to continue. I've relived the dreams I had about her so many times that I know them by heart.

"In one dream, we're going public for the first time, and you're afraid. I like that you're afraid. It turns me on. We've been working up to this moment for months, and everyone is there for your first public scene." I want to look at her, to gauge her reaction, but I'm too afraid of what I might see. "I make you take off your robe, but you're hesitant, shy, which is so unbearably sexy. Your hands tremble as you tug on the tie, but you do what I tell you to do because I'm in charge. You've ceded control of your pleasure to me. I have you sit on a table that's in the center of a big room, and we talk about your safe word, which is still Fluff. I put your legs in stirrups and bring your bottom to the edge of the table. You ask me what I'm doing, and I tell you I'm going to shave you because I prefer you bare. We've talked about this before, but I haven't told you I plan to do it tonight."

She takes a deep breath that interrupts the cadence of my story.

I venture a glance at her and see that her cheeks are flush with color and her lips are parted. My story is turning her on, which gives me the confidence to continue. Every time I think about these dreams, I get so hard, I ache. This time is no exception.

"As I shave you, your thighs quiver and tremble. Your entire body is flushed and heated. Your pussy is so wet I can see and smell your arousal. I lube up my fingers and press them into your ass, preparing you to take a plug. You protest and fight me. 'Not there,' you say. I tell you to hush and remind you of your safe word. If you don't want this, that's the only way to stop it. This is the first time I've touched you there, and I can see that you are shocked but also aroused."

She shifts in her seat next to me.

"Do you want me to stop?" I ask, not certain if she's uncomfortable or shocked or what.

"Don't you dare stop."

Those four words fill me with an unreasonable amount of hope. She's intrigued, interested and maybe even aroused. She's not pushing me away or telling me I'm sick or depraved.

Fueled by hope, I continue. "You try to keep my fingers out, but I make you take them. I want you to know everything that's possible. It's a battle, but I'll always win unless you stop me with the one word that ends it all. When my fingers are buried deep inside your ass, I lick your pussy, focusing on your clit until you're squirming and moaning. I remind you that your orgasm belongs to me and only me. I say when, not you. You're begging me, using my name and I also remind you of what you're supposed to call me there."

"What?" she asks in a hoarse whisper.

"Sir. I'm your master, and you'll afford me the respect I deserve while we're in a scene."

"W-what about when we're not in a scene? Am I supposed to call you that all the time?"

"No, sweetheart. I'm not into the whole master-and-slave thing at all. This is about sex and the emotional connection we find through sex. It's not about the rest of our lives. I have no desire to dominate you anywhere but in the bedroom." I smile at her. "Well, the dungeon and the club and a few other places maybe, but only in regard to sex. I have a feeling you might be capable of dominating me outside the bedroom."

That draws a smile from her. "You never know."

I bring our joined hands to my lips. "I can't wait to find out."

She glances at me hesitantly. "Was there more? To your dream?"

Nodding, I say, "A lot more. You want to hear the rest?"

"Yes, please."

"So polite. That pleases me greatly."

She lowers her eyes in perfect supplication. "I aim to please you."

I'm electrified by both her actions and her words. "Natalie… God."

"Is that the wrong thing to say?"

"No, it's fucking perfect. You're perfect." Because I can't resist her for another second, I take her in my arms and kiss her with the wild passion that has grown and multiplied inside me as I described my erotic fantasies to her.

She returns my passion with her own, meeting my tongue stroke for stroke until we're once again prone, me on top of her, wrapped up in each other.

I end the kiss slowly, in stages, reluctantly. "You're not running from me in fear."

"No. Quite the opposite, in fact."

"What do you mean?"

"I'm dying to hear the rest. Will you tell me?"

I press my rock-hard cock against her pubic bone. "Can I stay here?"

She runs her fingers through my hair. "I wish you would."

I nuzzle her neck. "I ask you if it's turning you on to have other people watch as I fuck your ass with my fingers."

She draws in a sharp deep breath.

"You try to deny it, but you're so wet. Your body can't lie to me. I ask you if you know what happens to sweet subs who lie to their Doms. Your eyes are wide with fear and desire and curiosity as you shake your head no. They get their asses spanked until they are red and rosy and too sore to sit on for days. You deny it when I ask if that turns you on, so I do it to prove you wrong. I spank your upturned ass so hard, it echoes through the big room." To make my point, I reach under her and squeeze her ass cheek, drawing a deep moan from her that makes me crazy with wanting her. "I fuck your ass hard with my fingers, and then I withdraw them, almost to the point of removing them before driving them back in as I suck on your clit. You come so hard that your ass muscles almost break my fingers, and I love it. But I didn't give you permission to come, so you know what that means."

She looks up at me, flushed and feverish, her lips swollen from our kisses and damp from the drag of her tongue. "I have to be punished?"

"That's right," I say, delighted by her.

"How?"

"I pull my fingers free of your ass so quickly that you gasp from the loss. You've quickly grown to love the way it feels to have my fingers there. Imagine what it will be like to take my cock there?"

"It would never fit."

"Oh, sweetheart," I say with a low rumble of laughter, "yes, it would."

She shakes her head.

I smile at her, and my heart is full of the possibilities. "I'd make it so good for you, you'd beg me for it again and again."

"Never."

"Are you challenging your Dom, little sub?"

"Maybe. Is… Is that how you'd punish me? By making me do that?"

"No, honey. I would never make that a punishment. That's something that has to be done carefully and with lots of preparation so you won't be hurt."

"Oh," she says, seeming relieved. "How could it not hurt?"

"I didn't say it doesn't hurt, but the goal is not to injure you. See the difference?"

"If it hurts, why would anyone want to do it?"

God, I love her so much, and I love that we are lying here together talking about things that seemed so far outside the realm of possibility only yesterday. "Because after it stops hurting, the pleasure is unlike anything you'll ever experience."

"How do you know? Have you done it?"

"Do you mean have I had it done to me?"

"Yeah."

"No."

"Then how do you know it feels good after it stops hurting?"

"Because people who love it, truly love it, will tell you it's an orgasm unlike any other."

She ponders that in her thoughtful way. "How do you punish me?"

"I clamp your nipples, which makes you scream from the painful pleasure. When I ask if you need your safe word, you shake your head even as tears spill down your sweet cheeks. I'm so proud of how courageous you are, and how focused. You've forgotten all about the people who are watching us, and you're thinking only of me and what we're doing together. You've made me very proud." I kiss her softly, sweetly, because I sense she needs some sweetness right now.

"What happens next?"

"I turn you over so you're bent over the table, and I spank you until your ass is red and hot. And then I make you take a plug. It's big, but not as big as I am, and eventually I want you to be able to take me. Again, you fight me, you struggle against the invasion, but you can't resist me. The plug settles into place, and you cry out from the shock of it. I lick you, from your clit to your ass, loving the way the plug stretches you. And then I fuck you, which isn't easy with the plug taking up so much space. It's a tight fit, and your muscles fight me, which feels like you're coming nonstop. It feels incredible. I mess with the plug to remind you it's there."

"As if I could forget," she says dryly, making me laugh.

"I fuck you harder than I ever have before, and you take me right to the edge of madness. I want you with me when I get there, so I reach around to play with your clit. With my other hand, I release the clamps on your nipples. I give you permission to come, and you come so hard, screaming from the pain of the blood returning to your nipples, that I come, too. You make me see stars. It's unlike it's ever been before with anyone else. There's only you."

She's moving under me, in time with me as I press rhythmically against her.

"Flynn…"

"What, honey?"

"I want you inside me. Right now."

Because she's naked under the robe, it takes very little effort to push down my sweats and slide into her. "God, you're so wet. So incredibly hot and wet."

"I've never been more aroused in my entire life."

"So you're not disgusted?" I ask, thrusting into her repeatedly while her fingers dig into my biceps.

She bites her bottom lip and shakes her head. "What else is there? What else do you like?"

Keeping up the steady, driving pace, I lose myself in her as the words pour out of me. "I want your hands wrapped in red ribbon that reminds me of how beautiful you look in your red coat. I love you in red. I want you bound and open to me, to take whatever I want to give you. Your nipples and clit are clamped with a chain connecting them. As I fuck you, I tug on that chain whenever I want to remind you who's in charge. You scream every time, your pussy gripping my cock so hard. I've never felt anything like it. You are the woman I love, the perfect sub I've waited all my life to find. I make you go down on your knees to suck my cock, to take me deep into your throat and swallow. We do everything. Everything we can think of."

I come out of the fog of desire I've slipped into to realize I've been fucking her harder than I ever have before, but she's right there with me, taking everything I give her. Looking down at her gorgeous face, I see only love and passion, but no sign of fear. "Do you trust me?"

"With my life."

"Do you love me?"

"I'll love you forever."

Knowing that gives me the courage I need so badly right now. I have given her my truth, and she still loves me. It is the most priceless of all the priceless gifts she's given me. "I want your hands."

Without taking her gaze off mine, she lifts her arms, offering her hands to me.

"Bring them together."

She flattens her palms against each other.

Watching her face intently, I wrap my hand around both her wrists and bring them up over her head, pinning them to the cushion. We're both well aware this is a major test. If we can do this, maybe, just maybe, there could be more for us.

I give her plenty of time to voice her objection, but my strong, brave Natalie never blinks. Instead, she raises her hips, asking me to move. I pick up the pace, stroking into her while watching her carefully for any sign of trouble. When I see none, I risk looking away to suck on one of the cherry-red nipples that stands at full attention.

Then I do something I haven't done before. I close my teeth over the nipple, tight enough to cause a sharp bite of pain.

She gasps, and her pussy clamps down on me, nearly triggering my orgasm. But I've learned how to delay my gratification, sometimes for hours, so I'm able to power through it. "Talk to me, Nat. Tell me how you feel. If you talk to me, I can keep doing this." I drag my tongue over the nipple that is now darker red than it was before. "Rather than watching you to make sure you're okay."

"I'm okay. Do that again… What you did before…"

I switch to the other side and begin with soft strokes of my tongue, adding a bit of suction after a minute or two. "This?"

"More."

"Tell me. I want your words."

"Bite it. Like you did before. Please…"

"You kill me when you're polite, Nat."

"I'm going to kill you if you don't do it."

I clamp down on her nipple, harder this time than the last.

She screams as she comes.

I drive into her one more time, taking my own pleasure in the midst of hers. Releasing her hands, I cup her breasts, running my tongue gently over the tips, soothing and caressing as she goes soft under me, her body yielding to me.

"Flynn…"

"Hmm?" I'm very busy enjoying her gorgeous breasts.

"I want to do what you dreamed about."

Her words stop me short. I raise my head to meet her gaze. "How much of it?"

"All of it. I want everything that you want. More than anything, I want to be everything you've ever dreamed of having in a wife and lover."

I'm stunned and humbled to have somehow won the love of this amazing woman. "Christ, Nat, you already are."

"Not quite yet, but I will be. Will you teach me how to be everything you want and need?"

I'm so overwhelmed by gratitude, I can barely speak. "Yes, sweetheart, I'll teach you."

CHAPTER 4

Natalie

"So what happens now?" I ask much later as we consume our favorite dinner from the nearby Italian takeout place—chicken piccata and Caesar salad. Flynn opens a bottle of chardonnay and pours a glass for each of us. We slept for hours after our life-altering conversation earlier, and woke starving—for food and each other.

It's dark now, and the wind is howling outside. The delivery guy told Flynn there's more than eight inches of snow already on the ground and more coming overnight.

"Now," Flynn says after taking a drink from his glass of wine, "we hammer out a contract."

"Like a real contract?"

"Yep. Hold that thought." He gets up and crosses the room to his office.

I watch him go, enjoying the view of him wearing only formfitting boxer briefs and nothing else. He's magnificent and all mine. Though I'm still reeling from everything that happened earlier, I'm no longer agonizing over what will become of us. We're in this together, and that's all that matters.

Flynn returns, a packet of papers in hand. "The contract between you and me is not legal, but it's a binding agreement for our relationship that outlines our hard and soft limits—in other words, things you absolutely won't do as well as things that make you nervous but you'd be willing to try. It's all negotiated in advance so there can be no misunderstandings during a scene."

"Could I ask a question?"

"Always."

This one requires some liquid courage, so I take a big sip of wine. "Will this… arrangement… involve other people?"

"No."

"Just no? No discussion? Haven't you done that before?"

"Yes," he says tightly. "I've done it, but there's no fucking way I'm sharing you with anyone. The thought of another man touching you… That's a hard limit for me."

"Okay…" I'm moved by his fiercely protective reaction, but that doesn't mean I'm not interested in pushing his buttons a little. "What about another woman?"

His eyes widen, and he starts to say something that dies on his lips. "Sorry, I'm just a little startled that you asked that."

I begin to laugh and can't seem to stop. "After everything you said to me today, *that* shocks you?"

"Coming from you, yes."

"I'm sorry. Have I shattered your illusions about your sweet, innocent wife?"

"I'm discovering my sweet, innocent wife may not be as innocent as I thought she was."

"Oh, she is, trust me, but I've done my research."

"Is that right?"

"Uh-huh. I'm wondering why all the secrecy surrounding this lifestyle. Why does it matter if people know?"

"Most people keep kinky preferences secret because society, as a whole, doesn't understand them. Too many equate kinky with perverted, and it's not perverted if two consenting adults are doing things that were agreed to in advance. The need for secrecy in my case and that of my partners is because that kind of judgment would hurt our careers."

"That's kind of sad when you think about it."

"It's reality," he says with a shrug. "People fear what they don't understand. It's easier and cleaner to keep it private. Plus it's none of anyone's fucking business."

"True."

"Another thing that people don't understand is it's not all about sex. It's much more about the emotion. When two people are fully invested in a scene, it can be the most intensely emotional experience you'll ever have—and that's before anyone has sex." He cups my face and slides his thumb over my cheekbone. "That's magnified a thousand times when you're in a scene with someone you love."

It's hard to imagine our lovemaking more intense than it already is, but I take his word for the fact that there is more—much more. "What else is in that contract of yours?"

"A checklist of possibilities. But first, I want you to look at this and see what you think. Most of the time, these things are hammered out verbally. But because of who we are and what we have to lose, we do paper contracts at Quantum. Everything about this lifestyle and our agreement is based on three core beliefs—safe, sane and consensual. Everything we do will be all three of those things or it doesn't happen."

He hands me two pages that outline our Dominant/submissive relationship. The Club Quantum logo sits at the top of both pages.

"Who has access to the clubs?"

"The five principal partners as well as our staff and the members we've admitted over the years."

"How do you keep something like this a secret in your business?"

"We are very selective about who we admit, and it costs a million dollars to join as a regular member. Everyone who's admitted into the club would have something big to lose if they talked about us or our activities or the club. We have people locked in custody battles, people with huge, prominent jobs outside the entertainment business, people with families who have no idea they're in the lifestyle."

"Does your family know?"

"No."

"Does Addie know?"

"Nope."

"She must suspect something after working so closely with you for so long."

"Not to be flippant about our recent troubles, but you married me, slept with me, made love with me, spent weeks with me and only me, and you didn't know."

"True, but then again, I didn't even know such a thing existed until I found Hayden's room."

"I'm not sure that Addie knows it exists either."

"Is this why Hayden doesn't pursue his feelings for her?"

"Yes."

"So many things make sense in this new context."

"And yet I still feel I have to say again—Hayden's business is his and his alone. Until you, I have never told another living soul about his involvement in the lifestyle, just as I'm confident he's never told anyone about mine."

"I'm honored to be trusted with all of this, Flynn. I swear to you again that I will never speak of it to anyone. You have my word on that."

"Even if our marriage disintegrates into a Hollywood disaster?" he asks with a wry grin that doesn't quite touch his eyes. I know he has no desire to discuss the possible demise of our marriage, but he's wise to be concerned nonetheless.

"Even then."

He takes my hand and brings it to his lips. "Thank you for that, for everything today, for giving me the chance to explain, to bring you all the way into my life. I'm so full of gratitude where you're concerned."

"It's odd because I felt so close to you before this, but now… It's even more so than it was before. Thank you for letting me the rest of the way into your world, even though you didn't want to."

"It's not that I didn't want to. It was my misguided attempt to protect you, which backfired badly and undermined everything we've built together."

I squeeze his hand, which is still wrapped around mine. "This isn't something I would've thought I wanted, but listening to you describe it to me…" I fan my face, making him laugh. "I don't know if I can do all of it, but I'm definitely curious and interested."

"That's an important first step. Now finish your dinner and read the contract."

"Yes, Sir."

My reply makes his eyes get very dark, and the connection between us in that moment is absolutely incendiary.

"*Read,*" he says in a low growl.

I smile at him before I return my attention to the documents.

The contract begins by outlining the timeframe for our agreement, which has been left blank. It goes on to cover a number of safety-related items, such as the hard and soft limits he's already mentioned and the use of what's referred to as a traffic-light system in which green means go, yellow means the sub is approaching his or her limits, and red means everything needs to stop right now. It covers the importance of open, honest communication between the Dom and the sub, and the proper form of address between a sub and the Dom.

Next is the availability of the sub, which is pretty much all the time, except for when the sub is at work or sleeping or otherwise engaged in his or her own activities. Then I read a line that says the terms of the agreement are enforceable by the Dom whether the couple is at home or in public.

I glance up at Flynn, who is watching me intently. "What?" he asks.

"At home or in public?"

He laughs, which softens his entire demeanor. "That's where you get lucky. Because of who I am to the rest of the world, I won't make you blow me in the men's room at LaGuardia."

"Thank goodness for small favors."

"I believe you once said there's nothing small about it."

His comment cracks me up. I love that we're laughing our way through what could've been a tense, uncomfortable conversation. It's anything but that. With every clause and sentence I read in the agreement, I feel closer to him, to understanding the real him and what makes him tick. I want to know that. I want to know everything about him. "So define public for me, then. What does that mean for us?"

"Possibly, down the road, when you're ready and I feel confident that you can handle it, we'd do a scene at the club."

"In front of people we know."

"Yes." He eyes me with his head tipped in inquiry. "What do you think of that?"

"I-I don't know if I can do that."

"Okay."

"That's it? Just okay?"

"We'll put public scenes on your soft limits list for now, and we can revisit it later. I have no intention of plunging you into this thing all at once, Nat. We're going to ease you in and take it one step at a time. At first it will just be us, experimenting, playing, trying new things in private. A public scene at the club would only happen much later, if or when we both decide it's time."

"What if I never get there?"

"Then you never get there, and I'll still love you with all my heart and be thankful every day that you're my wife as well as my sexual submissive."

"Could I… could we… maybe sometime… go to the club? Together?"

"That could be arranged."

"I'd love to see it and to better understand what goes on there."

"Then that's what we'll do."

His assurances help me relax some as I read about the exchange of respect between the parties as well as the expectations and rights of the Dom. These include the right to discipline his sub at any time but makes assurances that the Dom will never do anything that could be considered unsafe or that would leave permanent marks on the body of the submissive or create injuries that require medical intervention.

"How does punishment work?"

"Well, there are a variety of different ways that can be approached. It can be a spanking that's intended to hurt more than arouse. I can make you stand naked in a corner for a period of time during which you're expected to think about whatever behavior brought on the punishment in the first place, and then we'll talk about it afterward. Sometimes it might be both those things together—corner time followed by a spanking. There are Doms who bring in canes and whips and all sorts of other implements to discipline their subs, but I'm not really into inflicting that level of pain. The worst you'd get from me is a flogging for really serious offenses."

"There were whips in your playroom, or at least they looked like whips to me."

"Those belong to a friend."

"Oh." I swallow hard at the thought of being whipped. "And what would count as a really serious offense?"

"Disrespecting your Dom, talking back, refusing to do what you're told, failing to please me in some way." He pauses before he says, "I can see your wheels spinning. What're you thinking?"

"I can't imagine what it would be like to be spanked for talking back to you."

"This is only during sex. Feel free to sass me all you want the rest of the time. When we're in there," he says, pointing to the bedroom, "I'm in charge, and you do what you're told or face the consequences. That's how this works. By entering into this agreement, you're ceding the power over your sexual satisfaction and personal well-being to me, which means you have to do what I tell you and trust me to know what you need. That's how I do my job and ensure your safety—and your satisfaction."

I think that over from every angle and can see where it makes sense. "What if…" I shake my head. "Doesn't matter."

"Whatever you're thinking, just say it. Put it out there and let's talk about it. I don't want you to have any worries or concerns about how this will work."

"What if I'd come back, after learning everything I now know about you, and I just wasn't interested in this? What would've happened then?"

"If that had been the case, I would've been sad to not get the chance to explore this world with you, but we would've gone on like before only with no secrets left between us."

"How long would you have been satisfied with that?"

"For the rest of my life. I had already decided I could live without the lifestyle before I could live without you." With his hands on my shoulders, he looks directly into my eyes. "If what you're asking me is if I'd turn to someone else to fulfill these needs, the answer is an emphatic no. I will never cheat on you, Nat. Ever. I've been down that road, and I never hated myself more than when I stooped to Valerie's level by giving her a taste of her own medicine. I will never do that again, especially not to you. If I'm not having sex—of whatever kind—with you, I'm not having it with anyone else either. I swear to you. If you never believe another thing I tell you, that one you can take to the bank."

"I do believe you, because you already told me, a long time ago, how that incident made you feel."

"It sucked. It was the lowest point in my life, or it was until you left me yesterday."

"I had to do that, Flynn. I couldn't think this through and be with you, too."

"I know, but let me ask you something…"

"Anything."

"If I hadn't been here when you arrived, were you going to call me?"

Nodding, I say, "I would've called you today. I was as messed up without you as you were without me."

He puts his arms around me, and we hold each other for a long time. "Can we promise each other to never again walk away when the going gets tough? That we'll stay together and work it out no matter what it is?"

"I'll make that promise."

"So will I."

Pulling back, he kisses me, framing my face with his big hands and caressing my cheeks with his thumbs. He makes me feel so cared for and loved.

Looking sleepy-faced, Fluff comes strolling out of the bedroom and right over to my stool, jumping up on her hind legs to try to reach me.

"I bet someone needs to go out to pee," Flynn says, getting up from his stool. "I'll get someone to take her out, since neither of us can do it without being surrounded."

"How long do you think that'll last?"

"I don't know. The school sort of blindsided us with the announcement they made about offering your job back. We think they were trying to save some face with the public. Liza is dealing with it. We need to talk about that, too. And I want to hear everything about your visit with Candace. I started to ask you earlier, but we got sidetracked."

"Sidetracked," I say with a laugh. "Is that what we're calling it?"

He leans in to kiss me again. "It's more like we got back on track." Nodding to the contract, he says, "Keep reading. Take notes. We'll be back." After a trip to the bedroom to put on jeans and a long-sleeve T-shirt, Flynn whistles for Fluff, who goes running to him when she hears him pick up her leash.

I have to laugh at how she's taken to him when at first it didn't seem like she'd ever let him near me without having to listen to her snarl and growl. After the elevator comes to collect them, I refill my wineglass and return to my assigned reading.

The next section is on the roles and responsibilities of the submissive, which includes words that raise my hackles, including "obey," "serve" and "property" of her master. Yikes. I also stop short at the phrase that requires the submissive to ask permission before she touches her Dominant.

"That'll have to go," I say out loud. It is then that I realize I have power in this arrangement, too. I have the power to say no at any time. I have the power to negotiate the terms that suit me. This is what Flynn meant by the term "exchange of power."

Finally, the contract spells out the Dominant's requirements for his submissive in the areas of health, hygiene, birth control and masturbation, which is not allowed without permission from the Dom. That's not a problem for me, because I've never indulged in self-pleasure. Until I met Flynn, I avoided sex in all its many forms. Now I find myself craving the connection with him as well as the searing pleasure I always experience in his arms. I've gone from never having had an orgasm in my life before a month ago, to having more than I can count with him. As my sexual awakening is still quite new, I can't yet imagine wanting that without him there with me.

An addendum includes an exhaustive list of limits. The instructions at the top tell me to label each as a hard or soft limit and include precise definitions of the two terms that match what Flynn told me earlier. Someone, I assume it's Flynn, has drawn a line through many of the choices, and after reading them, I can see why. Some of these things are downright disgusting to me, and apparently to Flynn, too.

Of the ones he's left open for discussion, I stop at blindfolding and gagging. I don't know if I could handle being blindfolded after having been assaulted. The thought of that makes me queasy and anxious, so I mark it as a hard limit. Next to gagging, I mark a question—how will I use a safe word if I am gagged?

Spanking is a soft limit, as is anal play. I never would've believed I'd like that, but Flynn has already shown me otherwise. The thought of actual anal sex is a little less certain because I'm not at all convinced it would even be possible, but again, he has assured me otherwise. I mark that a soft limit as well. I'm willing to try it.

I discover there's a bevy of varieties when it comes to bondage. I mark light bondage and scarf play as soft limits and the rest as hard limits.

I set medical play and examinations as a hard limit as I can't imagine any scenario in which I would find that arousing after suffering through the trauma of a rape exam. Voluntary and forced masturbation are both soft limits, as are nipple clamps. After hearing Flynn's fantasy earlier, I admit to being intrigued by what that would feel like. Painful pleasure is a new term to me.

How do I feel about orgasm control? Meaning I would give up control of my orgasm to Flynn. He would say when, and I'd be at his mercy. I think about that for a minute before marking it as a soft limit.

Oh God, the next one on the list is rape fantasy.

"Mark a line through that one," he says from over my shoulder, startling me. I was so engrossed, I didn't hear him return with Fluff. "That's off the table."

I do as I'm told.

"I should've crossed that one off the list before I gave it to you. Sorry."

"That's okay."

"No, it isn't. My job is to take care of you, and by leaving that as an option, I didn't take care of you."

"It's really okay, Flynn. You gave me the option to make it a hard limit, which it is, so we're good." I glance up at him. "Have you…"

He shakes his head. "I've never done it, but I hadn't put it on my list of hard limits, which is why it's still there. It's a hard limit from now on." Scanning the page, he checks what I've marked so far.

I've gotten to the part on sex toys, including dildos, butt plugs, vibrators and beads, as well as the public use of any or all of them.

"How does that work?" I ask, pointing to the word public.

"I could, for instance, insist that you wear a butterfly vibrator inside your panties when we're going somewhere, and then use the remote control to turn it on at any time during the outing."

I cross my legs. "Oh. Wow. Well…"

He laughs at my reaction. "Don't knock it until you've tried it, sweetheart."

"It does sound rather… interesting. What's another example?"

Sliding his arms around me from behind, he nudges my hair out of his way and presses his lips to my neck. "I could insert a plug before an event such as the Oscars, for example, and you'd spend the entire evening sitting next to me, your ass being stretched by the plug so I could take you home after and replace the plug with my cock."

A tremble ripples through my body at the thought of such a scenario.

"My baby likes that one, huh?"

"I don't know. I'd be mortified."

"No one would know except for you and me. That's part of the thrill of this arrangement. You step outside your comfort zone with me and only me the wiser, and the reward is pleasure like you can't imagine."

As I raise my pen to mark the toys as a soft limit, he touches his lips to my ear. "Some of the plugs vibrate. That's the ultimate."

After a brief hesitation spent imagining a vibrating butt plug as part of my Oscar attire, I mark the toys as a soft limit as well as voyeurism, which sounds interesting as well. I think I'd enjoy watching others have sex, even if I'm not convinced I could let them watch me.

"That's my girl," he whispers. "So brave and fearless."

"Hardly fearless, but what did you tell me? Try everything once and twice if we like it?"

"Words to live by." After taking a closer look at the page of limits, he points to the question mark I've placed next to gagging. "What's the question?"

"How do I use a safe word if I'm gagged?"

"That's a great question, and the answer is we renegotiate the safe word so it's a gesture. Perhaps you snap your fingers twice for slow down and once for stop? Or you do thumbs-up for good, when I ask you, and thumbs-down for bad. We work that out ahead of time."

"Oh, okay."

"You should know I'm not a huge fan of gagging. I like to hear my partner's reaction to whatever I'm doing, and I especially like to hear *your* reactions, so let's cross that off our list." He takes the pen from me and draws a line through the word. "There're a lot of other things people do in this lifestyle, but if it's not on this list, it's not of interest to me. In our club, every Dom has their own list of things they enjoy, and the sub can determine his or her limits based on the Dom's list."

"So guys can be subs and women can be Doms?"

"Yep. Marlowe is a Dominatrix. She's in hot demand by male subs who get off on her brand of domination and humiliation."

"Marlowe is a Domme."

"Uh-huh."

"Wow, that's amazing."

"Wait until you see her in action. Suffice to say that none of us would dare fuck with her when she's wielding a whip." He returns to his seat next to me, and tops off both our wineglasses. "One more thing I want to add to our personal contract. May I?"

Still processing what I've learned about my new friend, Marlowe Sloane, I slide the pages across the bar to him.

He takes the pen from me and begins to write on the back of the second page. When he's finished, he pushes it over to me so I can see what he's written. It is, I realize, the first time I've seen his distinct handwriting. "That could be a font. The Flynn Godfrey font. It would be a huge bestseller."

"Just read it," he says, laughing.

The passage he has added says, *This contract between Flynn and Natalie Godfrey is binding for the purposes of enhancing their already spectacular sexual relationship. If, at any time, Flynn or Natalie should choose to end this contract, it shall have no bearing whatsoever on their life contract as best friends, lovers, husband and wife or parents to their future children. Flynn and Natalie's marriage vows take precedence over all other contracts and agreements set forth here.*

"That means," he says softly, looking at me as he speaks, "that you can get out of this at any time without endangering other more important agreements already in place between us."

"Thank you for that. It's incredibly sweet of you to know I'd need that assurance."

"You always have an out, sweetheart, whether it's through safe words or deciding the whole thing isn't for you or that your limits have changed. Despite how it may appear, you're the one who's actually in charge here."

"I like that," I say, giving him a sassy grin.

His low growl makes me laugh. "I'm going to like paddling that sweet ass when you get mouthy with me."

"Maybe I'll get mouthy with you *just so* you'll paddle my ass."

"*Fuck*, Nat," he says, the breath escaping from him on a long hiss. "You have no idea what you do to me when you say things like that, when you play along with me. You're my perfect match in every possible way." He reaches for me and brings me close enough to kiss. "I have a feeling you're going to make for a spectacular sub."

"I want to be the best sub you've ever had."

"You already are, my love. Just by talking to me about this, by reading the contract and considering all of it without judging me or deciding something has to be wrong with me to want this stuff... You're perfect."

I sign my name on the line Flynn has drawn for me under the paragraph he added. It is the first time I write the words Natalie Godfrey, and it gives me a thrill to see my new name in black and white.

Judging by his wide smile, Flynn likes it, too.

"So what happens now?" I ask him, tingling with anticipation.

"Now, I want to talk about your job and what we're going to do about it."

Chapter 5

Flynn

I can tell I've taken her by surprise with my reply. She thought I'd want to get right down to business now that we've hammered out the details. There's another detail that has to be seen to before we play, but I'll address that after we talk about her job.

"I thought you'd want to… you know, now that we've agreed to everything…"

"Are you in a rush?" I ask with a teasing smile intended to put her at ease.

"No, well… I'm curious, I guess."

Her curiosity is a huge turn-on for me. That she's interested and willing to try… I can't think about that right now when other decisions need to be made. "We'll get there, but we have other things to talk about, such as your job and your visit with Candace. How was it to see her again after all these years?"

"It was like no time had gone by. We picked up right where we left off. And then Livvy FaceTimed us, so we all got to be together." Her eyes sparkle with joy as she talks about her long-lost sisters. "They're so grown up and fun and beautiful."

"Of course they are. They're related to you, aren't they?"

She smiles at the compliment. "I missed so much with both of them, but we've promised to stay in close touch from now on. Livvy says she can visit next month when she has a long weekend."

"We'll set that up. You'll see her soon."

"We had fun at the hotel."

"I hope you ran up a big room-service tab."

"We sure did. Candace said if you were making us stay there and paying the bill, we ought to take full advantage."

Laughing, I say, "I can see I need to be concerned about these new sisters-in-law of mine. They sound like characters."

"They're great girls, and they're looking forward to meeting you. You'll love them."

"I have no doubt." I take her by the hand. "Let's go get comfy." We carry our wineglasses and the nearly empty bottle to the sofa. When we're snuggled under a warm blanket and Natalie is curled up in my arms, I rub my lips over her hair. "Talk to me about the job, Nat."

She leads with a deep sigh. "I'd love to go back to my class and finish out the school year, but I don't think I can."

"Why do you say that?"

"The school announced that they'd offered my job back, and now my apartment, your place, the school… We're overrun, and there's a freaking blizzard going on. And they're *still* staked out. For a while, when we were waiting to hear what would happen, I really thought I could go back if they asked me to and things would return to normal. But after the interview with Carolyn and the SAG Awards, I realized my normal has changed, and there's no going back to who I was before I became your wife."

Her words are like a spike to my heart, reminding me that while my life has changed for the better since we met, hers has been tipped upside down. "I'm so sorry, sweetheart."

"Please don't be sorry. It's not your fault. I knew what I was getting into when I took you on. Well, I mostly knew…"

A laugh rumbles through me. I'm glad she can joke about the thing that nearly ruined us. I started this day wondering if I'd ever see her again, and now anything is possible.

"I'm mostly afraid that if I go back, things will get crazy again with the paparazzi surrounding the school, and the board will regret asking me back. If that happens and I have to leave again… I can't do that to my kids, as much as I miss them and want to be with them. I can't jerk them around like that."

"I wish you could have everything you want and have me, too. Remember when we first met, and I tried to describe the downside to celebrity? This is it."

"There's something else…"

"What's that?"

"The foundation. Ever since you asked me to be part of that, it's all I seem to think about when I'm not thinking about you and everything that's happened with us. I'm so excited to be involved with such a worthwhile cause, and as much as I wish I could return to my classroom, being part of the effort to address childhood hunger in this country is so exciting."

"You have no idea how happy it makes me to hear you say that. I knew I was asking the right person to head up this effort. You should also know that my management team has been overrun with inquiries as to whether you're interested in modeling, acting and a wide variety of other offers, including interview requests from every major name you can think of."

"No way."

"Yes way. I told you you'd be in hot demand after the interview with Carolyn."

"Wow. They really want me to *model*? What do I know about that?"

"They love your look, and I can't say I blame them. I do, too. I can have my manager, Danielle, send over the most interesting offers, and you can take a look."

"I don't know about that, Flynn. Show business is your thing, not mine."

I shrug. "It can be your business, too, if that's what you want. You don't have to decide anything right away. Focus on the foundation for now, and see what happens."

"I suppose I could do that. It's so weird that people know who I am and are interested in me. That's going to take some getting used to."

"You've got the rest of your life to get used to it. Take all the time you need." I kiss her forehead and then her cheek. "Is it okay to say that I'm thrilled and relieved that we won't be spending any time on opposite coasts?"

"It's okay to say that," she says with a smile. "I'm relieved, too."

"So you're going to tell the school you're declining their offer to return?"

Nodding, she says, "I'll write to each of my students and explain why I'm not coming back and give them our address so they can write to me. That would be okay, wouldn't it?"

"We can't give out our actual address, but I have a PO box you can use."

"That'll work." She eyes me with excitement and anticipation. "So does this mean I'm officially moving to LA?"

"Eventually. In case you haven't noticed, we're somewhat snowed in for the time being." I nod to the windows, where the driving snow is highlighted by the orange glow of security lights from an adjacent building. "We're not going anywhere for the next day or two."

She runs her finger up the inside of my thigh, sparking an immediate reaction. "Whatever will we do with all that time?"

"Well, I've got that drawer full of movies and the tub you love so much."

Turning so she can see me, she takes a good long look to gauge whether I'm serious. "I'll admit to being confused."

"I'll admit to being incredibly aroused by the fact that you're so eager to proceed with our plans. I can't fucking wait to play with you. But before we do that, we need to talk to someone about whether it's a good idea in light of what you've been through in the past."

"I'm fine, Flynn. I talked to Doctor Bancroft last week."

This is news to me. "You didn't know the full picture last week."

"But still, we talked about sex… and everything."

I would give everything I have to know how that conversation went down. "You talked about kinky sex? About dominance and submission and everything that goes with those things?"

"Well, no, but—"

"No buts, sweetheart. We have to be certain it won't set you back before we try it. *I* have to be certain of that. We need to see your Doctor Bancroft or someone else who specializes in PTSD and sexual assault counseling."

"He does both those things, which is why the court sent me to him."

"You're already familiar with him, so I'd be fine with talking to him."

She glances up at me, seeming to gauge my sincerity. "You're very… private… about this part of your life, so private you didn't even tell me. You're really willing to talk to a stranger about it?"

"If it means being confident that you can truly handle what we're considering, then yes, I'll do it in a heartbeat. We've got to figure that we've met our quota of disreputable professionals for this lifetime with Rogers."

"True. I know Curt very well. We can trust him. He saved my life, Flynn. There's no way I'd be sitting here talking to you, capable of this relationship, without him."

"Then I owe him a tremendous debt of gratitude. Will you reach out to him and set up a time when we can talk to him?"

"Yes, I will, and thank you for being so concerned about me."

"I'm very concerned about you."

"I'll text Curt now and see if he can talk to us tomorrow."

I love that she wants to get on with our plans, that she's curious and interested rather than turned off and appalled. That makes her as different from my first wife as it's possible to get, but I already knew Natalie is made of much stronger stuff than Valerie could dream of being. Valerie… I need to do something about the trouble she caused between Natalie and me. I'll take care of that when I get back to LA. In the meantime, I take advantage of Natalie going to get her phone to look at mine for the first time in a while.

A message from Liza catches my attention. *Pictures of Natalie arriving at LaGuardia cropping up online. You won't like them. Will send pics in next message if you want to see.*

"Son of a bitch," I whisper as I scroll through the pictures of her looking cornered, frightened and very small next to the hulking men on either side of her. I begin to wonder how I'll ever let her out of my sight again. The thought of my precious love being afraid or surrounded makes me twitchy.

"What's wrong?" she asks when she rejoins me on the sofa, pulling the blanket back up over us.

Because I've learned there's no point in trying to hide anything from her, I hand her my phone and watch her closely as she studies the three photos Liza sent. "What're you thinking?"

"I look like I did during Oren's trial."

"I hate that you look so afraid."

"I wasn't really. Josh and Seth were right by my side, and they moved fast to get me out of there. I was never in any danger. I think I was surprised more than anything. It happened so quickly."

"This is why I always want someone with you going forward. If I can't be there, then someone else needs to be to make sure you're never hurt or overwhelmed. I'd lose my mind if anything ever happened to you because you had the poor sense to marry me."

She puts down the phone and climbs into my lap, straddling me.

Pleasantly surprised by her assertiveness, I cup her ass and pull her in tight against my instant erection.

"Marrying you was the best thing I've ever done. I don't expect to ever regret it."

"Did you regret it yesterday?"

Shaking her head, she runs her fingers through my hair, arranging it to her liking. "Not for one second. The time we've spent together has felt like a fairy tale. No matter what else happens, it will always feel like that to me."

"It's been like a fairy tale for me, too. After you left yesterday, I was out of my mind. I threw a vase through a window, and then the doorbell rang. I thought it was you, but it was that FBI agent. I wanted to kill him for not being you."

"Wait, why was he there, and why haven't you told me?"

I sweep away her concerns with my hand. "He was following up on Rogers's wife telling him Rogers had felt threatened by me. I assured Vickers the only way I threatened Rogers was legally. Why in the world would I kill him when I could've had the pleasure of watching him twist in the wind for years because of what he did to you?"

"Did you say that to Vickers?"

"Yep. I told him I was disappointed that Rogers had been murdered, because I'd been looking forward to making his life a living hell."

"So where did you leave it with him?"

"That I need to remain available for follow-up questions, which I said was fine. Neither of us has anything to hide where Rogers is concerned."

"I have nothing at all to hide, thanks to him," she says bitterly.

"I hate him for what he did to you, Nat, but in a way, I'm grateful that we have no more secrets between us."

She lays her head on my shoulder. "So am I."

"I hated keeping things from you. It felt wrong to me from the very beginning. You'll never know how badly I wanted to either tell you the truth or leave you to spare you from having to deal with something I didn't know if you could ever understand. We all know how successful my attempts to leave you were."

"You can't leave me after all this. I was able to move on from everything that happened to me before, but something tells me I'd never get over losing you."

I tighten my arms around her. "That's one thing you'll never have to worry about."

She rolls her hips suggestively over my cock. "Can we go to bed? Please?"

As if I'll ever say no to that question coming from her. "Anything you want, sweetheart."

CHAPTER 6

Natalie

We arrange to have Fluff taken outside, but she refuses to pee in the snowstorm. I hope we don't awake to a mess, but Flynn tells me not to worry about it. He says he wouldn't pee outside in this shit either.

In the bedroom, Flynn unties the robe I've lounged around in all day and pushes it off my shoulders, leaving me bare as his heated gaze travels from my face to my toes and back up again. He drops his shorts and raises the covers for me to get into bed ahead of him.

I'm freezing until he wraps his warm body around mine, pulling me in tight against him.

"You know what the worst part of yesterday was?" I ask him.

"What's that?"

"Sleeping without you last night. I hated that."

"I never went to bed at all, because I couldn't bear to sleep without you."

"You must be so tired."

"I am." His hand moves from my belly to land between my breasts. The hard column of his erection is pressed between my buttocks.

Despite his obvious arousal, despite my never-ending desire for him, neither of us is compelled to move. This is all about comfort and security. The feel of his skin against mine is all I need to release the deep breath I've been holding since I left LA yesterday, not knowing when or if I'd see him again.

In the last couple of weeks, my whole world has been turned on end by this relationship. Now, settled in his arms, with no secrets between us, and decisions made about our future, I feel ready for this next step we're planning to take. I'm excited. Of course, I'm also nervous, but I'm more excited than nervous.

I trust Flynn to make whatever we do together amazing for me, because that's what he's done from the beginning. I want to make it amazing for him, too. I want to give him everything he's ever wanted in a lover. I want to be perfect for him in every way.

Thinking about all the things I agreed to try, I drift off to sleep wondering how long he'll make me wait before our contract becomes a reality. I dream of things I'd much rather forget—the horrific weekend with Oren Stone that claimed my innocence and changed my life forever. I watch the scene unfold as an observer in my dream. I get a front-row view of my own assault, every lurid detail played out before my horrified eyes.

It was such a long time ago that many of the memories have faded somewhat. The overall horror has remained, though. As a witness, I'm forced to relive it once again. He is on top of me, inside me, hurting me, making me bleed, making me scream from the pain until I lose consciousness, floating, hurling through darkness so deep I may never find my way out.

I wake to Fluff's frantic barking and the low rumble of Flynn's voice.

"Nat, honey, what's wrong?"

Though my heart is racing, I'm sweating and undone, I know right away that I can't tell him I dreamed about the attack for the first time in years. He'll see the timing as a sign that I'm not capable of what we agreed to earlier. "N-nothing. Just a weird dream. I'm sorry if I woke you."

"You were screaming." Propped up on an elbow, he reaches over to stroke my face. "And you're crying." He kisses my shoulder. "Sweetheart…"

"I'm okay." I reach for his hand and hold on tightly.

"Are you sure?"

"Mmm. Uh-huh." Fluff curls up against my legs and lets out a huff of indignation at having been so rudely awakened.

"You're trembling, baby."

"I'm cold."

"That I can fix." He brings me in tight against him, wrapping his arms around me and intertwining his legs with mine. "Better?"

"So much better."

I was young and alone when Stone attacked me. I'm not alone anymore. Flynn's love and devotion only make me stronger than I was on my own. But the dream and the timing of it have me wondering if I'll be able to uphold my end of our agreement.

Once again a ringing phone wakes us early in the morning. Flynn groans as he reaches for his phone on the bedside table.

"Yeah, Emmett. You're up early."

Since he curls back up to me immediately, I can hear Emmett's side of the conversation, too.

"I just got a call from Vickers."

I feel Flynn go tense behind me. "What'd he want?"

"He'd like to see you and Natalie as soon as possible."

"What the hell for?"

"All he'd say is 'follow-up questions.'"

"This is bordering on harassment. Should we make some calls to Washington?"

"I wouldn't, Flynn. Calling in favors looks like you have something to hide when you don't."

"I don't like that he wants to see Natalie, too."

"They're ruling out both of you. My advice is to meet with him and get it over with. How soon can you get back here?"

"I don't know if you heard, but we had somewhat of a blizzard here last night."

"Yes, I heard," Emmett says with a laugh. "It's all over the news."

"I'd say it'll be tomorrow at the earliest before we can get back there."

"I'll make an appointment for Monday morning, then. Is that okay with you?"

"I guess it'll have to be. Let him know that if my name or Natalie's gets linked to this guy's murder in the press, I'll be after his job."

"I've already let him know that."

"You're good, Em."

"Just doing my job. See you soon."

I turn to face Flynn, looking for some assurances that we have nothing to worry about. He's got his glasses on, and he's typing frantically on his phone.

"What're you doing?"

"Asking Addie to get us back to LA tomorrow, so we can deal with this once and for all."

"Are you scared?"

"No, sweetheart. I'm not scared. We have nothing to worry about because we didn't do anything." He sends the text and puts the phone on the table. "Come here."

I curl up to him, my head on his chest, his arms around me. I trace my finger over the light scar on his ribs from where he was attacked by a deranged fan last year.

"It's all going to be fine. They're on a witch hunt. That's all this is. I handed them an easy lead with what I said on Carolyn's show, so they're taking the easiest and most obvious path straight to me. If they think we had something to do with this, then let them prove it." He strokes my hair. "We know people in DC, right up to and including the president. He and my dad are friends. If this gets any more out of hand, we'll call in some favors."

"So you've actually met the president?"

"Many times. You might get to meet him, too, as I've requested a meeting with him to discuss the foundation. I want him to throw his support behind it."

"Holy smokes. You don't fool around."

"You didn't already know that from the way I married you not even two weeks after I met you?"

"I suppose there were signs of this trait of yours."

His fingers trail down my ribs, digging in just enough to tickle me.

"Stop!"

Nuzzling my neck, he says, "What if I don't want to?"

"Fluff."

His hand drops to the mattress. He raises his head to look down at me. "See how easy that was?"

"I don't like to be tickled."

"How about I kiss it better?"

"Kissing is good. Tickling is bad."

"Mmm, I like to think I can be trained." He kisses his way down the front of me, between my breasts to my ribs, where he retraces the path his fingers had taken.

"And here I thought you were going to train me."

"We'll train each other. My goal is always your ultimate pleasure."

Moving back up, he tends to my breasts, moving slowly, lazily, as if we have all the time in the world, which apparently we do since we're snowed in. His tongue circles my left nipple while his fingers pinch the right one, just tight enough to draw a gasp from me.

"I love the way you respond to me, Nat," he says, his voice a hoarse whisper, his breath hot against my damp nipple, "every time I touch you. I love how you arch into me, trying to get closer. And the moan that comes from the back of your throat... It makes me crazy every time I hear it, knowing I made it happen. And that I'm the only one who will ever get to touch you this way makes me so fucking grateful that you chose me."

"Like you gave me a choice," I say with a teasing smile.

"The choice was always yours, my love." His teeth clamp down on my nipple as his fingers delve between my legs, where I'm hot and ready for him. Always ready for him.

"*Fuck*, Nat… God, you're so wet for me." He replaces his fingers with his cock and presses into me, stopping immediately when I wince. "Does it hurt?"

"I'm a little sore from yesterday."

He pulls out.

"No, Flynn. Don't stop. Please don't stop."

"I don't want to hurt you."

"You won't. Just go slow at first." I run my hands down his back to cup his tight, muscular ass. I love the dimples at the bottom of his spine and feel for them with my thumbs.

He gasps. "Natalie…"

"You like that?"

"I fucking love the feel of your hands on me—anywhere, but when you drag your nails over my ass like that…" A shudder rocks him.

Knowing I can do that to him fills me with delight and pleasure.

He moves into me slowly, in small increments, pressing in and then retreating, giving me time to adjust. He's big and I'm sore, which should make for a bad combination, but his slow, steady entry has me forgetting all about the soreness as I crave the fullness, the connection, the magic.

Propped on his elbows above me, his forehead resting on mine, he watches me in that intense way of his, making sure that nothing hurts me. I wrap my arms and legs around him, raising my hips to take him deeper.

His low groan makes me smile as I tighten my internal muscles around him, knowing that drives him crazy.

"*Fuuuuck*," he says on a long, low exhale.

I do it again and again and again until he forgets all about how he wanted to go slowly and begins to pound into me in the way I love best, wild and unfettered. One set of fingers digs into my shoulder while the other reaches below me to grasp my ass, to hold me still. Then he bends his head and bites my nipple, which sparks my orgasm.

He thrusts into me, pushing hard as he comes, too, and then he sags against me, breathing hard. "Shit."

I push sweat-soaked strands of hair off his forehead. "What?"

"I was rough, and you're sore."

"You were perfect, and I loved it. I love you."

"I love you, too. I wish you knew how much."

"I have a pretty good idea."

For a long time, we stay right where we are, arms wrapped around each other, still joined as we pulse with aftershocks, his sweat merging with mine. "I can't imagine this getting any better than it already is."

"It's not about better so much as it is about *more*. There's more I want to share with you, more I want you to experience." He kisses my neck and jaw on his way to my lips. "You know what I want to do now?"

"I really have to guess?"

Smiling down at me, devilishly handsome first thing in the morning, he says, "I want to fuck you in the shower."

My entire body reacts to his gruffly spoken words. "I am feeling rather dirty." To make my point, I tighten my internal muscles around him again. That's when I realize he's already hard again.

"Shower. Right now."

I discover I'm a big fan of shower sex after being pressed face-first against the tile wall and thoroughly taken from behind by my ravenous husband. His fingers dug so deep into my hips that I have no doubt there will be bruises, but I loved every second of it. But now I'm really sore.

"There's other stuff we could do," he reminds me when I tell him we're out of business for the rest of the day.

"What other stuff?"

Still standing behind me, he delves his fingers between my cheeks to press against my back door. "We could play here."

Every time he touches me there, I go lightheaded with desire and burning curiosity.

"Play how?"

"Fingers, toys, my tongue, my cock…" His erection is hot against my back, as if he hasn't just come twice in half an hour.

"Now?"

"Not until we talk to your doctor friend."

Moaning in frustration, I say, "I'm calling him right after we get out of this shower."

Laughing, Flynn shuts the water off, making me laugh, too.

I towel off, put my robe back on and head straight for my phone, where I see I've received a reply from Curt. *Working in the home office tomorrow—we got snow, too. Call me any time. Happy to chat with you and Flynn.*

"He says we can call him any time."

"What're you doing right now, Mrs. Godfrey?"

"Calling Curt."

Wearing only a pair of tight boxer briefs, Flynn heads for the door.

"Where're you going?"

"I need coffee for this conversation, and I'm going to get someone to take Fluff out for us."

"Put more clothes on. I don't want anyone to see you like that."

He comes to me. "Feeling possessive of what's yours?"

"Yes. Is that allowed?"

Tipping my chin up, he kisses me. "Everything is allowed, sweetheart."

While he tends to Fluff and makes coffee, I return Curt's text. He suggests a Skype session and sends me the info we need to connect.

"Are you okay with that?" I ask Flynn.

"Sure, whatever works."

"Okay, I'll tell him we'll call in half an hour." I return to the bedroom to dress in jeans and a turtleneck sweater. Opening the blinds in the bedroom, I look out on the winter wonderland New York has become overnight. Naturally, there's a sea of yellow taxis sloshing through sludge the plows left behind.

I join Flynn for a quick breakfast of coffee, cereal and fruit.

"You okay?" Flynn asks.

I realize I've been staring off into space, thinking about my dream last night. I've decided the timing was a coincidence. If I contemplate the possibility that it wasn't… "I'm fine. Shall we make that call?"

"Let's do it."

I scoop up Fluff as I leave the kitchen and follow Flynn into his office, where there's a big monitor that he plugs into his laptop. He brings a second chair into the room from the kitchen, and I sit next to him.

A minute later, Curt pops up on the big screen before us. He looks the same as I remember, maybe a little grayer around the edges.

"Ah, there you are," he says. "You look wonderful. And there's Fluff, too."

"She's going strong at fourteen. Curt, this is my husband, Flynn." I laugh. "And I think that's the first time I've introduced him as my husband."

"I'm honored to be first," Curt says, "and it's a pleasure to meet you, Flynn. I'm a big fan of your work."

"Thank you, it's nice to meet you, too. Thanks for being there for Natalie when she needed you."

"It was always a pleasure to work with her. What can I do for you today?"

We exchange glances, and Flynn nods for me to go ahead. "I know it goes without saying that we're a little leery after what happened with David Rogers."

"Which was unfathomable. I knew him a little, and what could've driven him to betray you so badly… You have nothing to worry about where I'm concerned. I assure you of my utmost discretion."

"I told Flynn we could count on you. Thank you for that." Suddenly nervous, I clear my throat. "Since we spoke last week," I say haltingly, "I've discovered some additional facets of my husband's personality. Specifically, he's a sexual dominant."

"Oh, I see."

"I kept that from Natalie before we were married because I had myself convinced I could live without that before I could live without her."

"And how did Natalie find out?" Curt asks.

"Through a series of unfortunate events," Flynn says. "I take full responsibility for failing to tell Natalie something she should've known about me before she bound herself to me for life, and I take full responsibility for her hearing about it from someone other than me."

"How do you feel about that, Natalie?"

"While I agree that he should've told me, I understand why he didn't. He was thinking of me above himself, and it's hard to be angry with him when he was willing to sacrifice so much to be what I need."

"Since all of this came to light, Natalie has expressed a genuine interest in exploring the lifestyle with me. Though we've had in-depth conversations about what it would entail and have gone so far as to negotiate a consensual contract, I'm reluctant to move forward before we have some professional advice about what, if any, impact it could have on her ongoing recovery from the assault."

"I think you're very wise to ensure that base is covered before you proceed," Curt says. "Natalie, can you tell me about your interest in the activities Flynn has proposed?"

"I'm curious," I say, glancing at Flynn, who's watching me the way he always does. "I'm intrigued."

"I notice you don't say you're frightened."

"I'm nervous, of course, and a bit anxious about what might happen if I don't like it or can't be what he wants—"

"I have to stop you right there, Nat. You *are* what I want." For Curt's sake, he adds, "I've told her that in every way I can think of. We've already had sex twice today—great sex, the kind of sex people dream about having. The connection between us is nothing less than combustible. The things we're talking about adding would only complement an already amazing sex life. But if all we ever have is what we already have, that would be enough for me."

"Then why add this element?" Curt asks.

"Let me," I say, my hand on Flynn's arm. "I recently told Flynn that I feel like I've been asleep my whole life until he awakened the part of me that's been asleep. With him, I've discovered desire and passion and satisfaction that I never dreamed possible. I've gone from thinking I'd never have a normal sexual relationship to having sex multiple times a day and enjoying it more than I ever thought I would."

"The honeymoon stage does wear off after a while," Curt says with a smile.

I glance at my husband. "I don't know if it will in our case." I squeeze his arm, drawing a smile from him. "Flynn tells me there can be more, and I want it all. As long as I'm with him, I know I'll be cared for and treasured and loved at every step along the way. I trust him more than I've ever trusted anyone in my life."

Flynn wraps his hand around mine and squeezes. "What's your take, Doc? Will Natalie be okay if we proceed down this road?"

"PTSD in all its many forms can be a tricky thing. You think you're fine, and then something happens, such as the thing with your hands on your wedding night, and it rears its ugly head. I'm reluctant to provide any assurances that Natalie will be totally fine. There are apt to be bumps, moments of genuine fear, flashbacks or even triggers that bring back the past trauma. That said, it seems that you have been able to get past these challenges before and may be able to do so in the future."

"*May* be able to," Flynn says. Trust him to home in on that one word. "What if Natalie can't get past it?"

"Then I'd recommend that whatever activity caused the reaction be ceased immediately and possibly permanently."

"But you're not recommending we don't try this at all?" Flynn asks.

"Natalie says she's intrigued, curious, interested. Never once has she said she's afraid. That's important."

"I'm not afraid." I swallow hard, trying to suppress the memory of the dream that reopened old wounds. I know I should tell them both about the dream, but I'm so tired of revisiting the past. I want to move forward with my amazing husband. I want us to have everything we want and deserve. "I want to live fearlessly."

"You see why I love her so damned much?" Flynn says softly.

"I do," Curtis says, smiling. "I encourage you to live fearlessly, Natalie, but I also urge you to proceed cautiously. Baby steps. Ease your way into this a little at a time to see what works for you and what doesn't. Don't be afraid to use whatever word you've agreed upon that stops everything. And keep the lines of communication wide open. Talk about it afterward, what you liked and didn't like, what you'd like to do again and what you wouldn't. That's going to be critical to ensuring a successful experiment."

"We're getting pretty good at the talking thing," Flynn says, glancing at me.

I nod in agreement.

"That's an excellent place to start," Curt agrees. "I'd like you to check in with me, Natalie, perhaps weekly for a while, if that works for you."

"Sure, that would be fine."

"I'm only a phone call away if you should ever need me—day or night. Don't hesitate to call."

"Thank you so much, Curt."

"Yes, thank you," Flynn says, "and I'll text you where to send your bill."

"There's no charge. It's my pleasure to see you settled and so in love, Natalie. I can't think of anyone who deserves that kind of happiness more than you."

Flynn puts his arm around me and kisses my temple. "I couldn't agree more."

"Thanks again, Curt. I'll call you next week."

"I'll look forward to hearing from you."

Flynn pushes the button to end the connection. "He's great and obviously very fond of you."

"He got me through a nightmare."

"For that, he shall always have my gratitude as well as yours."

"Do you feel better now that we've spoken to him?"

"I feel less worried than I was."

"Soooo… What now?"

Once again, he leans in close to me, his lips touching my ear. "Now, I need to do some work."

"Oh. Okay."

"But tonight at eight o'clock, I want you naked and on your knees at the foot of the bed. Your hands will be folded in your lap and your head down in submission as you wait for me to tell you what I want. Do you understand?"

My entire body heats as his words register. "I… Yes, I understand."

"Today, I want you to reread our contract and go over every detail we negotiated so you're reminded of what could happen later."

"Okay."

"What's the proper way to address me in this context?"

"Yes… Sir."

"Better. Now kiss me and let me get to work."

I expect a quick peck, but I should know better by now. He kisses me senseless and then leaves me reeling when he pulls back. I put Fluff down, get up from the chair, which I take with me when I leave the room on trembling legs. Eight o'clock is more than ten hours from now. How will I stand the insistent throb of desire between my legs for that long?

Chapter 7

Flynn

I'm hard as concrete as I watch her walk away. Her reaction to my instructions makes me want to forget all about the power of anticipation and begin playtime right now. But I've promised Hayden I'll work for part of every day, so I start by diving into the email that has accumulated during the time I've spent with Natalie.

I participate in a conference call with the production team on the film that has defied naming, and dismiss a lengthy list of ideas our marketing team presents to us at the end of the two-hour meeting.

Hayden reminds me we're long overdue with making decisions on our next project and forwards me an email containing his short list of suggestions.

"I'll take a look and get back to you with my thoughts."

"Great, thank you. Nice to have you back, even part time."

"Good to be back."

The call ends, and I immediately call Hayden on my cell.

"Didn't I just talk to you?"

"I wanted to speak to you privately, and I didn't trust everyone to hang up if I asked to do it during the call."

"Good thinking."

"Especially in light of what I want to talk about. So Natalie knows."

"What does she know?"

"Everything." I let that one word do the talking for me.

"How?"

"Our old friend Valerie decided she needed to know."

"You're shitting me, right?"

"I wish I was."

"Wow, she's got some brass balls. You gotta give her that."

"Perhaps so, but when I get back to town, we need to do something about her. It wouldn't take much to ruin her career, for one thing. Hardly anyone wants to work with her anyway."

"I can't believe she'd have the nerve to fuck with you this way. So, how did Natalie take it?"

"We had a rough couple of days, but we're better now. A lot better. She wants to come to the club."

"So she's interested?"

"Intrigued and curious were the words she used."

"A lot better than depraved and disgusting."

"I much prefer Natalie's words."

"Wow, Flynn… Congrats. You hit the jackpot. You found a woman who genuinely loves you *and* is willing to be part of the lifestyle, too. You're a lucky bastard."

I can hear the yearning in his tone. Perhaps someone who doesn't know him as well as I do would've missed it, but I don't. "You never know what's possible unless you try."

"Not gonna happen."

"How do you know—"

"I gotta go. Another call coming in. See you when you get back."

The line goes dead, and I shake my head in amusement and frustration at my best friend's dismissal of my suggestion. He and Addie would be great together, but Hayden's too afraid of what might happen if she found out about his involvement in the lifestyle. More than anything, I think he fears losing her friendship, not that he's ever come right out and said that. Hell, he's barely admitted his interest in her to me, let alone anything else.

I hope he can get out of his own way and decide to take a chance. I, for one, would tell him the rewards far outweigh the risks, but then again, I wasn't risking a longtime friendship with Natalie. It's a tough situation, especially because I believe Addie would welcome being more than friends with Hayden—again, not that she and I have actually talked about it.

Natalie appears in the doorway, and every other thought leaves my head except for those that involve her. "Sorry to interrupt."

"You're not. What's up?"

"I talked to Aileen, and she doesn't sound too good. She had chemo on Friday, and the kids are home today because of the snow. I was thinking I might go over there and entertain the kids so she can rest. Would that be okay with you?"

"Only if I can come with you."

"I thought you had to work."

"I did, and now I don't have anything else scheduled until eight o'clock tonight."

Her eyes drop and her cheeks flush at the mention of our date. "Oh, well, if you want to come, I'm sure the kids would love that."

"You should check with Aileen first. I don't want to make her feel uncomfortable."

"I'm sure she won't mind, but I'll ask her if we can hang out with the kids for a while so she can rest." She sends a text and receives an immediate response. "She says they'd love it and that neither of us are to look directly at her or at the condition of the apartment."

I laugh at the cute but sad reply. "We can't drive, though. With everyone home because of the snow, we'll never be able to park. We'll take a cab."

"How will we get out of here undetected?"

"I have the perfect solution."

"I won't wear Russian fur on my head."

"I wouldn't dream of making you do that. I've got something even better." He disappears into the bedroom and returns carrying two hats. When he hands one to me, I see they are knit ski masks with holes for the eyes, nose and mouth that cover the entire face. "No one will look twice at us in these today, because everyone will be wearing them."

"I've always thought they were kind of creepy when I saw people wearing them on the street."

"They do come in handy on days like this. And this way we can leave the security guys at home."

"Where are they when we're here?"

"In an office in the building next door. I call them when we need them."

"That must cost a fortune."

"It does, but it's well worth it."

We suit up in the warmest clothes we can find and head out a short time later with Fluff leading the way. In addition to the snow masks, we're wrapped up in scarves, warm parkas and gloves. "I wish I had my boots." The best she was able to do is a pair of black Nikes.

"I'll carry you over any puddles."

The doorman hails a cab for us, and as we're on our way out the door, Fluff stops right on the sidewalk to pee. Natalie and I lose it laughing, which draws the attention of the photographers camped outside my place. "Quick." I gesture to the waiting cab. I scoop up Fluff the second she quits peeing, and we make a break for the car before the photographers can get themselves organized.

Once inside the cab, we remove the masks.

"I can't believe they stand out there in the snow hoping for a glimpse of you," she says.

"And you."

"But mostly you."

"I don't know… Liza says pictures of you are going for a pretty penny these days, too."

After a slow ride through slush and ice, we arrive at Aileen's building. The snowdrifts are so high that I have to make good on my promise to pick up Natalie—and Fluff—and carry them over the snow to the vestibule.

"Our hero," she says.

"I specialize in damsels in distress."

We go up a flight of stairs, and Natalie pushes the button for Aileen's place. A buzzer sounds to admit us. Outside their apartment, Logan is waiting for us and lets out a happy squeal when he sees Natalie. She catches him up in a big hug.

"You've grown a foot since I saw you."

"That's not possible, Ms. Bryant."

She keeps him in her arms as we enter the apartment. "You can call me Natalie now that I'm not your teacher anymore."

"*Miss* Natalie," a weak voice from the sofa says.

With one glance, it's obvious Aileen is in rough shape. Her face is ghostly white, and she doesn't get up when we enter the living room, which looks as if a cyclone has gone through it.

"We're a wreck," she says.

"You're not going to be my teacher anymore?" Logan asks mournfully. "They said you were coming back."

I squeeze Nat's shoulder as I help her out of her coat.

"Logan, honey," Aileen says, "let Natalie take her coat off before you start asking questions."

Natalie sits on the love seat and pats the cushion next to her, inviting Logan to join her. "So here's the deal… You know that my husband, Flynn, is famous."

"He's in movies that Mom says I'm not old enough to see."

"That's right."

"So he's like SpongeBob, only for adults, right?"

Natalie fights a losing battle with laughter. "Exactly," she says, glancing at me, the laughter making her eyes dance with joy. "Because I'm married to him now, there's a lot of interest in both of us that would be a huge distraction for all my students."

"What's a districtión?"

"A *distraction* is when things happen that take our attention off our schoolwork."

"Like video games?"

"That's a great example."

Watching her patience with the little boy, I can't wait to see her with our kids. She's going to be an amazing mother.

"I'm afraid of coming back and then having to leave again when the distractions prove to be too much. I'd never want to put you guys through that, so I've decided not to come back, as much as I'd love to. But, I'm going to give you all my address so we can write to each other, and I'll Skype with you and your mom and Maddie. Okay?"

"I guess," he says, though he's clearly crushed. Who could blame him? I felt the same way when Natalie left me, and that was only for a day.

"I'm so sorry about all this, buddy."

"I know."

"Hey, Logan," I say, anxious to end this conversation for Nat's sake, "do you and Maddie want to go play in the snow?"

His eyes light up as his sister lets out a squeal. "Can we, Mom?"

"You don't want to do that," Aileen says.

"If I didn't, I wouldn't have asked. I'd love to take them to the park, if it's all right with you."

"Sure, they'd love that. They've been asking to go out all morning, and I just…" Her eyes fill. "I couldn't."

"No problem. I've gotcha covered. Why don't you come, too, Nat, and we'll let Aileen get some sleep?"

"I don't have boots."

"What size are you?" Aileen asks.

"Seven."

"I'm a seven and a half. Use mine."

"Okay, then, I'm in!"

While I help get the kids bundled up, Natalie walks Aileen to her bedroom and tucks her in for a nap. She comes out of Aileen's room with tears in her eyes and the boots in hand. "Hard to see her this way," she whispers.

"I know." I kiss her forehead and let her pass me in the hallway. The kids' rooms are cluttered with toys, the beds are unmade, and dirty clothes are on the floor. While the kids pull on their snow pants, I withdraw my phone from my pocket and fire off a text to Addie.

We're at Aileen's, and she needs some help. Can you please check into an agency here that does nurses/nannies/housekeepers? Get one of each if you would.

Got it. On it.

You truly are the best.

I know! J

I love her cheeky reply, and I love her, too. I'd be lost without her. Nothing I ever ask her to do is too much for her, and she's endlessly efficient and organized. I make it well worth her time and effort, but the truth is I'd pay her twice as much to keep her.

I stash my phone and go to help Natalie with the kids. On the way out the door, Logan produces a plastic sled from the front closet. We clomp down the stairs in a noisy group, Natalie and I with our ski masks covering our faces. The kids think they're hilarious, which I suppose is better than scary.

On the sidewalk, I load the kids onto the sled and pull them behind me down the snow-covered sidewalk, extending my free arm to my wife. We've left Fluff sleeping in a ball on Aileen's sofa. At the park, we spend more than an hour making a snowman, having a snowball fight and making snow angels. When the kids begin showing signs of tiring, we load them back up and set out for home, stopping on the way for pizza and hot chocolate.

The startled restaurant staff immediately recognize us, but I ask them not to make a thing of it in front of the kids. Thankfully, they respect my wishes. I'll ask Addie to send them a signed photo to show my appreciation.

We return to the apartment with two tired, well-fed kids who had a great time.

"Thanks for this," Natalie says as we follow them up the stairs.

"It was fun." And it was. Life's simple pleasures tend to get lost in the sea of celebrity madness that surrounds me. I like that Natalie and her friends have helped to remind me of what's really important.

"Guys," I say to the kids, who are preparing to barge into the apartment. "Your mom is probably sleeping, so let's be really quiet, okay?"

"Okay, Mr. Flynn," Maddie says solemnly.

We help them out of their snow clothes and boots outside the door. "One other thing I want you to do for me."

"What?" Logan asks.

"I want you to go in your rooms and pick up all your toys and put them away. Then you need to make your beds and gather up your dirty clothes. Can you do that?"

"If we hafta," Logan says glumly.

"Let's see who can get their rooms picked up the fastest." The contest sparks some interest in them, and they scurry into their rooms.

"You're going to be an awesome father," Natalie says.

"Funny, I was thinking the same about you earlier." I kiss her nose. "An awesome mom."

"That's going to be fun," she says, smiling at me.

"I can't wait."

"Really?"

"To see you round with our baby?" The thought of it does weird things to my heart and stomach. "I. Can't. Wait."

She wraps her arm around my neck and kisses me. "Love you," she whispers.

"Love you, too."

"I'm going to clean up the kitchen."

"I'll check on the kids and then take on the living room."

"This is way, *way* above and beyond the call of husbandly duty."

I lean in close so my lips are touching her ear. "You can reward me later."

I leave her with that thought and go to pick up the toys, pillows, blankets and newspapers that are strewn about Aileen's living room.

Natalie

While I tend to the mountain of dirty dishes in Aileen's sink, I think about how great Flynn was with Logan and Maddie. From pulling them on a sled to supervising the building of a snowman, to engaging in a snowball fight, he was incredible with them, and they loved every minute of the attention he showered them with.

I'm not sure what the deal is with their dad, just that he's not in the picture.

When I finish in the kitchen, I go to find Flynn, who's stretched out on the floor of Logan's room with both kids pinning him down.

"Natalie, help! I've been taken hostage!"

The kids giggle madly as he tries to tickle his way out of the bind they have him in.

Aileen joins me at the doorway, smiling at the sound of her children's laughter. "That's a very nice thing to hear."

"We had the best time," I tell her.

"Apparently, they did, too." She takes a closer look at Logan's room. "Did you *clean* his room?"

"Nope, he did."

"How did you pull off that particular miracle?"

"Flynn gets all the credit. He made it a brother-sister race to see who could clean their rooms the fastest."

"Wow. He's good."

"I think so, too. Are you feeling better?"

"So much better. I can't thank you enough for this today."

"Believe me when I say it was our pleasure. We had a blast playing in the snow with the kids."

"Logan, go easy," Aileen says. "God forbid we damage that priceless face."

"That's right," Flynn says. "It's insured for millions."

I roll my eyes and share a laugh with Aileen. As we prepare to head out a short time later, Flynn lets her know help is on the way.

"You've already done more than enough," she says in protest, referring to the half-million dollars he donated to the fundraiser for their family at school.

He puts his hands on her shoulders and kisses her forehead. "Let us help. There's no need for you to try to do this alone. You have friends who care, and if we lived here full time, we could come by every day and check on you guys. But since we don't, this is the next best thing, okay?"

"Are you ever able to say no to him?" she asks me.

"Rarely," I reply with a saucy wink that makes them both laugh.

"Thank you," she says, gesturing to the spotless apartment and the two kids on the sofa, quietly watching a movie. "I'll never forget this, and neither will they."

"We had a great time." I hug her, and the feel of her sharp bones under my hands unsettles me as I lean down to gather up Fluff. "Call you tomorrow, okay?"

"I'll be here."

"Bye, guys," I say to the kids.

"What do you say to Flynn and Natalie?"

"Thank you!"

"You're welcome. We'll see you soon."

Flynn has summoned an Uber car that is waiting for us outside Aileen's building. He holds the door for me and follows me inside.

After a long period of silence, I reach for his hand. "I'm worried about her."

"Me, too."

"Her bones… She's…"

"I know, sweetheart. I felt them, too. My dad has a friend who's a big-time surgeon here. I'm going to ask him to get a name for us. I want the top breast cancer doctor in the city for her."

I lean my head on his shoulder. "I'm scared for her. For all of them."

"We'll do everything we can for them."

"Thank you for making my friends your friends."

"Aileen and the kids are easy to like. I've enjoyed getting to know them."

Flynn asks the driver to take us into the garage to avoid the photographers still staked out in front of the building. The driver makes all the usual noise about the Bugatti, but while he's friendly, Flynn doesn't offer photos.

In the elevator, he says, "I feel like steak tonight. I need some protein to build up my strength." He waggles his brows, reminding me of our plans for the evening. As if I could forget. All afternoon with the kids, I've been thinking about how this night might unfold.

But after seeing Aileen in such poor condition, I'm not sure if I can get my head straight to concentrate on him.

"Nat?"

"Hmm?"

"You okay?"

"Sure." I force a smile for his benefit, but he's not buying it.

"Tell me what's wrong."

The elevator opens into the foyer, and he takes my coat, hanging it next to his in the closet.

"Nothing's wrong. I'm just worried about Aileen."

Flynn withdraws his phone from his pocket and places a call. "Hey, Dad, what's up?" He glances at me. "We're good. In New York for a couple of days but heading back your way tomorrow. You can tell Mom to go forth with her party planning. We have to go to London for the BAFTAs next weekend, so the weekend after that?" He looks to me for confirmation.

We're going to London next weekend? I want to squeal with excitement. I've always wanted to go there.

"Nat? Is that okay?"

I nod in agreement. Stella is excited to throw a party to celebrate our wedding, and since I already adore my new mother-in-law, whatever she wants is fine with me. This will be their big show, as I don't have many people to invite.

"So listen, Natalie has a friend here in New York who has breast cancer. She doesn't seem to be doing so well, and I wondered if you would ask your friend Jared about a recommendation of someone who could see her. I want the top doctor in the city."

While he talks to his father, I take advantage of the opportunity to text my former roommate, Leah.

So I've decided to decline the school's offer to return. Too much of a circus comes with me now, and it's not fair to the kids.

I sort of wondered if that would happen. We'll miss you, but I understand. I'm a short-timer there myself. They asked me to train to be a manager at the bar, and I'll do that while I figure out what's next.

Keep me posted.

Will do. How's married life with the hot movie star?

It's hot. If only she knew.

I hate you.

No, you don't.

Yes, I really do! LOL! You can make it all better if you invite me to some fabulous Hollywood party.

I'll see what I can do.

Squeeeee! How's Fluff?

She's good. I think she's starting to fall in love with her new daddy.

Awww too cute! Miss you guys.

We miss you, too. See you soon I hope!

Tell the hot movie star I said hello.

Will do. xoxo

"My dad is going to call his friend tonight and get back to me tomorrow," Flynn says when he finds me in the kitchen.

"Thank you for that. Leah says to tell my hot movie star husband she says hello."

"How is she?"

"Good. I wanted to tell her about not going back to school so she doesn't hear it through the grapevine."

"How'd she take it?"

"She totally understands."

"You could, if you wanted to, that is, send an email to Mr. Poole tonight to officially close that circle."

"Is that your way of saying you're glad I'm not going back?"

He props his hands on the counter, on either side of my hips. "I'm glad you made a decision you're comfortable with, and selfish bastard that I am, I'm *thrilled* you'll be coming home to LA with me, moving in permanently and sleeping next to me every night."

Looping my hands around his neck, I say, "I'm thrilled about those things, too."

"Yeah?"

I bite my bottom lip and nod, watching his eyes home in on the movement of my mouth.

"Are we really going to London?"

"Uh-huh."

"So why are we going back to LA tomorrow when London is in the opposite direction?"

"Oscar nominees' luncheon is Monday, and the nominees' party is Monday night." He's still staring at my mouth. "I was on my best behavior all afternoon with the kids. I think you owe me some thanks for that."

"I *owe* you?"

"Uh-huh." He swoops in and captures my mouth in a kiss full of hours' worth of pent-up desire. His arms band around me as he explores every corner of my mouth with his tongue. I'm left reeling when he ends the kiss as suddenly as he began it. "Food first. More of that later. Steak? Yes?"

"I'm expected to function after that?"

A satisfied smile stretches across his face. "I'm expecting a lot of *functioning* tonight." Another kiss has me clinging to him, but he pulls away before we lose control again. "Food. Now. Steak?"

"Mmm, okay."

"Stop trying to manipulate our agenda by looking at me that way."

"What way am I looking at you?"

"You know damned well what you're doing to me." He takes my hand and pushes it against the hard column of his erection. "Any questions?"

I squeeze him. "That feels uncomfortable."

"Tormenting your Dom, sweetheart? Are you trying to top from the bottom? Because that could get you a very sore ass later."

I'm almost ashamed by how aroused I am at the thought of him spanking me.

"Don't do that."

"What did I do?"

"Look away in shame because you like the idea of being spanked. Don't ever be ashamed of the things you want. And don't ever hold back from telling me what you want."

"It might take some time before I feel comfortable asking for those things."

"We'll get there, love." He kisses me. "All in good time."

"What did you mean when you said 'top from the bottom'?"

"That's a Dom/sub thing when the sub tries to take control of the Dom. I don't recommend it, my sweet."

He attempts a stern face, but his eyes twinkle with pleasure and delight. He's happy to be able to speak freely about these things, and that makes me happy, too.

"Tonight, I want to see your eyes, Nat, without the contacts. Will you give me that?"

"Yes," I whisper.

He kisses me again and then withdraws his phone to place the food order. It arrives a short time later, and we eat in silence, the anticipation building with every minute that goes by. I'm almost too nervous and excited to eat. But knowing I need the fuel, I consume half of my dinner without tasting much of anything before pushing the rest across the table to him.

He eats all of his and half of mine.

Apparently, I'm the only one too nervous to eat much.

After we do the dishes, Flynn says he wants to take a shower. "I'll be quick so you can use the bathroom."

I refill my wineglass and take advantage of the alone time to get my head together and calm down. No matter what happens tonight, it's still Flynn and me and no one else. There's nothing to worry about. I already know I'll probably love everything he does to me, even if the context has changed.

He comes out fifteen minutes later, his hair damp, his face freshly shaven, a towel wrapped around his waist. "All yours."

I swallow the last of my wine and turn to him. "Thanks." I feel his eyes on me as I walk into the bedroom and then the bathroom, which is lit by candles. He has filled the tub for me, and I'm touched by the thoughtful gesture. He knows how much I love that tub. As I remove my clothes and put up my hair to keep it dry, my hands tremble ever so slightly. I have twenty minutes until our "appointment." I spend half of those minutes in the tub, soaking in the warm water, trying to relax. I shave my legs and then contemplate the hair between my legs. Part of Flynn's fantasy was to shave me there. Does he want to do it himself, or would he mind if I do it?

As I sit on the side of the tub and lather the area with soap, I decide I'm willing to risk the potential punishment to make one of his fantasies come true.

I've left my phone where I can see the time. At five minutes to eight, I get out of the tub, towel myself dry and wrap the towel around my body. Standing before the mirror, I permanently remove the contact lenses I've worn for cosmetic reasons since I changed my name and became Natalie. As always, the rare sight of my green eyes is a reminder of how far I've come since I left April behind.

Despite the long road I've traveled since then, she's still part of me. Her heart still beats inside me. Her trauma is with me always but no longer defines me. I'm determined to live my life as I see fit, without giving the man who ruined April's life any more power than he's already had.

I brush my teeth and hair, cover my body in scented lotion and take the deep, cleansing breaths Curt taught me to use whenever I feel overwhelmed or anxious. I'm neither of those things now. I'm fearless and determined—and extremely aroused from thinking about this all day. I bring the candles from the bathroom with me and place them on the bedside table, before assuming the position he has requested—on my knees, hands folded and head down.

And then I wait.

CHAPTER 8

Natalie

And I wait. My knees begin to hurt, but I stay where I'm supposed to be as I wonder what kind of game he's playing. Is making me wait part of it? The longer I stay there, on my knees, awaiting his arrival, the more turned on I seem to get. I'm throbbing between my legs and my nipples are tight, perhaps from the chill of being right out of the tub and naked. But I know that's not why. My entire body is alive with anticipation.

Right when I think I can't take the waiting any longer, he appears in the doorway. He closes the door, leaving Fluff in the hall. Her plaintive whimpers tug at my heart, but she can't be in here for this. She'd go ballistic. She whines for a few seconds before seeming to get it's pointless to protest. I picture her on the floor, head on her paws, watching the door.

My head is down, as instructed, so I see his feet first. Have I ever noticed before how big they are? The thought nearly makes me laugh, and my ass tingles at the thought of the punishment I might receive for laughing right now.

"You look lovely, sweetheart."

"Thank you, Sir."

"Are you nervous, Natalie?"

"No, Sir."

"Are you lying?"

"No, Sir."

His low chuckle makes me smile, but I don't let him see that. I feel his hand stroking my hair and then his finger on my shoulder, his touch so light I barely feel it, but it sets me on fire nonetheless. I shudder and try to maintain my position until he tells me what he wants.

"Are you aroused, Natalie?"

"Yes, Sir."

"Do you remember your safe word?"

"Fluff, Sir. As well as yellow to slow down and red to stop."

"Very good. Sit up taller now and look at me."

I do as he asks, and that's when I see he's naked and fully aroused. My mouth waters at the sight of his beautiful body, hard and strong and ready for me.

He takes me by the chin to tilt my face up more and studies my eyes. "They're lovely, Natalie. Thank you for letting me see them."

"You're welcome, Sir."

"Stroke me, Natalie. Use your hand and mouth."

I'm thrilled to get my hands on him, to make him feel as good as he makes me feel every time he touches me. I stroke him the way he's taught me to, aggressively, keeping my hand wrapped tightly around him. Then I take the wide head into my mouth and suck while I lash him with my tongue.

"Yes," he says on a hiss, "like that. Just like that."

Knowing I'm pleasing him is the greatest thrill I've ever experienced, a natural high. I open my mouth wider and let him slide in deeper, controlling my gag reflex to let him into my throat.

"Swallow," he says harshly, his hands pulling tightly on my hair.

I swallow twice, making him groan. Then he withdraws so quickly, I nearly topple over.

Flynn catches me and helps me up.

"Why did you stop?"

"You don't ask questions when we're playing, sweetheart. You can ask them later, but not now."

"Do I get punished for asking?"

"Do you want to be punished?"

I shrug as I look up at him, going for the picture of innocence.

Growling, he turns me to face the bed. "Bend over, sweetheart, and put your elbows on the mattress."

I prop myself on my elbows and drop my head, waiting, tingling...

His hand on my bottom makes me gasp. My every nerve ending hovers at the surface of my skin, electrifying me. He squeezes and strokes my cheeks, spreading them and testing the wetness between them where he discovers the impact this is having on me.

"Talk to me, Nat. How're you feeling?"

"Hot."

"Do you want me to turn the fan on?"

"Not that kind of hot."

His fingers slide into me from behind. "This kind?"

"Yes. *Sir.*" Something buzzes an instant before it connects with my most sensitive place. It takes me right to the edge of ecstasy.

"Don't come, Nat. Your orgasm belongs to me and only me."

God… I grit my teeth, trying to hold back as the vibrating thing connects again. It feels… I don't have the words. "Flynn…"

His hand cracks against my bottom.

When it becomes too heavy to hold up any longer, I drop my head to my hands as the flash of pain turns to heat that spreads through me like wildfire.

"What do you call me here?"

"Sir. I call you Sir."

"Four more spanks to help you remember my name. Are you ready?"

"Y-yes, Sir."

"What's your safe word?"

"Fluff."

"Do you need it?"

"No, Sir."

He bends over me to drag his lips down my backbone. "You're doing great, Nat. I'm so proud of you." To punctuate his words, his hand comes down on my bottom, in the same spot as before, and the flash of pain makes me gasp. Then he switches sides for the next two before returning to the original spot for the fifth one.

His hard penis is wedged between my cheeks as he squeezes and strokes them.

I'm dying for him. I want him inside me, thrusting and driving me to the orgasm I crave. His fingers again slide through the dampness between my legs. "Tell me what you want, Natalie."

"You. I want you."

"How do you want me?"

"Inside me. I need to come."

"Will you always tell me what you want?"

"Yes." He pinches my clit but doesn't give me permission to come. It takes all my concentration to hold back the orgasm that's trying to break free. I'm lost in the moment, in the sea of sensation, carried away by desire.

His hands are on my hips when he pushes into me, giving me all of him in one deep stroke that makes me burn as I stretch to accommodate him. He reaches around and applies the vibrating thing to my clit again while holding perfectly still inside me.

I'm going to die from the need to let go of the pressure that's building. I've never felt this sort of desperate need for fulfillment before. I'm grasping the comforter so tightly, my hands have begun to ache. Then he suddenly withdraws, and I collapse onto the bed, my entire body pulsating.

"Turn over, sweetheart. I want to see your face."

He helps me to turn over, brushing my hair back from my face. "Hi," he says.

"Hi."

"How're you doing?"

"I'd be better if you'd let me come. Sir."

When he smiles, his eyes twinkle. I like the way happiness looks on him. He holds up his hand where I see something attached to his index finger. "What do you think of my little friend here?"

"I'd like him better if *he'd* let me come. Sir."

"Are you looking for some more punishment, my love?"

"Perhaps I am."

"Are you enjoying this?"

"Define *enjoying*."

"I've never loved you more than I do right now, Natalie. Seeing you willing to try, enjoying yourself so much…"

"Now you want to talk, when you've got me ready to explode?"

"Patience, my love." He begins to kiss my belly, paying attention to each of my ribs. "I promise it'll be worth it." Continuing down, he nibbles on my hipbone, all the while dragging his fingers lightly over my abdomen.

What should tickle doesn't. It only takes my arousal to yet another level. I squirm on the bed, trying to get closer to him.

"Stay still, sweetheart, and spread your legs."

I ease my feet apart.

"More. I want them as wide as they'll go." He looks down to watch and his eyes go wide. "You shaved…"

"Yes. Sir. Does that please you?"

"You're not asking questions, remember?"

Moaning, I let my head fall back to the bed.

"Put your arms over your head."

I raise both arms and lay them on the bed behind me.

He stands and drags his gaze from my face to my breasts and below. "Your pussy is so wet, it's dripping." His finger moves over my inner thigh, and that's when I realize it's wet, too.

I'm mortified and close my eyes so he can't see that.

"No," he says. "You'll never be embarrassed by the desire you feel for me. Do you understand?"

"Yes, Sir."

"Say it. Say I'll never be ashamed by the desire I feel for my husband."

"I-I'll never be ashamed of the desire I feel for my husband."

"Or my Dom."

"Or my Dom."

"Put your hands under your knees and hold them open for me."

My hands are sweaty and trembling as I grasp my legs.

He bends over me, touching me only with his tongue, lapping up the wetness but avoiding the one place I need him most.

"What do you want, sweetheart?"

"You. Inside me. *Please.*" I roll my hips higher, trying to get him to focus.

He takes advantage of the opportunity to spank me, reminding me again of who's in charge. Then he's back inside me and the vibrator is on my clit, the combination taking me up again so quickly I can't seem to get air to my lungs.

"Come, Natalie." As he says the word, he pinches my clit, and I come, screaming and thrashing as he continues to press into me, withdrawing and driving in again until he's coming, too.

I release my legs because I can't hold them any longer. My thighs are quivering, and every inch of my body is vibrating.

Flynn holds me close, kissing me everywhere he can reach. "Shhh, sweetheart."

He kisses my face, and I feel dampness. My tears.

"It's okay. I'll never forget the expression on your face when you came undone. You were so beautiful."

"I-I… It was…"

He frames my face and uses his thumbs to wipe away my tears. "Tell me."

"Incredible."

"Your favorite word to describe me. I like that."

I bite my lip and nod. "It fits."

Flynn turns on his side, taking me with him, our bodies still joined. He keeps his arms around me, stroking my hair and rubbing my back. "Are you okay?"

I nod.

"I need words, Nat."

"I'm good. Great, in fact."

"So you liked what we did?"

"You couldn't tell?"

"Yes," he says, laughing, "I could tell, but I want you to say the words. This is no place for virtuousness."

"Virtuous. That's the word Leah used to describe me because I wasn't willing to have sex with just anyone."

"She didn't know why."

"No. She didn't know I was waiting for you."

"Nat… You're so sweet and so sexy. The way you looked on your knees waiting for me… God, that was hot. I'll never forget it."

"Why did you make me wait so long?"

"Anticipation makes everything more intense."

"I wondered if that was why."

"By thinking about it all day, we were both on the razor's edge before we stepped foot in here." He kisses my forehead and continues to stroke my hair. He's in full caretaker mode now. "You were going to tell me if you liked what we did."

"I loved it. I loved turning over control of my pleasure to you and knowing you'd make it great for me."

"I'll always make it great for you. You can count on that."

"Tell me the truth about something."

"Anything."

"Did you go easy on me tonight?"

"Easy?"

"You know what I'm asking, Flynn."

"I told you we'd start slowly."

"And it was good for you, too?"

"Walking in here and seeing you in position… I'll never forget my first sight of you submitting to me so willingly and perfectly. I've never been more turned on in my life. Christ, Nat, if it'd been any better, I might've died from the pleasure."

"Please don't do that. I need you here with me."

"I'm right here, and I'm not going anywhere. There's nowhere else I'd rather be."

CHAPTER 9

Flynn

Before we leave the apartment in the morning, I prepare a text that I plan to send to Natalie while we're in the car on the way to Teterboro.

When the plane reaches cruising altitude, get up from your seat and go into the bedroom. Remove all your clothes and get on the bed facedown. I want two pillows propped under your hips so your luscious ass is the first thing I see when I walk in the door. Present that ass to me to do with as I please.

Holy shit, if writing the text makes me this hard, what will it feel like to walk into the bedroom on the plane to see her posed for me? While this is very new to Natalie, it's new to me to be doing it with someone I love as much as I do her. The love makes it much more intense and exciting than it's ever been before.

All morning, I've thought about how she looked on her knees for me last night, how sweetly submissive she'd been. I'd been on the lookout for any signs of trouble in the form of flashbacks or triggers, but there'd been nothing but pleasure. She'd loved it.

We woke wrapped up in each other, and I made slow, lazy love to my gorgeous wife, delaying my own pleasure until she'd come twice. She probably thinks we're done for the time being after that. I can't wait to see her reaction to my text.

When we're packed up and ready to go, I alert the security detail. They pick us up in my garage a short time later and whisk us away in a black SUV with tinted windows. I much prefer to drive myself, but the upside of being driven is I get to snuggle with my wife in the backseat. The window between the front and backseats is closed, giving us some privacy.

Fluff is wedged between us, snoring like a buzz saw as usual.

"It feels like I'm really leaving this time," Natalie says when we're on the Hudson Parkway headed for the George Washington Bridge. The traffic is heavy but moving.

"How do you mean?"

"Last time I left New York, there was still a possibility I might come back to school and my apartment."

"We can send movers to your apartment to get the last of your stuff."

"That would be good."

"Did you send the email to Mr. Poole?"

She nods. "This morning. He wrote back pretty quickly, thanking me for letting them know and offering me a severance package that includes the salary I would've made if I'd finished out my contract."

"That's fantastic, sweetheart. That's the least of what they owe you."

"I guess."

"You're not happy about it?"

"It just feels weird to take all that money for not doing my job."

"Natalie, what Mrs. Heffernan did to you was wrong. It was borderline illegal, and the board knows that. If we chose to sue them, they could potentially be on the hook for millions. Buying out your contract is more than fair. In fact, it was the very least they could do."

"The upside is I'll be able to pay off my student loans myself, which is important to me."

"Ummm, about that…"

She spins in her seat to look at me, disturbing Fluff, who lets out a grunt of annoyance. "What?"

"I, um… You're going to be mad."

"Did you pay off my loans?"

"I, well… Yes, I did."

"Flynn! I told you I didn't want you to do that!"

"I know, honey, and I only did it so you wouldn't worry about it. You lost your job. How were you going to make the payments?"

"I would've figured something out. Eventually."

"In the meantime, you would've missed payments and your credit would be affected. I didn't want that for you."

"So you went behind my back and did something I specifically asked you *not* to do?"

"I took care of my wife."

"I agreed to be submissive to you in the bedroom, but *only* in the bedroom."

"You think that's what this is? Me dominating you?"

"That's how it seems to me."

"Well, it's not. It's me taking care of you."

"It's you doing something I told you *not* to do."

"Put yourself in my place, Nat. If I'm stressing out about something you can easily fix, what would you do?"

"I'd respect your wishes."

"Well, sorry to be such a bastard that I couldn't stand to see you upset about something I could fix for you with a phone call."

"I'm going to reimburse you."

"No, you're not."

"*Yes*, I am!"

"If you think I'm going to take your money, you're crazy."

"But I'm expected to take yours like the dutiful little wife?"

"Now you're just trying to piss me off."

"Good, then we're both pissed off."

As much as I wish I hadn't made her mad, I love that she feels free to say anything she wants to me. I love that she's mad at me. I'm far more accustomed to women who go out of their way to please me rather than challenge me and risk losing my affection. None of them ever figured out that all I really wanted was for them to be *real* with me. With Natalie, it's as real as it gets. And she's furious with me. I can tell by the rigid set to her shoulders as she stares out the passenger-side window.

I reach for her hand. "I'm sorry, Nat."

She pulls her hand free. "No, you're not."

She's so cute when she's pissed. "I'm honestly sorry that I did something you told me not to do and that it upset you."

"Save it. You're just sorry you got caught."

I decide this would be the perfect time to send the text I've drafted. I press Send and wait for the chime of her phone.

She pulls it from her pocket, reads the text and then looks at me, incredulous. "Are you *for real* right now?"

"As real as it gets. You know how to say no. If I don't hear the word, I expect you to follow my instructions." I lean in close so I can see her green eyes, so different from what I'm used to but still my Nat. "To. The. Letter."

She shakes her head and resumes giving me the cold shoulder as she stares out the window. In this case, silence is golden. She doesn't say the word that would put a stop to my plans before they get started.

I flatten my palm over my coat pocket, where I've zipped the items I brought from my stash in New York. She has no idea what she's in for on this flight.

Natalie

He's crazy if he thinks I'm going to have sex with him after finding out he went against my wishes and paid off my loans. I'm appreciative of his desire to care for me and take away my worries. He's incredibly generous and thoughtful. But it worries me that he thinks it's okay to do something I specifically asked him *not* to do—without even talking to me about it first.

That's a dangerous precedent, even more so than his propensity for buying me extravagant gifts. I have to make him understand that I won't put up with him disregarding my wishes on important matters. That's not the kind of marriage I want to have. We're capable of better than that.

I want two pillows propped under your hips so your luscious ass is the first thing I see when I walk in the door. Present that ass to me to do with as I please.

I want to growl from the frustration that accompanies the slow drumbeat of desire that has me shifting in my seat. He knows exactly what he's doing to me with that text, which he obviously prepared in advance and then sent while we were in the middle of an argument. Does he think that scrambling my brain with sex will make me forget I'm annoyed with him?

Well, his plan is working, because rather than thinking about how angry I am, I'm thinking about my ass presented to him as his own personal plaything. I recall the times he's touched me there before and how much I loved it. I admit to being intensely curious about what he has planned.

We don't say another word to each other as we cross the bridge into New Jersey and arrive at the airport a short time later. We're loaded onto the plane with the usual efficiency, and greeted by yet another flight attendant who tries to pretend she's not freaking out that Flynn Godfrey is on her plane.

With Fluff on my lap, I settle into the seat by the window so I can continue to watch the world go by while trying to figure out what to do about my current dilemma. Do I give him what he wants even after he directly went against my wishes? If I give in to him now, will that be rolling over? Or can I separate the sex from the larger life issue that now stands between us?

I'm extremely confused but also extremely turned on by the demand he has made of me via text message.

The flight attendant offers drinks, and Flynn requests Bloody Marys for both of us. I've never had one, but I'm willing to try one if it means I don't have to speak to him to tell him I don't want it. I want him to admit he was wrong to pay off those loans without talking to me about it first. After the drinks are served, the attendant tells us she'll be back after takeoff to check on us.

I have to admit I like the taste of the spicy drink as well as the heat of the liquor as it travels through my veins.

As the plane races down the runway and soars into the sky, my heart begins to thud in my chest, again like a bass drumbeat that echoes in my ears and pulses in my throat. Every pleasure point in my body is on full alert, beating in sync with the drum. With the plane gaining altitude by the second, I'm running out of time. Any minute now, the seat belt sign will go off and I'll have to either use my safe word or follow his orders.

The chime of the seat belt sign turning off ricochets through the cabin like a gunshot, startling me even though I knew it was imminent.

"Good afternoon from the cockpit, Mr. and Mrs. Godfrey, and welcome aboard. You're now free to move around the cabin. We expect a relatively smooth ride but ask you to use caution as unexpected turbulence is always a possibility. For now, sit back, relax and enjoy our five-hour flight to Los Angeles."

Decision time. As if there'd ever been a decision to make. I will submit to him sexually, but I'll not be submissive in the rest of our life. If he won't take my money, I'll find a way to reimburse him the same way he went about paying off the loans in the first place—behind his back.

I can feel Flynn's eyes on me, waiting to see what I'll do.

I unbuckle my seat belt and move carefully to settle Fluff's sleeping body in my seat. Without so much as a glance at my husband, I make my way to the back of the plane to follow his orders. I use the bathroom to freshen up before removing my clothes and crawling onto the bed, reaching for the pillows to position them under my hips.

Part of me can't believe I'm doing this. A month ago, I was untouched by any man other than the one who attacked me so long ago. Now here I am, preparing to offer my ass to my husband. It's surreal, to say the least.

I lean over the pillows, my legs parted to hold me up, my head resting against my forearms. I try not to think about what he'll see when he comes into the room. Once again, the position coupled with the anticipation has the intended effect on me. My entire body is humming with desire.

Just as I'm beginning to wonder if he'll make me wait as long as he did last night, the door opens.

My skin prickles as I imagine him looking at me laid out for him this way. I wonder what he's thinking, if he's pleased with what he sees. The door closes, and the snick of the lock sliding into place makes my heart pound. It's the not knowing, the wondering, the speculating, the desperate desire that make me crazy. It's a heady combination, as he well knows.

He doesn't say a word, and if he's doing anything, I can't tell because he's doing it in utter silence. The only sound is that of the low hum of the plane engines. My legs begin to tremble from the effort to hold myself up and open to his perusal. I *know* he's looking. I can *feel* his eyes on me, which somehow makes this hotter than the hottest sex we've ever had, and he hasn't even touched me yet.

The scrape of his zipper breaks the silence and ramps up my already rapid heartbeat. Again the bass drumbeat thumps through me, awakening every part of my body in preparation for him.

By the time I feel air pass over me as he approaches, I'm ready to weep from the relief. Waiting for him to touch me, I break out in goose bumps all over.

My nipples are so tight, they ache, as does my clit, which throbs in time with the drumbeat. Even the soles of my feet are in on this, vibrating and tingling.

Oh *God*. Is that his tongue on my ass? *Yes!* Oh my God… I can't breathe. I can't think. I can't do anything but feel as he traces a path up one side and down the other. He touches me with nothing other than his tongue, which is more than enough to make me whimper from the need for more. I don't even know what I need. I just need *more*.

Then his hands are on me, holding me open to his tongue. I can't believe he is actually licking me *there*. And holy shit does it feel amazing. His tongue is everywhere, circling, delving, coaxing. I'm shaking like a tree in a storm, on the verge of begging him to do anything he can think of to me, as long as it slakes the desperate ache.

And then he's gone, leaving me hanging on the precipice of something huge. I want to cry from the frustration, from being left unfulfilled and needy. I hear the click of a cap opening and the sound of something liquid. He knew what he was doing by putting me in this position so I won't know what to expect next.

His finger presses against my back entrance, insistent and determined to breach the tight muscles.

My impulse is to fight back, to deny him, but he doesn't take even a silent no for an answer. His finger slides in as far as it can go as my muscles tighten around it. Like the other times we've done this, I can't deny the dark, forbidden thrill of it. Before him, before us, I wouldn't have thought I could enjoy being touched or penetrated there. But enjoy is too tame a word for how it feels to allow him to take me there, to welcome it, to crave it.

He withdraws his finger, and I want to cry out from the loss, but I maintain my silence. Unless he speaks directly to me, I'm not to question him.

He's back again, this time with two fingers, and the fit is decidedly tighter, less comfortable. The bite of pain causes my clit to throb, which surprises me. How can pain and pleasure coexist?

He strokes his fingers in and out.

I widen my legs and move my ass in time with his strokes. I begin to realize I could come from this and have to remind myself I'm not allowed to.

"Talk to me, Nat. How does it feel?"

"I'm not talking to you."

He spanks my ass with his free hand—harder than he did last night. "What goes on out there does *not* come in here, you got me?"

"Yeah."

"Excuse me?"

"Yes," I say through gritted teeth. I'm still so angry with him.

"Yes, who?"

"*Sir*. Yes, Sir."

"Don't get sassy with me, Natalie, or I'll have to spank this sexy ass until it's so sore you won't be able to sit for a week without remembering how it got so sore."

I have so much I'd like to say to that, but I bite my tongue. I have a feeling I'll be sore enough from the other things he has planned without adding that pain to the mix.

"Tell me what I'm doing to you right now."

He wants me to say the words? Of course he does. "You're putting your fingers in me."

"Where am I putting them?"

"In my ass."

"And what am I doing with them?"

"You're stroking me."

"What's the word I would use?"

Though I'm not a prude about swearing, I've trained myself to avoid those words in my career as an elementary school teacher—training that is no longer necessary. "Fucking."

"That's right. Now say the whole thing."

"You're… You're fucking my ass with your fingers."

"Mmm," he says, nibbling on my right ass cheek, "I love when you talk dirty to me."

I roll my eyes, which of course he can't see. I only talk dirty to him when he makes me.

He gets me to say the words, and then he's gone again, leaving me trembling and weak with need. I've never felt quite so needy in my life. It's the not knowing what to expect that has me right on the edge, ready to implode. I hear the click of the cap again and the squishy sound of liquid. *What is he doing?*

Then I feel pressure again, only this is something other than fingers. The pressure is intense.

"Push back, sweetheart."

"W-what is it?"

"No questions, remember?"

I exhale before drawing in another deep breath, trying to breathe my way through the pain of my muscles fighting the intrusion. Whatever it is, it's much bigger and wider than his fingers were. I'm not at all sure I can take it.

"That's it, sweetheart, you're doing great. This is the widest part now. You can do it."

Wider? How is that possible? All of my focus and attention are on the tight stretch of my ass struggling to take the object, which is how he is able to catch me completely off guard when he chooses that moment to stroke my clit. Forgetting all about where we are, I scream from the bolt of pleasure that takes my mind off the intrusion in back and allows him to fully seat the object in my ass.

Oh. My. *God.* If he doesn't let me come, right now, I'm going to lose my mind.

"You did so great, Nat. I wish you could see how amazing your ass looks stretched around the plug. It's the sexiest thing I've ever seen."

I feel the head of his penis pressing into me, and the fit is so tight because of the plug that I don't think I can take him.

"Easy, sweetheart. You can do it. Relax and let me in." He goes slowly, giving me small increments, stretching me beyond the point of pain and into a realm I never knew existed until he showed me how it could be. Then the object in my ass begins to vibrate, and I come undone.

Flynn is right there with me, driving into me hard and fast as I yield to him. It's the hottest thing I've ever experienced. I give myself over to him completely. I'm his in every possible way, to do with as he pleases because I know that whatever pleases him will please me, too.

His hands slide under me to cup my breasts and tweak my nipples, and I can't hold back any longer. The orgasm crashes over me like a huge wave, sucking me under and stealing the breath from my lungs as every part of my body reacts to the overwhelming release.

Flynn pinches my nipples again, triggering a second smaller orgasm, as he comes with a groan. The plug makes it so I feel everything so much more acutely, including the heat of his release that fills me deep inside. He comes down on me so his chest is pressed against my back, his hands still cupping my breasts.

"I don't recall giving you permission to come."

"I couldn't help it."

"You're going to need to learn to help it."

"How do I do that?"

"With practice. For now, you've earned a punishment." His words, whispered close to my ear, make me tremble. He pulses inside me, reminding me he's still there, as if I could forget. Raising himself up, he places his hands on my hips and withdraws from me slowly, tapping on the plug, which makes me gasp from the sensation that travels through me. "Your punishment will be keeping the plug in place until we get home to LA."

"That's hours from now!"

"Which will give you plenty of time to think about how you'll better control yourself next time." He removes the pillows from under my hips. "Turn over. I want to see your face."

When I'm on my back looking up at him, he kisses me. His erection is already coming back to life between us. "That was so hot, sweetheart. I love your sweet ass. Did it feel good for you, too?"

"Again, you have to ask? The screaming orgasm wasn't proof enough?"

"I like to hear the words."

"I loved it."

"I'm glad to hear that. Were you scared at all?"

"Not in the way that you mean. I was anxious because I didn't know what to expect and couldn't see what you were doing."

"That's part of it. Denying one sense heightens the others. Because blindfolding is a hard limit for you, the position today is a way around that. You can't see me, but you're not in the dark."

"You're very clever."

"I've been practicing for years. I've learned a few tricks along the way."

It pains me to think of him practicing with other women.

"What? Something just upset you."

"It's just the thought of you doing this with other women..." I close my fist and rest it on my breastbone. "Hurts right here, as unreasonable as that may be."

"It's not unreasonable. The thought of any other man touching you makes me crazy, so I get it. But you should know, every woman who came before you was the dress rehearsal for the main event. They were getting me ready for you."

"That's sweet of you to say, but if we ever run into any of them, don't tell me. I'm better off not being able to picture them."

"I thought you knew everything about me before we met?"

It's funny now that I thought I knew him so well before we met, when I knew only what was reported about him. The real man is so much more complex than even the paparazzi who stalk him relentlessly could ever begin to imagine. "I know about the famous ones. I'm sure there were legions of others."

"Not *legions*..."

I poke his belly, making him grunt with laughter.

"You're the only one who has truly mattered, Nat. You have to know that."

"I do, but I never get tired of hearing it."

"I'll have to tell you more often, then." He rubs his stomach and stretches. "I don't know about you, but I'm starving. Want to get up and eat and watch a movie?"

"How am I supposed to do all that with this *thing* in my butt?"

"You'll get used to it."

"*When* will I get used to it?"

"You earned this punishment fair and square, sweetheart. Don't make me add to it by complaining about it."

"I think it's only fair that you should have to do this sometime so you know how it feels."

"Nope."

"That's so hypocritical."

"It's not something that interests me. It *is* something that interests you. Thus there's nothing hypocritical about it."

"You were a lawyer in your past life, weren't you?"

He gets out of bed and pulls a pair of gym shorts from his backpack. "Funny, my mother used to say the same thing when I would argue everything to death with her and my dad."

"I can so picture that."

"Come on, lazy girl. Time to get up and have dinner with your husband." He disappears into the adjoining bathroom to wash up.

I move carefully, aware every second of the plug that's lodged in my ass. At least it's no longer vibrating. I'm thankful for small favors. In the bag I brought with me to New York, I find clean panties, a pair of sweats and a long-sleeve T-shirt that I put on without a bra. There is definitely something to be said for traveling in luxurious comfort. The cross-country flights are beginning to feel routine to me.

He comes out, and I take a turn in the bathroom. With my pants down, I turn to look in the mirror at the plug, which is red. The flat end is visible between my cheeks, and the sight of it there is oddly arousing.

I join Flynn in the salon, sitting slowly and gingerly. When I catch him smiling at me, I scowl in return, which only makes him laugh. I'm glad one of us thinks this is funny.

The flight attendant comes out with menus and wine lists for each of us.

"I'm in the mood for seafood and chardonnay," he says after a quick perusal. "What do you think, sweetheart?"

I study the menu while the attendant waits to take my order. When I decide, I look up at her, but before I can give her my order, the words are stolen from my lips as the plug begins to vibrate again.

"Nat?" Flynn asks, the picture of innocence.

"I… um, I'll have the same."

"Very good," the perky woman says, taking our menus. "I'll be right back with your wine."

"I can't believe you did that," I whisper to him the minute we're alone, which is when the plug miraculously stops vibrating.

"What did I do?"

"Don't act all innocent. You turned on the *thing* and made it so I couldn't speak."

"How does a plug in your ass make it so you can't speak?"

"Don't say that out loud! She might hear you."

His low rumble of laughter makes me want to smack him.

"You're enjoying this, aren't you?"

"You bet your *ass* I am."

"Enough already with my ass."

"I'm just getting started on your ass, sweetheart."

"Clearly, I've made a deal with the devil."

"You're just figuring that out now?"

The flight attendant returns, bringing our wine and salads. I take a sip from my glass and nearly choke when the vibrating begins anew. Somehow, I manage to swallow the wine. "*Flynn!* Stop!"

He's laughing too hard to speak.

Then the buzzing shifts up a notch, becoming more intense and incredibly arousing. God, how is it possible that I'm getting so turned on from a vibrating plug in my ass? It's unfathomable that I should like this as much as I do. Just as I'm really getting into it, the buzzing stops, and I collapse into my chair.

"Eat your dinner, Nat."

"I hate you right now."

"No, you don't. You love me."

"First you pay off my student loans behind my back, and now this."

"I'm sorry, honey. I'm an awful bastard."

"Well, at least you know it."

"You're still mad about the loans?"

"Yes, I'm still mad. You can't sex me out of being mad at you."

"Damn. It was worth a try." He turns in his seat so he's facing me. "Nat, listen, I know you're pissed about the loans, and I get why. I suppose I can't have it both ways—"

"Have what both ways?"

"I love that you couldn't care less about my money, but with that comes your fierce independence, which I also respect."

"I'm not with you because of your money."

"I know that, sweetheart. That's what I'm saying. I appreciate that you don't care about the money, but the fact is, I have more of it than I can ever spend in a lifetime. Hell, in two lifetimes. And seeing you worried or upset about paying off those loans after you lost your job because of me… I had to fix that for you. I hope you can try to understand my perspective."

"It was nice of you. I won't deny that, but the *way* you did it was wrong. We talked about it, I told you I wanted some time to figure out how to handle the loans, and you disregarded my wishes. I'm not going to put up with that, Flynn. I don't care who you are."

"Come here."

"What? We're going to eat, and we're having a conversation."

"Come. *Here.*"

Aggravated, I get up from my seat and stand in front of his. "I'm here. What do you want?"

He reaches for me and brings me down on his lap, the plug bouncing off his thighbone and making me gasp from the sensations.

"What has gotten into you?"

"You have. You're so deep inside me, I don't know where I leave off and you begin." He kisses me. "What you just said…"

"What did I say?"

"'I don't care who you are.'"

"Don't take that the wrong way."

"I took it exactly the right way. You don't care who I am, and I love you for that. I love you so fucking much."

"You're crazy, you know that?"

“Maybe so, but you can’t know how precious it is for me to love a woman who would dare to say those words to me.”

“Have I earned another punishment?” I ask with a coy smile. I’m deeply moved by what he said and that he’s not afraid to tell me how he feels.

“Nah. I could never punish you for being the perfect woman for me. Besides, that’s in there, not out here. I’ll never punish you for something you do in our regular life. That’s not what we agreed to.”

“Then no more buzzing in the butt?”

“I never said that. That’s part of your punishment, which you earned in there.”

He cups my ass cheek and squeezes. “Knowing you’re wearing my plug is such a huge turn-on, sweetheart. It makes me so hot.”

“It makes me pretty hot, too, especially when you turn on the vibration.”

“So you like it?”

“I’ll never admit to that out of fear of being forced to regularly wear one in public.”

His satisfied grin is positively sinister. “Too late. You basically already admitted it.” His fingers delve deeper between my cheeks to press against the base of the plug.

“Flynn, stop. She’ll be back any second, and you’ll embarrass her.”

He swivels the chair so it faces away from the galley. “She can’t see what we’re doing.”

“Come on… Not out here.”

“Someday,” he says against my ear, “you may end up naked and plugged and bound in public for me.”

His words send a shudder through me, making me forget all about the four orgasms I’ve already had today. Suddenly, four is nowhere near enough.

“Someday isn’t today,” I manage to say, even though my throat has gotten tight and my mouth has gone dry at the thought of being on display in the way he described.

“Does the thought of that turn you on?”

“No.”

His erection presses against my bottom. “If I were to put my hand into your panties right now, would I discover you’re lying?”

"Don't do that."

"Answer the question."

"Maybe."

He laughs at my reply and hugs me tightly. "You can feel what the thought of that does to me."

"Is that your ultimate fantasy? To do that, with me, in public?"

"One of them."

"What're the others?"

"I'd so much rather show you than tell you."

"You just want me unprepared and unaware."

"Doesn't the not knowing make it so much hotter?"

"I'm afraid to agree with anything you say out of fear of encouraging you."

"There's no real fear, though, right?"

He's so sweet in his concern for me. "No real fear. Everything we've done has been… well… indescribable."

"Try."

"Try what?"

"To describe it."

"Like in actual words?"

"That'd be good."

"You like making me say things that I'd never ordinarily say, don't you?"

"Uh-huh." His hand inches up my thigh until my hand on top of it stops its progress. "I want to talk about it, all of it. The talking helps to build the trust between us. It makes it more intimate."

"I'll give you the words *only* if you let me reimburse you for the loans you paid off."

"You drive a hard bargain, my love, but you've got a deal. These had better be some really *good* words."

I lean in as close as I can get to him and let my lips brush against his ear. I love when he jolts and his arms tighten around me. "What we just did… I loved everything about it. I loved the anticipation, the not knowing what would happen, but also the knowing that you would touch me there."

"Where?" he asks gruffly. "Where did I touch you?"

"My ass." I draw out the S sound until he groans. "I couldn't believe you licked me there. It was so dirty but so hot, so incredibly hot. When you used your fingers…" I shimmy on his lap, making sure to press against him in all the right places. "I never would've expected to like that as much as I do. And the plug…" I exhale, making sure my breath floats over his ear. "That was… *is*… crazy. It was so tight when you…"

"Fucked you. Say it."

"When you fucked me. There was hardly enough room—"

"Stop."

I pull back so I can see his face, which is tight and tense. "What's wrong?"

"If you say another word, I'm going to fuck you again right here in this chair, which will certainly shock the flight attendant."

"So they were good words?" I ask innocently, thrilled to know I've completely undone him.

"They were fucking awesome words."

I return my lips to his ear. "After we eat, maybe I'll let you fuck me right here in this chair."

"Stop!"

Chapter 10

Flynn

Just when I think she can't possibly get any more perfect, she takes me apart, piece by piece, with a description of our lovemaking that sets me on fire. Hearing those words from her sweet mouth is one of the most incredibly arousing things I've ever experienced—second only to the sight of her gorgeous ass on full display for me earlier. That's something I'll never forget.

Watching her blossom into the amazing, sexy woman she was always meant to be has been one of the most satisfying experiences in my life. That she's been able to overcome her painful past and put her trust and well-being in my hands is something I'll never take for granted.

That's especially true after spending a very long day and night thinking I might've lost her forever.

The meal of broiled scallops, rice and vegetables is delicious, but I barely taste a bite as I satisfy one kind of hunger only so I'll have the strength to satisfy the other kind.

Natalie shares her scallops with Fluff, who stares at her adoringly, waiting for whatever scraps she chooses to share. She's serene and relaxed while I'm as tightly wound as I've ever been after listening to her description of our sex. I want to tell her to hurry up, to eat already and be done so we can get on with it, but I don't do that because I'm almost afraid to show her what she's started.

Eventually, the attendant comes to collect our plates and refills our wineglasses. "Can I get you anything else?"

"No, we're all set. You can take the rest of the flight off."

"Oh. Okay, just hit the call button if you need anything."

"We won't." Hopefully she gets the message to stay out. I won't be responsible for anything she sees if she doesn't take the hint.

She takes the dishes with her and closes the door.

"That was kinda rude," my lovely wife says.

"Come back over here."

"Now?"

"Right now."

Natalie secures her wine in one of the cup holders and comes over to stand in front of me. "You beckoned?"

"Take off your clothes."

"Here?"

"Right here."

She glances over her shoulder at the closed door to the galley. Worrying about the attendant coming back will make this more intense for her, so I don't allay her concerns.

"Natalie… I wasn't asking…"

She looks at me again, as if trying to gauge what's afoot. She has to know that she set me on fire with what she said to me. But because this is new to her, I feel the need to remind her that she still holds all the power. "You know how to say no."

For a long moment, I wait for her to say the word that will stop everything.

After another tentative glance over her shoulder, she draws the T-shirt up and over her head, baring her breasts to my hungry gaze.

"Keep going."

The sweatpants travel slowly down her legs, inch by tantalizing inch, until she's left wearing only a skimpy pair of panties.

"Turn around."

She is hesitant but does as I request, but she's crossed her arms over her chest. That'll never do.

"Hands by your sides." I can almost see her gritting her teeth as she turns, bare breasted, to face the door that separates us from the flight attendant. Leaning forward, I run my hands from her calves to her thighs and up to cup her ass. The bright red base of the plug is visible through the thin layer of cloth that covers her.

"Flynn…"

"Shhh. No talking." I slide her panties down until they are snug against the bottom of her cheeks and make a circle of kisses on her bottom around the plug. I spread her cheeks, taking in the sight of her stretched to accommodate the wide girth of the medium-sized plug. I can't wait to move her up to the next size. All in good time.

Then I let my fingers slide through the flood of wetness to find her clit standing up at full attention. I'm satisfied to discover she's more than wet enough for what I have in mind. Her legs wobble.

While continuing to caress her clit, I put my arm around her waist to keep her from stumbling.

"Turn back toward me, sweetheart."

With her panties keeping her legs together, she moves stiffly.

"Take your panties off."

I can sense her hesitance as she bends to comply with my request. Any second now, she's sure the flight attendant is going to reappear. She's about to discover that the fear of getting caught can be a powerful aphrodisiac. I take advantage of the opportunity to remove my own clothes while keeping a close eye on her. I make sure to remove the remote for the plug from my pocket and place it under my leg so she can't see it. When she's standing upright, her panties on the floor, I hold out my hands to bring her onto my lap, straddling me.

Her hands land on my chest as she tries to find her balance. "Didn't we just do this?"

"That was before you talked dirty to me."

"You made me!"

I shrug as if that isn't true. I got exactly what I wanted—and then some. "Now you have to pay the consequences."

"This isn't fair."

"Are you looking for a spanking?"

"You can't spank me for doing what you told me to."

"I can spank you for doing it too well."

"There's no logic to that."

"Are you arguing with your Dom, little sub?"

"No."

"No, who?"

"Sir."

I fill my hands with her breasts and kiss a path up her neck to bite her earlobe. "I think you like pushing my buttons because you like being spanked."

"That's not true."

"Did I ask you a question? No, I didn't think so." She's so wet, I can feel her moisture collecting on the rigid length of my cock, which wants in on this—right now. "I want you to fuck me this time, Nat."

"Like this?"

"Just like this." I want to see the expression on her face when my cock squeezes into the tight space that's already compromised by the plug. I want to watch her come alive when the plug begins to vibrate. I want to suck on her nipples and completely overwhelm her senses.

She takes me in hand and guides me into her slick heat, coming down on me slowly, carefully. It's an effort for her to relax and allow me in when there's almost nowhere for me to go.

I grasp her ass cheeks and hold her open, hoping to ease the entry.

"I-I don't think I can," she says when she's only taken about half of me.

"Yes, you can." I stroke her clit and make her gasp. I also make her forget she's trying to resist me, allowing another inch to slide inside her. I love the way her head falls back in complete surrender and the way her breasts jut forward, riding the arch of her back. I can't resist the sweet temptation right in front of me. Cupping her left breast, I run my tongue around in circles and feel her inner muscles contract around my cock.

I draw her nipple into my mouth, sucking and tugging until it's hard and tight against my lips. Ever so gently, I begin to bite down on her nipple, giving her something else to think about other than the tight squeeze of my cock invading her.

Then her arms encircle my head, holding me to her chest. That's when I know she's on the verge of leaving all her worries behind and giving herself up to the moment. I reach under my leg for the remote and turn the plug on high. As the first vibrations register with her, she slams down on me, taking me to the root. She goes wild, crying out as her body adjusts to me. I wonder if she even knows she's having one orgasm after another. Between the tight grip of her muscles and the vibration that's right up against my cock, I'm fending off my own orgasm.

Time to bring her back to me. With my arms banding around her, I force her to be still and take her nipple back into my mouth, biting down again, and drawing a whimper from her that makes my cock expand inside her.

"Can't get bigger," she whispers. "No more." Her eyes are closed, her lips are parted, and a bead of sweat runs from her neck to the valley between her breasts. I'm completely and utterly mesmerized by her.

"Look at me, Natalie."

She forces her eyes open. They're glazed and unfocused. I wait until she blinks me into focus.

"How you doing?"

"I-I'm… I don't know."

"Feels good?"

"Feels full. Really, really full."

"What am I doing to you right now?"

"Fucking me with your great big dick."

Holy shit. She's incredible. Those words from that sweet, sweet mouth make me crazy. She gives me more than I ask for every damn time. "That's my girl," I say gruffly. "You know what I like. Now move your hips."

She rolls forward and then backward, sending me deeper than I already was.

"That's it. That's the way. Faster now."

Her hand curls around my neck, and she picks up the pace, the combination of her tight heat and the insistent vibration nothing short of combustible. When her eyes close and her head falls back again, she bites her lip. That's when I know she's trying not to come.

I reach between us and find her clit hard and full. The mere touch of my finger makes her gasp. "Not yet."

"Can't hold it back."

"Yes, you can. Don't stop." I leave my finger there to make sure that every forward stroke of her hips will bring her clit into contact with my finger.

"Please," she whispers.

"You can come now." I bring her lips down on mine to smother the sharp scream that accompanies her release. She thrashes against me, and I hold back as long as I can before I join her, letting go as she collapses into my arms, utterly spent. When I've recovered my breath, I pick her up and carry her into the bedroom, laying her down on the bed.

She opens her eyes and blinks twice.

"Welcome back."

"How do you do this to me every time?" Her voice sounds gravelly and rusty from screaming.

"What did I do?"

She laughs and shakes her head. "You know *just* what to do."

"Are you tired?"

"I'm wrecked. Utterly and completely ruined."

"Then I've done my job as your husband and as your Dom." I kiss her and look down at her, drinking in the sight of her flushed and worn and sweaty from our loving. Reluctantly, I withdraw from her. "Get some sleep. We still have a couple of hours to go."

"Only if you'll come sleep with me."

I have scripts to read, proposals to review… A million things I've let slide in the last few weeks. I'm so far behind, I may never catch up. But my wife wants me to sleep with her? I'm there.

"Let me clean up our clothes and check on Fluff. I'll be right back."

By the time I crawl into bed with her ten minutes later, she's out cold.

Natalie

It's raining when we arrive in LA, where we're met by Seth and Josh, who drive us home to Flynn's house in the Hollywood Hills. I guess his house is my house now, too, which reminds me of something I've wanted to ask him for a while now.

"Did Valerie live here?"

He pauses midway through opening a beer. "Not really. She never actually moved in. We spent most of the time we were married filming the only two movies we were in together back-to-back."

"So those aren't her plates? The sheets on the bed?"

"Mine and mine alone. Everything in this house is mine, and you should feel free to change up anything you want to make it yours, too."

"That's nice of you. Thank you." I pause before I ask the one question that has been weighing on me for days now. "If she never lived here, how did she know about the room in the basement?"

He puts the beer on the counter and leans his hip against it, crossing his arms. As always, the topic of Valerie raises his hackles. "After we wrapped the second film, we were talking about finally moving in together, officially, when I decided I should tell her about it. I showed her the room, which was much less elaborate then than it is now. Obviously, it was a huge mistake to take her down there, because she had no desire to understand me or what's important to me."

"She has no idea what she missed out on."

He stares at me in that intense way he does so well. "When you show me how badly you want to understand me, it gets me," he says softly, "right here." He lays his hand over his heart. "I actually *feel* it."

I go to him and kiss him, caressing the stubble on his jaw. "I know that feeling. I get it, too."

Putting his arms around me, he holds me for a long quiet moment.

"Have I completed my punishment?"

"Oh damn, I forgot all about that."

I raise my head, intending to chew him out for forgetting, but he's laughing. He hasn't forgotten anything.

"You've done a great job with your punishment, sweetheart."

"So how do I get this thing out of me?"

"Go into the bedroom and take off your clothes. Slide to the end of the bed with your legs as far apart as you can get them. I'll be right there to help you out."

"Are you serious? We've had sex—wild, monkey sex—three times today already. You're going to break me."

"Who said anything about having sex? You said you wanted the plug out. That's all we're doing."

Crossing my arms, I eye him skeptically. "Why do I find that hard to believe?"

He takes a drink of his beer. "I have no idea. Now isn't there something you're supposed to be doing?"

I shake my head in frustration and amusement. Clearly he enjoys keeping me off balance in this new arrangement of ours. Still wondering what he's up to, I go into the bedroom, where a rack of clothes is waiting for me—gorgeous dresses in various lengths and colors. And shoes… pair after pair of delicate, beaded, open-toed shoes, posed on top of their boxes.

"Flynn!"

He comes to the door, Fluff along with him. "What's wrong?"

"Nothing is wrong, but what's all this?"

"Tenley dropped that off for you. We've got the Oscar nominee luncheon Monday and the Nominees Night celebration at Spago Monday night. She'll be here that morning to help you get ready."

"Is there some sort of list I could get of all these events?"

"I'm sorry. Yes, of course. I'll ask Addie to get you something and make sure you're included on all the emails going forward." He pulls out his phone. "What's your address?"

"It was my school address. I need to get a new one."

"We'll set you up with a Quantum address. Addie will take care of that for us." He punches in a text and then grimaces. "Fuck."

"What?"

"Emmett texted me. The meeting with the FBI agent is on for Monday morning."

"Okay…"

"It's not okay. We had nothing to do with it, and they're wasting our time."

"Then we have nothing to worry about. Let's just talk to him and get it over with."

"It'll have to be early. I want you to have enough time to get ready for the luncheon."

"I can do early."

He sends off another text, presumably to Emmett, and puts the phone in his pocket. "I believe you were supposed to be doing something in here. I'll leave you to it."

"But… You still want to do that? Now?"

"Why not now? Your punishment has ended, and it's time."

"You're not angry? About the FBI?"

"No, I'm not. We didn't do anything, so we have nothing to be angry about, other than the inconvenience of it all. If you're asking if I'd ever take anger or frustration or anything like that out on you, the answer is a definitive no. If I were truly angry about anything, having to do with you or not, I'd never lay a hand on you. You have my word on that."

"Thank you for saying it, but I already knew that."

With a quick nod, he turns and heads for the door. "I'll be back. Be ready."

As an independent woman, it should raise my hackles to be told what to do in that brusque tone. But it doesn't raise my hackles. It turns me on because I know when he talks to me like that, pleasure will follow.

I go into the bathroom to brush my hair and teeth. Even though my body is sore and tired, I experience the now-familiar signs of arousal. I remove my clothes, and since I expect him to make me wait anyway, I decide to take a quick shower. After covering my body in the citrus-scented lotion that Flynn loves, I go to the bed and get into the position he's requested.

My bottom is at the edge, my legs are propped apart, and I'm staring at the ceiling, waiting. That's when the vibrating begins.

Damn him! He's taking full advantage right up to the bitter end. If the vibration weren't so arousing, I'd laugh at how he's playing the game. But there is nothing at all funny about the way the vibrating plug sets my body on fire. Even after everything we've already done today, I'm primed for more by the time he enters the room, stopping the vibration with his arrival.

He has also showered. His hair is damp, he's naked and fully aroused. "I love the way you do whatever I ask, that you're game for anything."

"I love that you're sharing this side of yourself with me."

"Even when I punish you by making you wear a plug for hours?"

"Even then."

"You've been a very good sport." He drops to his knees and flattens his hands on my inner thighs, pressing them farther apart.

I wince at the tug of overused muscles protesting the movement.

"Are you sore, sweetheart?"

"A little."

"We were kind of crazy today."

"We're newlyweds. We're supposed to be crazy."

"There's crazy—and then there's today. I don't want to push you too hard or too fast."

"I know how to put a stop to it if I need to."

"I like to hear you say that, to know you get it."

I feel the scrape of his stubble against my inner thigh.

My body immediately arches toward him. The impulse is automatic. I want to be close to him. I *need* to be close to him. He opens me to his tongue and strokes my tender skin gently, soothing as much as arousing. I'm floating on a wave of sensation, and then the buzzing begins again. The next stroke of his tongue takes me right to the edge of madness.

"Not yet," he whispers as he begins to pull on the plug, dislodging it and then reseating it. He does that again and again as he continues to tease my clit with his tongue.

I'm going to lose my mind if he keeps this up much longer. This is the slowest, easiest thing we've done all day and yet it's *more.* It's engaging every sense, every erogenous zone. My skin feels hot and too tight to contain all the things he's making me feel as the plug continues to move in and out of me until he removes it completely, replacing it with his fingers.

"You have permission to come, Natalie."

I explode, screaming and writhing, my hands fisting his hair to keep him from getting away.

Then he's screaming, too, and pulling away from me so abruptly that I come crashing back to earth to realize Fluff is attacking him.

"Fluff, *no*! Stop!" I jump from the bed on rubber legs that threaten to buckle under me to pull her off him. "Bad girl!"

"Oh my God, she bit me right on the ass!"

He spins around and tries to see behind him, his hard penis flopping as he jerks his body into contortions.

I can't help it. I begin to laugh. I laugh so hard that tears stream down my face and Fluff tries to lick them up, the way she's done so many times before. Those were heartbroken tears. These are joyful tears because my husband is so cute and funny as he tries to get a look at his wounded backside where there isn't so much as a mark.

"Don't worry," I say, gasping from laughing, "your career as a butt model hasn't been ruined."

"How can you laugh at a moment like this? She attacked me when I was going down on you! I had my fingers in your—"

I cuddle Fluff to my chest and put my hands over her ears. "Not in front of Fluff! You left the door open."

He advances toward us, a comically sinister expression on his face. "Are you saying it's my fault because I left the door open?"

"And you made me scream. You've known since day one that she's protective of me."

"She's certifiable!"

"She's my baby."

Fluff coos as I stroke her. "Naughty girl biting Daddy's booty. Those buns are insured for millions. You can't damage the merchandise."

"Do you know how close she came to my balls where our future children live?"

I bite my lip because I know he won't appreciate my laughter right now. "She's very sorry she bit you. Again."

"That's three times. You know what they say about three strikes and you're out?"

"If she's out, I'm out."

Through gritted teeth, he says, "Would you please remove her from our bedroom?"

"Don't worry, precious. Daddy's not really mad. You threatened his manhood, and boys are *really* funny about those kinds of threats. He understands that you were only protecting me." I kiss her face and send her to go lie down in the living room, closing the bedroom door. Turning to him, I find that he's nowhere near as amused by this as I am. "You have to admit it's kinda funny."

"It's not even sorta funny."

I pinch my fingers together as he advances on me. "Maybe just a teeny tiny bit funny?" I take a step back and encounter the wall.

"Nope. In fact, since you find it so funny, I assume you won't mind accepting Fluff's punishment for her. After all, I can't exactly spank a poor, *defenseless* old dog."

"You wouldn't dare."

"Wouldn't I?" He goes to sit on the bed and pats his lap.

I approach, planning to sit on his lap, but apparently that's not what he has in mind. He turns me, and I end up facedown over his lap, his intentions now crystal clear as he rubs a hand over my cheeks. "Flynn, wait…"

"You know what to say to put a stop to it. Now," he says, continuing to caress my suddenly sensitive skin, "how many spanks do we think your little wildebeest earned by biting me?"

"One."

"Ha-ha, try again. She could've unmanned me."

"She never came close to unmanning you."

"Depends on your perspective. If you give me a reasonable number, I'll let you decide. Otherwise, I'll decide, and I have a feeling my number won't seem reasonable to you. After all, it was my butt that got bit."

"Five?" I ask in little more than a squeak. The blood is beginning to rush to my head, among other places.

"Hmm, that's a little more reasonable than one, but not quite in the range that I was thinking. Want to try again?"

"Seven?"

"Getting closer, but I'd say nothing less than ten would do in light of Fluff's crime."

"*Ten?* Seriously?"

"You know how to say no…"

The word is on the tip of my tongue, but I bite it. I won't give him the satisfaction. "Fine."

"What was that you said?"

"I said it's *fine*."

"Ten it is, then. Are you ready?"

"Hurry up already. I'm getting a headache from hanging upside down."

"We can't have that." He helps me up and onto the bed, where he sits back against a pile of pillows and arranges me over his lap with my head cushioned by another pillow. His hard cock is pressed against my belly, which lets me know he's not unaffected by this, despite his businesslike demeanor. "Better?"

"I guess."

"Do we need to add to the number to address your attitude?"

"You have to admit this isn't fair!"

"It also isn't fair that your dog bit my ass."

"*I* didn't bite your ass."

"If you had bitten my ass, I wouldn't be punishing you. Trust me on that."

I'm intrigued by this insight. "Good to know."

"I'd also remind you that you laughed after my butt was bitten."

"It was funny! And you laughed the first time she bit you. How was I to know this was different?"

His hand comes down on my ass, the sharp cracking sound echoing through the big room. "Count them."

"One," I say, my teeth tight with the indignation, which is only exacerbated by the spread of heat from my bottom to my clit. *How* is this turning me on? My nipples tingle as well, which nearly makes me growl in aggravation. I feel like my body is betraying me.

His hand lands on the other side, near where my cheek meets my leg.

"Two."

By eight, I'm sobbing from the need for release. By nine, I'm on the verge of begging, and when the tenth spank lands in the same spot as the first, I can't hold back any longer. My entire body seizes from the explosive release that overtakes me.

Flynn's fingers delve between my cheeks to slide through the flood of moisture. "I don't recall giving you permission to come."

I don't even have the wherewithal to apologize, to beg for mercy, to do anything other than breathe and *feel.* Then he's turning me over. His hands slide up my legs, parting them as he settles on top of me, wiping away my tears with his fingers.

"I need to be inside you, Nat." His face is flushed, his eyes alive with desire.

I reach for him, wanting him as badly as he seems to want me. I'm sore and swollen, so he goes slowly, giving me time to adjust. This time isn't about playing. This is all about love. He never looks away from me as he makes slow, easy love to me. When he reaches beneath me to cup my sore cheeks, I wince from the bite of pain that morphs into pleasure.

"Natalie, God… I love you so much. I feel so lucky to have found you. Tell me you love me, too."

I put my arms around him, holding him as close to me as I can get him. "I do, you know I do."

"Tell me."

"I love you, Flynn, more than anything."

His low growl precedes his orgasm. He pushes into me, throws his head back and lets himself go. Seeing him lost in me, in the passion we create together, is the most beautiful thing I've ever seen.

He lands on me, gathers me up and holds me as we come down from the incredible high. "I came in here telling myself we'd remove the plug, I'd give you one good orgasm, and then it was off to bed."

"Didn't go quite as planned, huh?"

"You can blame your buddy Fluff for that."

"I'm sorry she bit you."

"No, you're not!"

I descend into giggles all over again. "Yes, I am! I'm genuinely sorry. I can't believe how naughty she's gotten as she gets older. She never used to be like this."

"Since I owe her a tremendous debt of gratitude for leading you to me, I'll let her continue to live here."

"Well, that's a relief, since you just talked me into moving here. I'd hate to have to relocate *again.*"

"You're not going anywhere."

"If Fluff goes, I go."

"I'll keep that in mind."

"You might want to remember to shut the door, too."

"I'll definitely remember that." He raises his head to look down at me, his sexy lips curved into a smile. "Had yourself a good little laugh at my expense, didn't you?"

"I can't wait to tell Marlowe and your sisters about this."

"You'd better not…"

"What's it worth to you?"

"A lot."

"No punishment for coming without permission?"

"Hmmm, I suppose that's a fair tradeoff, considering you could ruin my life by telling them your dog bit my ass while I was—"

I kiss the words off his lips. "Do we have a deal?"

"We have a deal," he says begrudgingly.

CHAPTER 11

Flynn

Long after Natalie falls asleep in my arms, I'm awake thanks to the nap on the plane that took the edge off for me. I stare into the darkness, reliving the incredibly decadent day we spent together. I've gone from fearing I'd lost her to bringing her fully into my life—and my kink—with astonishing results. Not only is she the perfect submissive, but she seems to love our new arrangement as much as I do.

For the first time in what feels like forever, I can relax and take comfort in knowing I'm exactly where I should be with the woman who was born to love me—and vice versa. Not to mention she's fun and funny and loving and sweet and smart and compassionate and strong and everything I ever wanted in one delicious, sexy, adorable package.

If only this shit with the FBI wasn't hanging over our heads, everything would truly be perfect. I can't figure out what more they could possibly want with us. We had nothing to do with the murder of the lawyer who sold Natalie's story to one of the Hollywood news shows. Did I want to kill him for the anguish he brought down on her? You bet I did. But that was as far as it went. Desire to see someone dead doesn't equate to murder.

When it becomes apparent that sleep is going to remain elusive tonight, I settle Natalie on a pillow, kiss her forehead and leave her to sleep with the wildebeest snuggled up to her. I still can't believe the little bitch bit my ass. I'll admit to myself—and only myself—that it was sort of funny. And the "punishment" that followed led to some of the hottest sex I've ever had. I should be thanking the little beast for that, except that my butt still hurts where she latched on, so I won't be thanking her quite yet.

I pull on a pair of shorts and a T-shirt and go into the kitchen to make some coffee, planning to take advantage of the sleepless night to catch up on work. Hayden is after me to make a decision on the next project we're going to take on after we complete the film he's currently editing, which still doesn't have a name.

I go over his list of potential names, add a few of my own and send that off to him. Then I lose myself in the screenplay Hayden has insisted I read first about a recovering drug addict who sets out to fix the damage he's left behind. The story is engrossing and compelling, and definitely has my interest.

As I read, I realize I'm spinning my wedding ring around on my finger. It's amazing how quickly I became accustomed to having it there and how right it feels, when only a few months ago, the thought of being married was appalling to me. That was before Natalie crashed into me and changed me forever.

Thinking about her makes me want to be near her, so I put down the script, shut off the light and return to the bedroom. I slide into bed next to her, snuggling up to her back. She doesn't wake but turns to me, cuddling into my embrace. God, she's sweet, and even when she's sleeping, I can feel how much she loves and trusts me.

I have so many things I want to do and explore with her. I can't wait for all of it. Soon, I'll take her to the club, where she'll get her first exposure to the public aspect of my chosen lifestyle. I hope someday we'll get to the point where scenes at the club are a routine part of our life together. But if we never get there, I'll be perfectly satisfied—and content—with what we already have.

We spend a lazy and relaxing weekend at home. Natalie's foundation notepad is never far from her side, and she adds to it regularly as we brainstorm ideas for programs. She wants to bring in the national teachers' union as a partner in helping us to reach the children most in need, which I think is a fantastic idea. Who would know better than the teachers who work on the front lines with the kids each day?

I love her passion for my passion project, and I'm thrilled to have her involved.

All weekend, I try to forget about the looming appointment with the FBI agent. That he wants to talk to Natalie, too, fills me with anxiety that has me tossing and turning on Sunday night.

At some point, I fall asleep only to be awakened by the alarm on Natalie's phone. It's way too early to be awake after being up most of the night stewing, but remembering why she had set the alarm so early puts me immediately on alert. The goal today is to end this bullshit with the FBI once and for all.

"Did you sleep?" Natalie asks.

"Some."

Fluff stands and stretches, spots me on the other side of Natalie and shows me her ten stumpy teeth. She gets a lot done with those remaining teeth.

"Stop it, Fluff. This is Daddy's bed. He can sleep here, too."

"When did I become her daddy anyway?"

"When you married her mommy." She says this as if it makes perfect sense, which is utterly adorable.

"I never signed on for that, and P.S., this is *our* bed, not mine. Ours." I yawn deeply, remembering the multiple events that lie ahead.

It's going to be a long day and nowhere near as much fun as the weekend was. I'm thrilled to finally receive an Oscar nod for acting, but I'd much rather spend today alone with my new wife than schmoozing at yet another Hollywood event. "I need a shower to wake up. Want to join me?"

"Only if you'll sign a no-sex waiver. I'm on hiatus."

"Says who?"

"Says my bruised and battered body. And judging from the bloated crampy feeling I woke up with, I'm due to get my period today, so we're out of commission for a while."

"No, we're not."

"*Yes*, we are."

"Have you forgotten that you signed over control of your sexual satisfaction to me, which means you don't get to say when?"

"I get to say not then."

"No, you don't."

"Yes, I do."

"No. You don't."

"Where's Fluff when I need her?"

"The dog or the safe word?"

"The dog. I want her to bite your ass again."

Emmett arrives about twenty minutes before our eight o'clock meeting with Vickers. Natalie and I are fresh out of the shower, where she was true to her word—no sex. That's okay. I'll let her make it up to me later. She hasn't yet dried her hair, and she looks fresh-faced and young as we meet with my attorney and close friend.

"What happened to Rogers anyway?" I ask him over coffee.

"You don't already know?" Emmett asks, surprised. As always, he's decked out in one of the custom bespoke suits he has made on twice-a-year trips to London's Savile Row.

"I suffer from a staggering lack of curiosity where he's concerned."

"He was stabbed in his office. No sign of forced entry, and whoever killed him made him suffer first. His left ear was cut off, his right pinky finger—"

When I see Natalie go pale, I hold up a hand to stop Emmett.

"Sorry. I figured you guys had read about it by now."

"We can't possibly be the only ones with motive," Natalie says.

"You aren't. The stories coming out of Lincoln tell a tale of a life gone totally off the rails. He was big into gambling and owed money all over the place."

"So we basically handed him the golden egg when Natalie appeared with me at the Globes."

"That's my speculation. And I believe it's possible that someone knew he'd come into the money and was looking for their share when he was killed. Our guy is working that angle right now—who did Rogers owe that would be interested in his big payday?"

I glance at Natalie. "You see why we love Emmett so much?"

"I can definitely see."

Emmett smiles at her. "Just doing my job and protecting my friends. This whole thing is bullshit."

The doorbell rings, and I go to admit Vickers. He takes a long look around at my house, which makes me wish I'd had this meeting at the office instead. This'll give him a story to tell in his retirement, the time he suspected the movie star of murder. If only he could've proved it, the case would've made his career.

As I have that thought, I begin to understand Vickers's motivation. Pinning Rogers's murder on me—or Natalie—would make him a star. Yeah, that's gonna happen over my dead body.

I bring him into the kitchen, offer him a chair and a cup of coffee, which he declines.

"Nice place you got here."

"I like it." When I sit next to Natalie, she takes hold of my hand under the table. And just that simply, I feel calmer, more prepared to keep my cool no matter what buttons Vickers decides to push. "This is my wife, Natalie."

"Pleased to meet you."

She smiles and nods but doesn't return the sentiment. That's my girl.

"And my attorney, Emmett Burke."

"What can we do for you?" Emmett asks.

"Do I have your permission to record this conversation?"

Emmett nods. "Go ahead. We have nothing to hide."

Vickers places a handheld recorder on the table and lists the parties present as well as the date and location. "As you know, we're looking into the murder of David Rogers. Mrs. Godfrey, could you please tell me about your association with him?"

She looks at me for reassurance. I wish I could spare her from having to talk about things she'd rather forget.

"I met him during Oren Stone's trial. He was acquainted with the detective who took me in after my parents… I was estranged from my family and…" She takes a deep breath. "David offered to help me establish a new identity."

"Was that his idea or yours?"

"It was his suggestion, but I was very anxious to leave the past behind. He didn't have to talk me into it."

"How exactly did he go about establishing your new identity?"

"I'm not sure of the exact steps he took. I was seventeen and looking for a fresh start after two nightmarish years. When he produced a new birth certificate, passport, Social Security card, a credit card, bank accounts, I didn't ask questions."

"Do you know if he actually changed your name or if he created a new identity?"

"He created a new identity because I didn't want some clerk in an office to be able to tie the two names to each other. That was very important to me."

"How much did you pay him for these items?"

"Five thousand dollars."

"And where did you get the money?"

"After Stone was charged with attacking me, some of his rivals and enemies came together to raise funds to support me during the trial. I used the money to pay for living expenses and tutors so I could finish high school from home. I paid for clothes and other expenses. I used part of it to pay David, and the rest went toward half of my college tuition."

"How did you pay for the other half?"

I reach my limit with that question. "What does that have to do with anything?" It's pure torture watching Natalie talk about this shit again. The experiences of her teenage years might always be part of her, but she shouldn't be forced to constantly relive it. I can't bear it.

"We're looking into Mr. Rogers's business dealings."

"All of them or just the ones that involve my wife?"

"All of them."

She squeezes my hand. "I paid for the rest of college with loans and by working two jobs."

"A run of your credit shows that your loans were recently paid off in full. Can you explain how that transpired?"

"Not that it's any of your business, but I paid off her loans."

"I was asking Mrs. Godfrey."

"What he said. How do you think I suddenly paid off thousands of dollars in loans when I recently lost my job?"

I bite my lip to hold back a smile.

"When was the last time you saw or spoke to Mr. Rogers?"

"More than six years. I never saw him again after he delivered the documents to the home where I was living."

"Talk to him?"

"No. I had no need to. I hired him to do a job for me. He did it. I paid him. End of story. Until…"

"Until?"

"Until I appeared at the Golden Globes with Flynn, and David sold me out to the media."

"And how do you know it was him?"

"He was the only one who knew me by both names."

"You never told anyone else what your new name is? Not even the family you lived with?"

"No. I told no one. I'm still April to the family I lived with and the few other people who remained in my life after the attack."

"In all the years after you changed your name, you never told anyone about your former name, your former life in Lincoln?"

"The point of changing my name was that I didn't want anyone to know who I used to be. I never told anyone. I hadn't even told Flynn the full story before it hit the news. He learned my birth name from reporters."

"Where did you live while you were in college?"

Again she looks at me, as if to ask what the meaning of this is. I'm wondering the same thing.

"The first year, I lived in a dorm and then in an apartment the other three years."

"Roommates?"

"A few. Here and there."

"I assume you made some friends there, in classes, jobs, activities? Boyfriends?"

"What're you getting at, Agent Vickers?" Emmett asks, saving me the trouble.

"Yes, I had some friends. People I did things with. But I didn't date, if that's what you mean."

"I'm just having a little trouble believing that in all that time, with all those people you came into contact with, lived with, did things with, you never told *anyone* about Stone or the trial or anything about your life before college. I have a daughter. She talks about everything."

Her eyes flash with anger. "Was your daughter attacked and repeatedly raped by a man she trusted when she was fifteen? Did your best friend lure her to his home, hold her down, take her virginity, her innocence, and ruin her life? Did your daughter's parents disown her when she refused to back down from bringing charges against your best friend and boss? If not, then you certainly have no place to judge me or the choices I made after I was attacked."

I want to stand up and cheer. I've never been more proud of her or more impressed by her than I am in that moment.

"You went to college in the same state in which you helped to send the governor to jail. No one recognized you?"

"I'd changed my appearance by then. I'd changed my hair color from reddish brown to the current color, and until this week, I wore brown contacts that changed my eye color. I was also older by then, and I had matured in the years since the attack and trial. No one ever so much as suggested that I might be April Genovese. They were college kids. What did they care about the girl who brought down the governor? Most of them probably didn't even know it had happened."

"When you heard the media was reporting that Flynn Godfrey's new girlfriend was the same girl who brought down the governor of Nebraska, what did you think?"

"I knew right away that David had cashed in on what he knew about me. It had to be him, because no one else knew."

"Since the story went public, have you spoken to anyone you knew before in Lincoln?"

"Only my sisters, who I hadn't spoken to since before the attack."

"You didn't speak to Rogers?"

"Why would I? Flynn's lawyers were handling the situation with him. I had bigger concerns, including the loss of my job and livelihood. I had no desire to speak to the man who'd given me a new identity and then stolen it from me when it served his purposes."

Both men look at my wife with admiration while my heart swells with love and respect. She's magnificent.

"Have we answered all your questions?" I want him gone so I can be alone with her.

"For now. We'd like you to remain available while the investigation continues."

"We're going to London for about forty-eight hours this weekend for the British Academy Film Awards," I say, "but we'll be back in LA early next week."

"We'd like to know what else is being done to find Rogers's killer," Emmett said. "Surely you have persons of interest by now other than my clients?"

"We're investigating a number of promising leads. The information you provided today is very helpful."

"It's safe to assume, then, that my clients are not suspects?"

"Not yet. This is an ongoing investigation, and we reserve the right to question your clients again."

"I'll show you out," Emmett says, tuning in to my need to have the agent gone.

The moment we're alone in the kitchen, I reach for her. "You were fucking magnificent." I realize she's trembling, which infuriates me. "I'm so sorry you had to go through all that again. I hope that's the last time you ever have to talk about it."

"I hope so, too."

"We can skip the lunch today if you're not up for it."

"We're not skipping it. You're an Academy Award nominee, and we're going to that luncheon."

I raise her chin and kiss her. "So proud of you, sweetheart."

She smiles weakly.

Emmett comes back. "That was awesome, Natalie. You handled him like a pro."

"I just told the truth."

"You did it brilliantly."

"See?" I tuck a strand of her hair behind her ear. "I'm not the only one who thinks you're fucking amazing."

"Don't forget I've had training on how to deal with hostile questions, cross-examination, the whole nine yards."

"I'm so turned on right now."

"And that's my cue to get the hell out of the love nest," Emmett says, laughing.

I get up to shake his hand. "Thanks for coming, man."

"You got it. Any time."

"We'll see you at the office tomorrow and at the club on Friday."

"Oh. Really?" He glances between Natalie and me.

"Really."

"Well, okay. See you soon."

"Keep me posted on anything you hear from the investigator."

"I will."

I see him out the door and return to the kitchen, where Natalie is staring out at the pool, lost in thought. Probably lost in torturous memories. If I could, I'd spend every dime I have to erase those memories for her.

"Are you okay, sweetheart?"

"Yeah, I'm fine. It's just that I've been forced to confront my past more in the last few weeks than I have in years."

"It's not lost on me that those are the same weeks you've known me."

She takes my hand, brings it to her lips and looks at me with gorgeous green eyes. The color is still new to me, but the warmth, affection and love are familiar by now yet no less humbling than they were when I first knew her.

"Just when I think I can't love you any more than I already do," I tell her, "I find out there's more, so much more."

The chime sounds to indicate the front door is opening. "Is it safe to come in?" Addie calls.

"Everyone is dressed," I say with a smile for Natalie.

Addie comes in, a tray of coffees in hand and a pile of mail that she places on the counter for me to go through when I have time. "Morning! How'd it go with the FBI?"

"Fine." I take two of the coffees from her and hand one to Nat. "Natalie ruined all his fun."

"I would've liked to have seen that," Addie says.

"It was quite a show." Right then and there, an idea comes to me that takes my breath away because it's that captivating.

"Flynn?" Natalie asks. "What's wrong?"

"Nothing. Just thinking about something for work."

"He does that," Addie says with a smile for Nat. "Spaces out in the middle of conversations when he gets a big idea. What is it this time?"

"It's…" I can't say it out loud or even entertain the possibility without first speaking to Natalie. "It's not ready for discussion yet. Early stages."

The doorbell rings. "That'll be Tenley," Addie says of the stylist who has been dressing Natalie for award season. She goes to open the door.

"You're sure you're up for this today?" I ask her.

"I'm positive. I wouldn't dream of missing a chance to celebrate my talented husband."

Natalie enjoys the Oscar luncheon at the Beverly Hilton and the opportunity to meet more of my friends and colleagues, who are equally fascinated by her. I take a lot of razzing about giving up my bachelor status, about strapping on a "ball and chain" and all the usual bullshit guys say to each other. But my "ball and chain" is absolutely stunning in a midnight-blue dress that clings to all her sumptuous curves. I'm the envy of every straight guy in the room and a few of the women, too.

After a delicious meal of tasty fish, rice and vegetables, we sit through the comments offered by the Academy's president as well as the producers of the show, who lecture us about keeping our acceptance speeches to forty-five seconds. I find that amusing. It takes months, sometimes years, to make a quality, award-worthy film, and winners are expected to boil down those years to forty-five seconds.

If I win, and I'm favored to after the run I've already had this award season, I suppose I can jam what I want to say into forty-five seconds.

I pose with the other nominees in this year's class, and the picture probably starts hitting social media before we leave the room.

After the luncheon, Natalie and I return to a suite upstairs, where we'll spend tonight after the Oscar Nominees Night party at Spago. I'm exhausted after the restless night without much sleep as well as the two glasses of Bowmore I had at the luncheon.

Natalie presents her back to me to unzip the dress. She's got another dress, a black one this time, hanging in the closet for tonight. She made a joke on the way into town that God forbid she show her face in Hollywood wearing the same dress at two different events on the same day.

I kiss her shoulders and the side of her neck. "How're you feeling?" I ask, really wanting to know if her period has arrived.

"I've still got cramps, but otherwise I'm fine. You?"

"Tired. I couldn't sleep last night."

"Do we have time for a nap?"

"You're reading my mind, sweetheart." While I remove my suit, she goes around closing the blinds. It occurs to me that every other woman I've ever dated would want to spend this afternoon by the pool, using me and my celebrity to see and be seen. Natalie is proving once again that she is exactly perfect for me—and with me for all the right reasons.

We remove the rest of our clothes and crawl into bed together, coming together in a tangle of arms and legs. Though I've yet to make love to my gorgeous bride today, the need for sleep is trumping my need for sex. "I love being naked in bed with you, even if all we're doing is sleeping."

"Mmm, me, too. Before I met you I didn't like being naked in the shower," she says with a laugh that makes me laugh, too. "Now I feel like I spend half my life naked."

"Want to go for three-quarters?"

She kisses me and runs her fingers through my hair. "Get some sleep while you can. It's going to be another late night."

I close my eyes, breathing in the scent of my love, and fall asleep, thinking about the special surprise I have for her tonight.

Natalie

I'm putting on the jewelry Flynn gave me before the Golden Globes when he comes into the bedroom carrying a small gift bag.

"For you." He holds out the bag, which I eye with trepidation.

"That had better not be anything sparkly."

"It might be kinda sparkly."

He is boyishly handsome in yet another well-cut suit that shows off his broad shoulders and trim waist. Looking at him is one of my favorite things to do. It doesn't matter if he's fresh out of bed or turned out for a night on the town, he's always stunning.

I take the bag from him. "I reserve the right to return this if it's too much."

"Okay."

I remove a small package wrapped in pink tissue paper, revealing a tiny piece of cloth. All I can see are the jewels encrusted on the fabric. "Those had better not be diamonds or anything in the diamond family."

"They're crystals. Hold it up."

I remove the item from the paper, and that's when I see it's not jewelry. It's lingerie. Very fancy panties. A thong, to be more specific. "It's beautiful."

"Will you wear it for me tonight?"

"Sure." I'm eager to please him even if I've never been a big fan of thongs. "Where did you get it?"

"A high school friend of Ellie's runs the most exclusive lingerie shop in Beverly Hills. That's where I get everything."

"And you trust her to keep your secrets?"

"Delany keeps *everyone's* secrets, which is why her business is booming."

"When did you go shopping?"

"I didn't."

"Let me guess—you made a phone call."

"Yep, and this one didn't involve Addie."

"Thank God."

"So you'll wear that tonight?"

"Yes! Now go away and let me finish getting ready."

"Yes, dear." He kisses me and leaves the room, Fluff trailing behind him. They seem to have gotten past their spat, which is a relief. Flynn didn't blink an eye when I brought her with me today. He certainly has people on his payroll who could take care of her for me, but I don't want others caring for her. Not when I can do it.

I reach under my dress and remove my panties and step into the thong. The string settles between my cheeks, which I normally don't like, but after having worn a plug for hours, the thong doesn't bother me as much as it used to. I finish getting ready and load the clutch Tenley said would go perfectly with the black dress. I take my phone, tampons (just in case) and lipstick.

The cramps have continued unabated all day, but so far there's been no sign of my period. Perhaps the birth control shot is throwing off my cycle. In the mail that Addie had delivered was a report on my test results, all of which were negative. I'm perfectly healthy, except for the cramps and an odd buzzing in my head that began during the luncheon. I send off a text to Doctor Breslow, asking if my period might be affected by the birth control shot.

She writes right back saying that it's possible I won't have periods at all during the next three months, which is good to know.

I thank her for the info and finish getting ready.

Tonight's event is at Spago, and we're driven to the iconic Beverly Hills restaurant by the security detail. Photographers pounce the second we emerge from the car, but Flynn keeps a protective arm around me. Cameras record every second of our walk into the restaurant.

Many of the same people who were at the luncheon are at this party, and we make the rounds. Flynn gets me a glass of chardonnay and the passed hors d'oeuvres are delicious. But the more I eat and drink, the queasier I become. I'm also overheating.

We're talking to Flynn's partners, Jasper and Kristian, and I'm about to ask him if we can find a place to sit when my panties begin to buzz. I manage to suppress a gasp, take hold of his arm and try to stay focused on the conversation despite the vibrator pressed tight against my clit. I'm going to kill him for this.

"Are you okay, Natalie?" Jasper asks in a crisp British accent.

"I'm… It's a little warm in here. Maybe we could sit?"

"Of course, sweetheart." Flynn guides me to a booth. When we're seated, he leans in close to me. "Are you okay?"

"I feel weird—and not good weird."

The buzzing stops immediately. "Define weird."

"I don't know. My head feels funny, I've had cramps all day, and now I feel sweaty, too."

He leans in to kiss my forehead. "Holy crap, Nat. You're burning up. Let's get you out of here."

"No! We don't have to go. This is important to you."

"The hell it is. We just had lunch with all these same people."

"I don't want to ruin your evening."

"You're not. I'm just sad it wasn't the panties making you flush." He smiles and winks and gets me out of there with the greatest of finesse. We leave through a different door than the one we came in and manage to escape the notice of the paparazzi on the way out, which is a relief. I can only imagine what they'd have to say about us leaving so soon after we arrived.

"Do you want to go home or back to the hotel?"

"We have to go to the hotel. Fluff is there."

"I could have her brought home if you'd rather be there."

"The hotel is fine." I need a bed, and that one is closer. He holds me for the short ride back to the hotel. In the few minutes it takes to ride the elevator to our top-floor suite, I feel a hundred times worse. "Flynn…"

"What, honey?"

"I think I'm sick."

"I'll send for a doctor. Don't worry about anything. It's probably just a bug."

"Don't want you to get it."

"Don't worry about me, sweetheart. I never get sick."

In the bedroom, Flynn gets me undressed and removes the panties. "We'll save these for another time," he says, tucking them into his suit coat pocket. He helps me into a regular pair of panties and pulls a T-shirt of his over my head. "Lie back and rest. I'll see if they can get us a doctor."

"Sorry."

"Don't be sorry. I'd so much rather be alone with you than in a room full of people, but I'm sorry you don't feel well. We'll get you fixed right up." He kisses my forehead and goes into the other room to use the house phone. I fall asleep to the low rumble of his voice on the phone calling for help.

Chapter 12

Natalie

I'm so hot. I have to be on fire. And then I'm freezing, my teeth chattering from the chills that torture me. Flynn pulls my hair back while I puke into what might be an ice bucket that he holds for me. My throat hurts too much to ask him what's wrong with me. Whatever it is, I've never felt this bad in my life.

All I can do is sleep when I'm not puking.

Fluff is there, too, whimpering, but it takes more energy than I have to comfort her. I hear Flynn telling her that Mommy is sick. I'll have to thank him for that when I can. He's nice to her even after she bit him—again. I love him for that.

I fall back into a restless sleep filled with dreams about things I'd rather forget. I'm at the governor's mansion, and Oren is there. He's attacking me, hurting me. I'm screaming and crying and telling him to stop. I beg him to stop, but he doesn't. Then Flynn's mother is there, telling me it'll be okay, that they're taking care of me.

But Oren pushes her away and tells her to get out before he hurts her, too. I want to protect Stella, but I can't move. My arms and legs are like lead pipes, refusing to follow my orders.

"Natalie." Flynn's voice breaks through the sound of my own screams. "Sweetheart, wake up. You're dreaming."

My eyelids seem to weigh a ton. I force my eyes open. He looks terrible. His hair is standing on end and his eyes are wild, as if he's been awake for days.

"You were dreaming," he says, wiping tears from my face. He kisses my forehead and both cheeks. "Do you think you can drink some water?"

I'm desperately thirsty, so I nod. Just that small movement sets off a painful blast in my skull that has me gasping.

He brings me a glass of ice water with a straw that he holds for me.

The cold water is like heaven to my parched throat, but it lands with a gurgle in my empty stomach. "What's wrong?" I ask him.

"You've got the flu."

"Your mom…"

"She was here to check on you yesterday."

"Yesterday?"

"It's been two days, Nat. You've been totally out of it. We came very close to taking you to the hospital, but the doctor came here to check on you so we wouldn't end up in the news again."

"Two days."

"Two very long days."

"Have you slept at all?"

"Not much. I was too freaked out to sleep."

I want to reach up to touch his tired face, but my arms won't cooperate. "So sorry to freak you out. And to puke all over you."

He cracks the faintest of smiles. "You didn't do that. Came close a few times."

"Ugh, how sexy." The thought of nearly puking on him makes me feel worse than I already do. "Sorry."

"You think I care about that, Nat? God, I was so scared that something was seriously wrong with you and everyone was missing it. I was afraid to sleep, that I would wake up and you'd be… Well, I was scared."

"I know I must smell gross and I'm probably communicable, but will you please get in bed with me and hold me?"

"I'd be very happy to do that." He gets up to go around the bed and gets in with me.

I turn away from him because I don't want to infect him any more than I already have.

"You don't smell gross. I got to give you a sponge bath yesterday. We enjoyed that very much."

"We?"

"You and me."

"So you took full advantage of my feverish state to get handsy with me?"

"You know it."

His arms around me are exactly what I need. With my head cushioned on his arm and the heat of his body warming me, I begin to feel the slightest bit better. And then I remember… I was expecting my period when I got sick. "Flynn…"

"What, honey?"

"I know we just got settled, but I could use the bathroom."

"No worries." He gets up, comes around to lift me right out of bed and carries me into the bathroom. "Take it easy. You're going to be really weak and wobbly."

I grasp the sink, hoping to stop the world from spinning. "I'm okay if you want to give me a minute."

"You can pee in front of me, Nat."

"I don't think I can, actually."

"I'm afraid to leave you."

"I'll hold on. I promise."

"Call me if you need help."

"I will."

As soon as the door clicks shut behind him, I get busy checking what's going on below. Nothing. I'm beyond thankful he didn't have to deal with that on top of the puking and the rest.

I immediately regret a quick glance in the mirror. I use the last of my dwindling strength to brush my hair and teeth before I call for Flynn to give me a lift back to bed.

"Do you think you could eat something?"

"I don't know. Maybe some soup. Later. First I just want to close my eyes for a minute while you hold me."

"We can do that."

The next time I open my eyes, sunshine fills the room and I'm alone in bed. I experiment with moving my arms and legs, which seems easier than it was the last time I was awake. My headache seems a bit better, too. I attempt to sit up and have to take a moment before the spinning stops.

Flynn comes into the room wearing a pair of basketball shorts and those sexy glasses that make him look so smart. His hair is standing straight up and he hasn't shaved in days, but he still makes my heart beat a little faster just by walking into the room with Fluff hot on his heels.

"You look better."

"I feel a little better."

"Thank goodness. How about some food?"

"That actually sounds good."

"Progress, Fluff. I told you Mommy would feel better soon."

"You guys are getting along okay?"

"We're living proof that you *can* teach an old dog new tricks. She's learned not to bite the hand that feeds her."

My heart melts at the adoring gaze Fluff directs his way. "Glad to see something good came out of me getting stricken with the plague."

"I also got a ton of work done, and I'm all caught up, which makes Hayden very, very happy."

"Oh good."

"Not good. I never want to see you that sick again—ever."

"Let's hope it was a one-time thing."

"The doc says you have to take it really easy for a week to ten days, so I canceled the trip to London."

"No! You have to go! I'll stay home while you go."

"Absolutely not. I'm not going anywhere without you."

"But you're going to *win*!"

"I can't believe you just said that out loud."

"This is no time for your superstitions."

"Natalie…"

"You have to go."

"I'm not going without you, and you can't go. That's the end of it."

I recognize defeat when I see it. Sighing, I say, "I was really looking forward to going to London."

"We'll get there. For now, we're going to chill at home until you're fully recovered, and that's that."

"I hope you don't get it, too."

"I won't. I seriously never get anything."

"With all your superstitions, you'd better be knocking on some wood with that statement."

He makes a big production out of knocking on the bedside table. "Now let's get some food into you."

True to his word, after we finally check out of the hotel, we don't leave the house at all over the next week. We watch him win the BAFTA for Best Actor on TV, and this time Marlowe accepts the award for him. During the week, Flynn works from his home office, participating in conference calls with the Quantum team in between checking on me and waiting on me hand and foot. He also oversees another meeting of the foundation board of directors, which I sleep through.

"You're like my butler," I tell him when he makes lunch for me on Friday, the day before the Valentine's Day party his parents are hosting to celebrate our marriage. This is the first day I feel somewhat normal, although I'm still far more tired than I should be.

"We can role-play that sometime. I'll be your faithful servant, and you can be the mistress of the manor who orders me to service her in more ways than one."

"Ohh, I like that. Could I dominate *you* in this scenario?"

"To a certain extent."

"When can we do that?"

"You might not want to light the fuse, baby. I'm feeling a little pent-up over here."

"Awww, my poor sweet hubby has been so neglected by his sick wife."

"You're racking up the demerits," he says with a teasing grin.

I rest my hands on his chest and look up at him. "Tell me the truth. Have you been taking the edge off on your own?" I can tell right away that the question has surprised and maybe shocked him.

"Whatever has become of my sweet, virtuous wife?"

"She married a sex-crazed maniac who has turned her into one, too."

"Is that right?" He zeroes in on my lips, his eyes heating with desire. "Maniac, huh?"

"Answer the question."

"Since you came down with the bubonic plague, I have not once touched the equipment except to pee and wash it."

"I don't believe you."

He takes my hand and covers his rock-hard erection. "He's all yours—and only yours—whenever you're ready to get back in the saddle." Kissing my forehead and then my lips, he says, "P.S., it's no fun without you. I hope you're happy that you've ruined a long career of monkey spanking."

"That's very gross and very funny."

"Also very true. I have no desire to 'take things in hand' when you're around."

"And this is a… *new*… development?"

"Very new. The hand and I go *way* back. It's been a jarring breakup."

I laugh so hard that my sides ache.

"This is the second time you've laughed at my pain. More demerits."

I resist the urge to roll my eyes. "If I were to help you with this pent-up situation you've got going on, would you let me leave the house?"

"Only if I can go with you."

"Will I get to drive?"

"That could be arranged."

"And will you take me to the club tonight?"

"Oh, well, um, you've been so sick. You might not be ready for that yet."

"I'm ready." I run my finger down his chest and hook it in the waistband of his jeans. "I'm more than ready."

"I'm afraid to touch you right now."

"How come?"

"The pent-up thing we previously discussed."

"So you're afraid you might scare me?"

He bites his lip and nods.

I lean close enough to touch my lips to his ear. "Do your worst."

His arms band around my waist as he lifts me up and over his shoulder.

I let out a squeak of surprise as he takes us into the bedroom, coming down on top of me. He breaks the contact only long enough to all but tear the clothes from our bodies before he returns, wrapping himself around me. "This is gonna be fast," he whispers the second before he captures my lips in a kiss that tells me how much he's missed being close to me while I was sick. His hands are everywhere, tweaking my nipples, stroking my back and bottom, caressing the slick heat between my legs.

"Need you so bad, Nat."

"Take me. I'm all yours."

As he slides into me fully in one deep stroke, I arch my back, needing to be closer, as close as I can get.

He takes my hands and holds them over my head, our eyes meeting as he makes certain this is okay with me. It's more than okay. I wrap my legs around his hips and meet his every stroke. He pulls out of me, leaving me reeling and on the verge of exploding.

"Turn over."

When I'm posed on all fours the way he wants me, he kneels behind me, grasps my hips and drives into me again. "*Yes*," he whispers. "I wanted to be deeper."

I drop my head to my forearms and submit to him completely. He's taken such tender care of me during my illness. I want to give back to him in every possible way.

"Ah, God, Nat…" His fingertips dig into my hips, and he picks up the pace. Then he reaches around to stroke my clit.

"Flynn…" He's not my Sir right now. He's not my Dom. He's my husband, and I love him desperately. "Please…"

"Yes. Now. With me."

It's perfect and beautiful, and the connection I feel to him is nothing short of spiritual. He has truly been there for me in good times and in bad, and we've had plenty of both in our first six weeks together.

He rests on top of me, the way he always does after he makes love to me. I love the way he holds me afterward while our bodies cool and pulse with aftershocks.

"Flynn."

"Hmm?"

"Thank you for taking such good care of me while I was sick."

"It was my pleasure to take care of you, but don't ever scare me like that again."

"I want you to know…"

"What, honey?"

"That marrying you was the best thing I've ever done in my entire life."

"Awww, sweetheart, me, too."

"A lot has happened since we met, and my life has changed completely—in some ways we both wish hadn't happened. But even knowing what we do now about what was in store for us, I wouldn't change a thing if it meant I got to be with you."

"I'm glad to hear that. Sometimes I wonder if you rue the day your wildebeest led you to me."

"Best day of my life. No question."

"Mine, too, sweetheart. Mine, too."

Flynn

I'm as thrilled as Natalie to be out of the house and cruising down the Pacific Coast Highway in the silver Mercedes sedan that will be hers when she gets her license. I've never given away one of my precious cars. It will be my pleasure to give this one to her.

"We need to schedule your road test. You're ready."

"Are you sure?"

"You're doing a great job. You'd never know it's been a while since you last drove." I punch out a text to Addie asking her to get it booked for the week after the Oscars.

"I'm more comfortable than I was before."

"While we're on the subject of your comfort, I want to talk to you about the club."

"What about it?"

"I want you to be prepared for what to expect there."

"Okay…"

"It's hard for me to talk about this because I'm so conditioned not to."

"I understand the need for discretion."

"It goes beyond discretion, as much as I appreciate that. You'll see people there you know and like. You'll see Marlowe possibly dressed in leather, brandishing a riding crop as she makes some dude her bitch. You'll see Hayden and his ropes, and perhaps Kristian and Emmett and Jasper in a variety of scenarios."

"You've mentioned they're all members."

"The thing is, you can't look at them with any kind of judgment, no matter what they might be doing or how shocking it might be to you. The club is their place to let loose. It's where they go to be totally themselves. Every single thing that happens there is done under the basic tenets of safe, sane and consensual. Everyone is there because they want to be, even if they're on the receiving end of something that might look awful to you. Everyone who is inflicting painful pleasure is doing so with the utmost care and concern for their subs. We don't let anyone in there who doesn't believe these things to be the core values of our lifestyle."

"I understand exactly what you're saying."

"I'm not accusing you of being judgmental or anything like that. You've been the opposite of judgmental, but this is still very new to you."

"Will they mind that I'm there?"

"No, sweetheart, they'll be thrilled to see you there and to know you've fully accepted me and my lifestyle. They'll be happy for both of us and eager to share this part of our lives and our friendship with you." I glance at her and find her pondering what I've said in that adorable, serious way of hers. "It's hard to explain until you're really part of it, but by sharing this aspect of our lives, our friendships are deeper and more meaningful. We give each other a safe harbor to get away from the insanity of our public lives. Taking you there will be one of the greatest thrills of my life."

"Even if we don't do anything?"

"We won't do anything. Not there. Not tonight. That's something we'll work up to. Tonight we're there to observe."

"What if…"

"Say it. There's nothing you could say or ask that would be wrong."

"What if I just can't ever bring myself to have sex with you in public?"

"Then we won't bring that part of our relationship to the club. But that doesn't mean we can't still be part of the club in other ways."

"What other ways?"

"Supporting our friends and their need for the public demonstrations. Some people get off, big-time, on getting busy in public."

"Do you?"

"I have, in the past, but it's not an essential ingredient for me. You and I are forging our own path that works for us. Nothing and no one who came before us figures into that. If you told me that all I could ever have is what we've already done, I'd be more than satisfied."

"But there's more, right? Things you want to show me and teach me?"

"The variety and options are endless. We're only limited by our own imaginations. But none of it has to happen in public if that's not your thing—and I'd completely understand if it isn't."

"I haven't decided anything yet. I'm reserving judgment until I have more information."

"That's a very wise way to approach it." I look up to see that while we talked, we've driven almost to Redondo Beach. "Want to go check out the beach?"

"Can we do that?"

"Sure." I grab my Dodgers ball cap from the backseat and put it on. "I'll just send Seth a text to tell him we're getting out." We find a place to park and manage to get onto the beach without anyone noticing us. Natalie has her long, distinctive dark hair up in a bun that makes her look much younger than her twenty-three years. I'm feeling brave and daring today, so after a long walk on the beach with her and Fluff, who had a nice nap in the backseat while we were on the road, I lead her to a beachfront café, where we sit outside and enjoy the warm sunshine, drinks and an appetizer with a minimum amount of fuss from the waitstaff.

Josh and Seth are at a nearby table, keeping an eye on things. They are close enough to get involved if need be but far enough away to give us some privacy.

"This was a really nice day," she says when we're heading back toward the city.

"It was good to get out and get some air." I'm driving because I want her to take a nap on the way home. I worry about her becoming overtired after being so sick. She truly scared the hell out of me with the way she went from fine to not fine in the matter of an hour and then spent two days in and out of it.

At one point, her fever had registered at one hundred and three. I was awake for two days keeping an eye on her and caring for her. I've never been so happy to see my mother as I was when she came to the hotel to check on us the second day. I hadn't wanted to expose her to the flu, but she'd cried nonsense and spent half a day with me, keeping me company as I worried obsessively about Natalie.

The doctor had to tell me more than once that it was "just" the flu, and I had to be talked out of taking her to the ER on two different occasions. Thank God she'd rallied and was now almost fully recovered, but I won't soon forget the fright of her illness or the loneliness of having her close by but unavailable. I hated that almost as much as I hated that she was sick in the first place.

I glance over to check on her and see that she's asleep with Fluff rolled up in a ball on her lap. The two of them are so damned cute together, even if one of them likes to bite me.

I can't wait for tonight, to take Natalie to the club and to introduce her to yet another facet of my life. I feel confident that she's ready, that we've talked it all through and she's prepared for what to expect. When I get home, I'll text the others and let them know I'm bringing her by. They'll appreciate the heads-up, and I fully expect them to be thrilled to welcome her.

Hayden, in particular, has expressed concern about me marrying someone outside our lifestyle, as that had been such a spectacular failure the last time around. That makes me think of Valerie, and I wonder if she has gotten the offer we arranged—to appear on a reality TV show about a fishing boat in Alaska.

Rather than confronting her and making her day with my rage over what she tried to do to Nat and me, Hayden suggested this route, and I have to admit it's fucking brilliant. I smile to myself when I picture her in an environment she will find so far beneath her, but I've made sure it's the only offer she'll get for the immediate future.

She'll have no choice but to take it, which will get her out of town and out of my hair for the time being. Our manager, Danielle, who took on Val only because I asked her to when we were married, was happy to facilitate something as far beneath Valerie's self-determined standards as she could find.

When Danielle came back to us with the Alaskan fishing boat show, Hayden and I laughed our asses off and told her to go for it. Make it happen.

I'm fairly confident Valerie will have no doubt how she ended up in Alaska. She might blame me until the cows come home, but it isn't my fault that she has no other options. Her reputation as a self-aggrandizing prima donna makes it so no one wants to work with her. That's on her. The affair she had with our director at the end of our marriage won her no friends either, especially when it came to light that she broke up the director's marriage to exact her revenge on me.

I haven't forgotten the one ace she still holds in her hand—her knowledge of my sexual preferences. The only reason I'd ever care if that got out is because it might embarrass my parents. Not to mention the potential impact on my career. But that's a much lesser concern. I don't even want to think about my parents catching wind of my preference for kinky sex. The thought of that makes me feel like *I'm* getting the flu.

Natalie is still asleep when we arrive at home, so I pick up her and the wildebeest and carry them inside, laying Nat on our bed and tucking her in for a while. We've got plenty of time. The club doesn't really get busy until after ten anyway.

I take advantage of the free time to play with some thoughts on the big idea I had the other day. Before it goes much further, though, I need to talk to Natalie about it because the story that's running around in my head is hers—and ours. Ever since the idea came to me, it's almost all I can think about. I've learned to trust my gut in this business. If a project gives me the chills, chances are it will resonate with audiences, too. Jeremy's story in *Camouflage* is a recent example of my instincts paying off in a big way. Not only is the film a huge critical and financial success, it's racking up the awards, too.

I reach for my phone to call Hayden. I want his take. If he thinks it's an awful idea, then there's no point in pursuing it with Natalie.

"What's up?" he asks when he takes the call.

"This and that. Did you get my text?"

"Yep. So are you doing a scene tonight?"

"No, nothing like that. We're taking baby steps, but so far, so good. She's curious about the club, so I figure I'd bring her by to get a feel for it."

"I gotta say… I didn't see that coming. In light of everything… From her past and all."

"She's got this inner strength that astounds me, and a determination not to let her past dictate her future."

"I know I've been kind of a douche about her and you and everything, but I hope you know how happy I am for you."

"Thanks, man."

"And despite how it might've appeared on occasion, I like her and I like her for you, even more so now that you're not hiding a big part of who you are from her."

"I like her for me, too," I say with a low laugh.

"I bet you do."

"So listen, I've been thinking about something that I want to run by you."

"Is it a title for the film that defies naming?"

"I wish."

"So do I," he says with a sigh.

"If it's any consolation, the early cut is amazing."

"I'm happy with it, too. I just wish we could name the fucker."

"We will."

"What's the other thing you're thinking about?"

"Natalie's story."

"What about it?"

"It's a powerful story that hits all the right notes."

"You're not seriously considering…"

"Not seriously. Yet. So far, it's just an idea."

"What does she have to say about it?"

"She's next on my list. If you think the idea is ridiculous, then there's no point in bringing it up with her."

"It's not ridiculous."

"Really?"

"It's an amazing story, Flynn. Why do you think you've got photographers camped outside every building you're known to frequent? They want a glimpse of it. People are captivated."

Captivated. That's the word I used to describe my feelings the day I met her, and nothing has changed since then. "That would make for a good title."

"Great, so you've got a title for a film we're not even making yet, but for the one that's almost done, you've got nothing?"

Laughing at his wry comment, I experience profound relief at being back on familiar ground with my closest friend and business partner after a rough few weeks. "I'm working on it. I swear."

"Yeah, yeah. Where have I heard that before?"

"I'll see you tonight."

"I'll be there. Cresley is in town. She's coming by."

"Oh great. I want Natalie to meet her. See you there."

"Later."

While I wait for Natalie to wake up, I prepare a light dinner of salad and pasta, feed Fluff and go out with her into the backyard so she can pee. I stare into the pool, which glows from within by lights on a timer, thinking about how Natalie's story might be told in a film.

Would I be violating her further by even suggesting it? That's my greatest fear. Along with my greatest fear goes my greatest motivation—to tell the rest of the world about the strong, resilient woman I had the good sense and even greater fortune to marry.

"There you are," she says when she comes out to join us.

Fluff bounds over to greet Natalie, her glee nothing short of puppylike.

Natalie scoops her up to give her a hug and receives joyful dog kisses to her face that make her laugh. "How long was I asleep? She's acting like I was gone a week."

"Every minute without you feels like a week to us, right, Fluff?"

Fluff barks in reply, and we both laugh.

"Are you and Daddy bonding?"

"We were just discussing an invitation to a father-daughter dance when you joined us."

Natalie puts Fluff down and wraps her arms around me from behind. "Is that right?"

"Yep. Fluff says she has nothing to wear, and I told her I'd take her shopping if she promises to never again bite my ass when I'm going down on Mommy."

"And what did she say to that?"

"What does 'going down' mean, Daddy?"

She pokes my ribs and rocks with laughter behind me.

"Are you hungry?"

"Starving."

"I've got just the thing for you." I turn to her, put my arm around her and lead her inside to eat.

"You made this all by yourself?"

"Sure did. I had to boil water and everything."

"I thought you didn't know how."

"I watched a video on YouTube."

She laughs while I pour us both a glass of chilled chardonnay, and we dig into the meal, which is surprisingly good, considering I made it.

"How're you feeling?"

"Great. The nap was just what I needed. I'm starting to feel like my old self again."

"I'm glad to hear it. I like your old self a lot."

"Sorry to be such a drag this week."

"Don't be sorry. You were sick."

I twirl pasta around my fork, but I lose my appetite thinking about the film idea I want to run past her.

"What's on your mind over there?" She's looking at me over the top of her wineglass.

"An idea that's been running around in my head."

"What sort of idea?"

"The kind you're either going to love or hate. I can't decide which."

"What sort of sexual torture have you dreamed up for me now?"

"Not about sex, although when you ask me things like that, it gives me other ideas."

Her cheeks flush with color. "Forget I asked, then."

"I won't forget, but the idea is about your story."

"My story? What about it?"

Here goes nothing… "It would make for a rather compelling film."

For a moment, she's expressionless, and then her mouth opens and closes again.

"You want to make a movie about what happened to me?"

"I would like to consider the possibility." I'm unable to determine her true feelings, because her expression is totally blank.

"You've gone from not wanting to talk about it in the interview with Carolyn to wanting to make a movie about it?"

"I'm only *talking* to you about making a movie. I'm saying I think it's an amazing story of resilience, perseverance, courage and determination with a happy ending for the ages. It's tailor-made for Hollywood."

Again she's silent as she contemplates what I've said.

"Of course, the only way anything happens with your story is if you want it to. I'm only suggesting that it could be a great film. I'm not saying it has to be."

"So you won't be disappointed if I don't want to do it?"

"Nope. As always, I want you to be happy. If it makes you unhappy to pursue it, then it won't happen."

"How would it work if I were interested?"

"First, we'd buy the rights to your story, which would give you that financial independence you're so fond of."

"Most people are fond of being financially independent."

Smiling at her predictably saucy reply, I continue. "Next, we'd hire a screenwriter to put the story together. Once we have a script that you and I approve of, then we get busy making it happen."

"You make it sound so simple."

"It's not. It's a long and involved process to take something from idea to the big screen, but it's also an exciting and energizing process."

"I can see that you're excited by the possibility."

"I am excited. Since the idea came to me the other day, it's been constantly on my mind. That's usually a good sign to me that I'm on to something. But as I said, it would be totally up to you."

"And no hard feelings if I choose not to go there?"

"Seriously, Nat? I could never have hard feelings where you're concerned."

"Seems to me you have *hard* feelings frequently where I'm concerned."

Her comment makes me laugh. "Very funny. But all kidding aside, I've got avalanching piles of scripts and potential projects on desks in three offices. I'll find something else that interests me. Don't worry about that."

"I'd like to think about it."

"Take all the time you need, and feel free to say no. I promise that if you do, that'll be the end of it." I reach for her and bring her onto my lap because I need to hold her right now. "If you're at all interested, it's something you should consider very carefully. By now you have a better idea of the kind of attention it would generate and whether or not you can handle that. I've already asked so much of you. I don't want this to be another thing you feel you have to do for me. This is about you and sharing your incredible story with the world. It's yours to tell or not tell, and that will always be the case."

"I appreciate that you find my story compelling enough to even consider something like this."

"It's an incredibly compelling story. I'd love to tell the whole world how lucky I am to be married to you."

She smiles and kisses me. "I'll think about it."

"Okay, then. You and I have a hot date tonight, and we need to get ready."

"Get ready how?"

"Come with me, and I'll show you."

CHAPTER 13

Natalie

Apparently, "getting ready" to go to the club involves a shower with my husband, during which he lifts me, props my back against the wall and takes me hard and fast as the steam rises around us.

"I've wanted to fuck you in the shower again since the first time we did it," he whispers in my ear as he pounds into me.

"You do some of your best work vertically."

He laughs and drops his head onto my shoulder. "Don't make me laugh when I'm trying to make you come."

"Where else have you wanted to do it?" I manage to ask.

The hands that are gripping my bottom tighten and spread my cheeks apart. "Here."

The thought of it makes my entire body tingle. "So you've said."

"I had another dream."

I open my eyes and find him watching me, gauging my reaction.

"Will you tell me about it?"

"After I make you come."

"Mmm, hurry."

That I'm curious and eager to hear about his dream seems to spark something in him, and he picks up the pace, driving into me repeatedly until we're both coming. He holds me close to him for several minutes before easing me back down to stand on wobbly legs.

We get out of the shower and dry off. I'm reaching for a robe when he takes my hand and leads me to our bed. He lifts the covers. "In."

"I thought we were going out."

"We are. Later."

"Okay…" I get into bed, and he follows me. We come together in the middle, arms and legs wrapped around each other in a routine that has become wonderfully familiar to me. I can't remember what life was like before I got to sleep in his arms every night. But we're not sleeping now, and judging by the fiery heat I see in his eyes, we're not going out for a while either. "Tell me. I want to know what you dreamed about."

"We were at the club. We'd been working up to this moment for weeks. Everyone was there to watch. You're bent over the spanking bench, and I've used my paddle. Your ass is hot and red, and your pussy is so wet, it's running down your legs."

I squirm to get closer to him. Even though he came not even ten minute ago, he's hard again. His hand cups my ass to bring me in tight against him, his finger dipping between my cheeks.

"You're wearing the biggest plug I have, and it was a struggle for you to take it. I tell you it's got nothing on me, and you begin to tremble. Your entire body is vibrating, and I haven't even turned on the plug yet."

His finger slides through the slickness between my legs and presses teasingly against my back entrance, making me burn with desire.

"Do you want to hear more?"

My mouth is so dry that I nod in response.

"I need the words."

"I-I want to hear more. I want to hear it all."

His low growl is hugely arousing to me. Knowing I'm turning him on by letting him speak to me about his fantasies excites me beyond belief.

"In my dream, I can tell you're scared. I want to take away your fear by showing you how amazing it can be to give up control to me, to trust me with your pleasure. I ask if you want to stop and remind you of your safe word. You're afraid it will hurt, and I tell you it will, but only for a short time. Then it will feel so good. So unbelievably good."

His finger dips inside me, making me tense and excited and eager all at the same time. I still can't believe how much I love being touched there. It sets me on fire every time he does it.

"I promise you the most powerful orgasm of your life."

I tremble at the thought of it. More powerful than what I've already experienced with him?

"First the plug has to come out, and it's as difficult coming out as it was going in. Of course I take my own sweet time and work you up until you're practically begging me to do it. Tell me what you want, sweetheart. Let me hear you say the words."

"I want you to… To fuck my ass."

"Fucking hell, that's so hot. Hearing you say those words… God, Nat…"

His finger pushes in deeper, and I strain against him, needing more. He lifts my leg up and over his hip, and enters me, giving me half of him as he continues to torture me with his finger. If talking about it is this intense, I can't imagine what actually *doing it* will be like.

"The plug finally pops free, and I move fast to lube up myself and you and begin to press into you. Right away, you panic. You tell me it's too big. Of course that only makes me bigger."

Despite the assault on my senses, I laugh.

"You make me laugh when I ask you if you're ready for more and you ask how there can be more. But you can't see what I can, that we've only just begun. I try to give you something else to think about by playing with your clit and nipples, and when you're distracted, I'm able to give you more."

I groan at the thought of what it will feel like.

"Jesus, Nat, you're so tight and hot. Your muscles are rippling around my finger."

And sure enough, he gets bigger inside me, stretching me nearly to the point of pain once again.

"You say, 'Holy fuck.' I've never heard you say that word before unless I was making you say it. It's so hot to hear you say it when I'm taking your ass. I ask you if it still hurts, and you say, 'Not like it did.' But it doesn't feel good yet. I'm determined to get you there. I tell you to relax, and you snap back at me, saying, '*You* try to relax when you've got a gigantic cock jammed up your ass.' You make me laugh, even when I'm trying to concentrate and make this good for you."

He withdraws his finger and presses it back into me. This time a second finger joins the party.

"I start to move in and out in small increments until I'm certain you're ready to take the rest. You scream when I press all the way into you, giving you the widest part of me. I start to fuck you, slowly, carefully, and the noises you make, Nat… God, I'm crazy, knowing you're finally enjoying it. I touch your clit… Do that now. Touch yourself."

I've never done that before, but I'm so desperate to come that I don't hesitate to reach down to where I'm stretched around him. I can't believe how wet I am. I circle the hard nub of my clit and gasp from the pleasure that zings through my entire body. Every sense is on full alert, and I'm so ready to come.

"Flynn…"

"Who am I in this scene?"

"Sir… Please… Let me come."

"We're not done yet."

I groan in response to that. How can there be more?

"I fuck you until I can't hold back anymore. I need you to come so I can, too. Come for me, Nat."

I press down hard on my clit as he slides deeper into me with both his fingers and his cock. The orgasm hits me like a tsunami, and I scream from the power of it. It's without a doubt the strongest one I've had yet, and that's saying something.

He groans as he comes, too. "Fucking hell, Nat. That was so hot and so amazing."

"I want to do it. What you described… I want it, Flynn."

A big shudder rocks his body. "We have to get you ready."

"Okay."

"Will you wear a plug for me tonight?"

"Yes."

"No hesitation?"

"None."

"I feel like I have to be dreaming, that I can share this with you, Nat… I can't even tell you what it means to me."

"I want to share everything with you."

"The plugs are downstairs. Will you come down with me?"

"Yes. Let's go."

Flynn

Her eager response is the most incredible aphrodisiac. I've had her twice in an hour, and I'm already ready for more. After a quick stop in the bathroom to clean up, I go into the kitchen to get the key to my room downstairs. I can't believe I'm about to take Natalie, my wife and the love of my life, into my most private world.

It's a dream come true. *She* is a dream come true.

We're both still naked when she follows me downstairs and stands in the middle of the big space, taking it all in again. Her nipples are tight and standing at full attention, her fingers linked together in front of her as her eyes move slowly from the implements on the wall to the spanking bench and cross, and then up to the ropes hanging from the ceiling.

"What are they for?" she asks of the ropes.

"Suspension and bondage. A lot of what I have down here requires pretty heavy bondage for it to be safe, so we won't be spending much time here. I can't play with you on the cross, for instance, unless I know you're safely attached."

"I might be willing to try it. Someday."

I shrug. "If it happens, great. If not, no worries."

"What's that?" she asks, pointing.

"That's a Tantra chair. Lots of cool positions. Deep penetration."

"Could we try that sometime?"

"Absolutely."

I go to the armoire and retrieve the largest plug I own. "Come on over here." I gesture to the spanking bench and tell her where to put her knees and elbows so she's bent over in the proper position. Opening a bottle of lube that warms on contact, I prepare her and the plug.

"Ready?"

"Yes."

"Remember your safe word?"

"Always."

"Grasp the leather handles. It helps to have something to hold on to."

She does as directed, and I press the plug against her, giving it to her slowly so she has time to adjust and adapt. The last thing I want to do is turn her off this before we even get started.

"How does it feel?" I ask.

"Big. Hurts."

"I know, sweetheart. Just keep breathing and press back against me."

It takes about ten minutes of stopping and starting before I'm able to slide the plug into place. By now she's sweating, and her entire back and ass are flushed with a warm rosy color. I desperately want to see her face, so I guide her up and into my arms.

Her eyes are closed, her lips parted, and her face is as flushed as the rest of her. She's the sexiest thing I've ever seen.

"Talk to me."

"Hmmm."

"That's not a word."

She nuzzles my neck. "Mmmm."

"That's not a word either. I want the words, Nat."

"My body feels like one big nerve ending. Everything is tingling, and I feel like I could come if you so much as breathed on my clit."

"I can do that. I can breathe on you anywhere you want me to."

She smiles, her face angelic and relaxed despite what we just did. "We need to go. Your friends are expecting us."

I can't believe I've forgotten all about our plans to go to the club. "We can do that another night if you want to stay home."

"I want to go. I want to see it and understand it."

"Okay, then. I think we need another shower first."

"Definitely."

We leave the house forty-five minutes later. Nat is dressed in a clingy top that leaves her shoulders bare and black pants that mold to all her curves. A pair of strappy black heels finishes off her sexy outfit. Her hair is a riot of curls, and she's gone with dramatic eye makeup that highlights her green eyes. She's worn the diamond chandelier earrings I gave her as well as the bracelet. I love that she's wearing the jewelry I gave her, especially the two diamond rings that sit on her left ring finger.

Part of me wants to cancel our plans because I don't want anyone, even my closest friends, to see my wife looking so hot. Knowing that underneath the sexy outfit she's wearing my plug only adds to my agitation.

"What's wrong?" she asks when we're on our way in the Aston Martin Vanquish.

"Huh? Nothing. What could possibly be wrong?"

"I don't know, but you haven't said a word since we left the house, and that's not like you."

I reach for her hand. "Nothing's wrong, baby. For the first time in my entire life, everything is just right."

"Then what are you brooding about?"

"Truthfully?"

"Always."

I blow out a deep breath. "I don't want my friends to see you looking so hot."

She looks down at her outfit. "Should I have worn something else?"

"No, sweetheart. You look beautiful—and sexy. Incredibly sexy."

"We're going to a sex club, Flynn. I thought sexy was the word of the night."

"It is."

"Then what's the problem?"

"I don't want other guys looking at you."

"And yet you want to have sex with me in public."

"It doesn't make sense to me either." I grip the wheel a little tighter, my knuckles turning white from the pressure. "Maybe I don't want things the same way I used to. It's different now."

"What is?"

"Everything. I've never thought twice about having sex with other women at the club, but the thought of doing that with you… In front of people… It's different. You're different. *We're* different."

"You said there're other ways we can enjoy the club short of actually having sex ourselves, right?"

"Lots of ways, up to and including sex. We have private rooms there."

"Are they like your room at home?"

"Some of them. Others are more like regular bedrooms with implements on the side."

"Implements on the side," she says with a laugh. "Like kinky room service?"

Smiling, I say, "Something like that."

"It's like you said—we can figure out what works for us. Just because you've done something in the past, doesn't mean you want to do it now. Perhaps all of that was about getting it out of your system so you'd be ready for me."

"That's very possible." I glance over at her and then back at the road. "It's so great to be able to have these conversations, to not have to hide this side of myself from you. I'm still sorry about the way you found out, but I'm not sorry you know."

"I'm not either. Everything we've done so far has been…" She shakes her head when she can't seem to find the words. "I would've hated to miss out on knowing you this way."

I'm humbled by her acceptance, her trust and her love. What I ever did to deserve the love of such an amazing woman is beyond me, but I'll do whatever it takes to make certain I'm always worthy of her.

We arrive at the Quantum building, and judging by the cars already in the lot, it's a busy night. "You ready for this?"

"Ready."

"Let's go, then." I take her by the hand and use the palm scanner to gain access to the building as well as the elevator that leads to the club in the basement. The doors open, and I lead her inside, my beautiful submissive wife.

CHAPTER 14

Natalie

I'm not sure what I was expecting, but I didn't anticipate a nightclub. Well-dressed attractive people in cocktail dresses and suits, others dressed in classy-looking leather, a few shirtless men, all of them with drinks in hand. There's a crowded dance floor and a packed bar along with stand-up tables as well as booths. The low bass thump of dance music vibrates through the room, mixing with the conversations taking place. The thump reminds me of the bass drum of desire that I've experienced with Flynn, and my body begins to react to the familiar sound, my muscles contracting around the plug.

The only thing that sets this apart from other nightclubs I've visited are the stages set in various spots throughout the room, the crosses, the benches and other equipment that identify this as not your average club. It's early yet, or so Flynn tells me as he keeps a hold on my hand and leads us to the bar. Everyone seems happy to see him, and several people greet me by name even though I don't recognize them. They all know me, which is something I still find bizarre even all these weeks later.

A shriek to my left draws my attention, and Marlowe swoops in to hug me. "It's so good to see you here, girlfriend."

"Thanks, Mo. It's good to be here."

"You look *amazing*!"

"Marlowe Sloane thinks I look amazing. Pinch me please."

"I'll leave the pinching to your sexy Dom. But seriously, I'm thrilled to see you here, to know you've accepted this part of him. It's so huge."

"It's been an interesting couple of weeks."

"I can only imagine. You know you can talk to me anytime. If you need an outside perspective."

"That's very sweet of you. So far, Flynn and I are doing pretty well with the talking. He *loves* to talk."

Her dirty laugh tells me she gets what I mean. "I remember that about him. We weren't together long, but that's one thing I remember."

I feel like I've been hit with a stun gun. Didn't Flynn tell me he and Mo were only friends? How many times have I thought about what a beautiful couple they might've made?

"Anyway, are you here to watch or to play?"

"Watch."

"I might be doing a scene later with a new sub." Adding with a wink, "He's young and hung, just the way I like them. I hope you'll be around to watch."

"I wouldn't miss it after that introduction." Though I'm still reeling from what she revealed to me, I can't help but laugh at that. Whatever might've happened between her and Flynn, it's long in the past. But I will ask him about it as soon as I get the chance.

"We'll see if he shows. I think he's scared of me."

Flynn leads me to a table out of the fray and hands me a glass of wine. He's got a glass of Bowmore, judging by the color of the liquid. "Enjoy it slowly. We've got a two-drink limit."

"How come?"

"We want everyone clearheaded for any activities they might decide to participate in. No one is allowed to get drunk here." He glances at me, his eyes soft but serious. "There's no place for large quantities of booze in a safe, sane, consensual environment."

"Makes sense."

We're interrupted by the arrival of a tall, gorgeous woman I recognize instantly as Cresley Dane, the supermodel.

"Is this the famous Natalie who took our friend Flynn off the market in such dramatic fashion?" she asks with a warm smile for me and a hug for Flynn.

"Cresley, meet my wife, Natalie.

Cresley surprises me when she hugs me, too. "It's so great to meet you. I'm an admirer."

"Oh. Thank you. That's nice to hear. Likewise."

Hayden joins us, slipping an arm around Cresley, who leans into him. "Nice to see you here, Natalie," he says.

"Nice to be here."

"You ready?" he asks Cresley, who nods in response.

"Let's go."

"See you later?" Cresley asks us.

"We'll be here," Flynn says. "We may even watch."

"Good," Cresley says with a smile that encompasses both of us before she lets Hayden lead her away.

"Where're they going?"

"To the dungeon."

I'm surprised by the pang of distress I feel in the area of my heart at knowing Hayden is going to have sex with Cresley when he's so obviously in love with Addie. "What will they do there besides the obvious?"

"He's a practitioner of Kinbaku, the Japanese art of erotic tying."

"What does that mean? Tying?"

"Ropes. It's an intricate practice designed to stimulate all the pleasure points."

"Could I see it?"

"Sure, we can go in there later. They'll be there for hours." He glances down at me, taking inventory in that intense way of his. "What're you thinking?"

"I just wonder how he can spend hours having sex with Cresley when he cares so much for Addie."

Flynn exhales a long deep breath. "It's complicated for him. He and Addie are really close friends, and he's not willing to risk what he has with her by exposing her to this. If she were to reject it—and him—the way Valerie did me, he'd never get over it."

"So he refuses to even try." The reality of Hayden's predicament saddens me.

"Yeah. We've talked about it a few times recently, and he's adamant."

"It's sad."

"On that we agree. I don't think he's giving Addie enough credit."

"Do you think she'd be upset to find out about this? About the fact that all of you are involved and she doesn't know?"

"I have no idea, but it's not something we share with just anyone. Other than you and my partners in Quantum, there's no one I'm closer to than my parents, my sisters and Addie, and none of them knows."

"Can I ask you something else?"

"Anything."

"Were you ever going to tell me that you were once with Marlowe?"

"I told you that."

"Um, no, you didn't. She did. She assumed I already knew."

"Oh. Shit. Are you pissed? It was years ago, before I married Val. And it was brief. We quickly discovered we're much better friends than we are lovers."

I gesture to the room around us. "Did you do this with her?"

"Some of it. We were all new to it then and in training. We practiced on each other on occasion. Does that make it weird for you with her?"

"No, not really. Like you said, it was a long time ago, and I know you had a life before me. A *busy* life."

He roars with laughter and tweaks my nose. "Cute."

"True. What about Cresley?"

"What about her?"

"Have you been with her, too?"

"I have, but only in threesomes with Hayden."

I take a drink of my wine, seeking fortification. That's what I get for asking—the painful truth. "She's beautiful."

"Yes, she is, but she's no Natalie Godfrey."

"Right," I say, laughing. "She's a freaking supermodel."

"Did you look at the stack of inquiries from Danielle that I left in the kitchen?"

"What about them?"

“There’re about ten offers from some of the top modeling agencies in the country, along with cosmetic companies, couture houses and advertising agencies, all of whom are drooling over the idea of landing Natalie Godfrey to represent their products.”

“They are not.”

“They are, too! I told you to look through the stuff I left for you.”

“I thought you meant my test results.”

“That was only one of several things I left for you. Did I also mention the interest from the casting directors? Ever since the Globes, Danielle has been overrun by them, too.”

“It’s insanity. What do I know about any of that?”

“Maybe nothing, but they know true, raw beauty when they see it.” He kisses me. “And so do I.”

“I’m not interested in any of that. I want to work on the foundation and be with you. That’s all I want right now.”

“Then that’s all you have to do. But you have to know that the whole world is interested in you.”

“I don’t care about the whole world. I only care about you, that you’re interested in me.”

He hooks an arm around me and brings my back in tight against his front so I can feel his erection. “Suffice to say, I’m very interested.”

“That’s all that matters.” The words are no sooner out of my mouth than the plug in my ass begins to vibrate. It’s a good thing his arm is around me so tightly, or I might’ve fallen off my four-inch heels.

Pressing his cock against my bottom, he groans from the vibration that he can feel, too.

“You’re making a scene,” I say when I notice people are watching us.

“It’s what we do here.” He kisses my neck and continues to grind against me. His hand, which has been flat against my belly, moves down, his fingers splayed open. “We make scenes.”

“Flynn…”

“Shhh, no one can see what we’re doing. It looks like we’re just standing here talking.”

The tall table hits me just below the ribs, hiding my lower half. I suspect that's the table's secondary purpose. His middle finger dips lower, parting me and pressing against my clit through my pants. I gasp from the pleasure that zings through me. "We can't do this here."

"We're not doing anything."

"You're touching me."

"You're my wife. I'm expected to touch you."

"*Flynn…*"

"What's my name here?"

Oh God. "S-sir."

"That's right. And what's your safe word?"

"Fluff."

"Use it if you need it, otherwise I expect you to remember the rules."

He just changed the rules on me, but I understand what he's doing. He's showing me how incredibly hot it can be to experience desire in a room full of people, most of whom are paying us no mind. But there are a few who are watching us closely, and I suspect they know exactly what he's doing to me.

The vibration in the plug goes up a notch, and I grasp the edge of the table.

"Let go of the table, Nat. I've got you." His voice is low and intense against my ear. He's asking me to trust him to know what's best.

I force my hands to relax their tight grip on the table.

"Fold them and rest them on the tabletop."

When I bring my palms together, I realize they're sweaty. With my hands settled where he can see them, he does nothing more than rock against me, his finger teasing my clit through my clothes. He takes me right to the edge of release in under a minute.

My hands tighten around each other. I can't possibly *come* here, in front of all these people. I can't. I won't. "Flynn…"

"Call me that again, and you'll earn a punishment at home."

"Sir… Please… Don't do this to me here."

"What's your safe word?"

If I say it, even in reply to his question, he'll stop. Is that what I want with my body primed to explode? This is insanity. It's the craziest thing we've done yet.

My heart is beating so hard, I'm afraid it will burst, and my lungs seem to have shrunk, making me feel like I'm hyperventilating.

"Natalie?"

I remain stubbornly quiet. If he wants this, I'll give it to him, even if I didn't intend to.

My head starts to drop forward. I'm hiding behind my hair so no one can see me come apart.

"Lay your head back on my shoulder."

I want to growl with frustration and embarrassment. Of course he knows I was trying to hide. Because I'm his submissive, I do as he asks and rest my head on his shoulder.

"Don't ever be ashamed of taking your pleasure."

"I told you I didn't want this here."

His finger grazes my clit as his erection bumps up against the plug. "You know how to make it stop."

I'm not sure what makes me do it, whether it's where we are or if I'm testing the system, but the word appears on my lips. "Fluff."

He withdraws immediately, and the plug ceases vibrating. Only his arm banded around my midsection keeps me from toppling over when my legs want to buckle under me. "Well done, sweetheart."

"So that was a test?"

"Of sorts." Nuzzling my neck, he says, "I want you to remember *always* that you have all the power. You say yes, you say no, you say not here, you say not that. It's all about you."

"You've left me all revved up."

"That was your call, not mine."

"What's the word for 'game back on'?"

"There isn't a word for that, but if you'd like to take this somewhere private and finish what we started, I could make that happen."

I'm about to accept his offer when I see Kristian lead a naked woman to one of the crosses. He's wearing only a pair of formfitting black leather pants, leaving his muscular chest, back and arms on full display. Part of me feels like I should look away, to respect the privacy of Flynn's friend. But that's not why we're here.

We're here to watch, which is both titillating and embarrassing. I'm dying to see what will happen but embarrassed at the same time.

"What's the verdict?" Flynn asks, his lips close to my ear.

"Could we find a private spot after we watch whatever Kristian is about to do?"

"Yep. Do you want me to talk you through what's going on?"

Breathless and aroused and curious, I nod.

"The name St. Andrew's cross comes from the crux decussata, or the diagonal cross that Saint Andrew was supposedly martyred on. A sub can be attached facing forward or backward, and some of the crosses spin, allowing the sub to be inverted."

"I don't think I'd like that," I said.

"I wouldn't either. It would make me feel seasick. So if they're facing forward with their backs against the cross, like Kristian's sub is going to be, that's more about teasing and slow seduction."

"What happens if they're facing the other way?" I ask.

"That's about whipping or flogging."

I shudder at the thought of being whipped.

"Don't worry, sweetheart. That's a hard limit for both of us. I don't find whipping fun or arousing, although many people do."

"How can they find that kind of pain arousing?"

"Some people get off on the pain of it, not to mention the humiliation."

"Do I know her from somewhere?" I ask of Kristian's sub.

"She's been on TV." He names a popular sitcom that has my mouth falling open. Of course! That's how I know her. She's tall and curvy, with long red hair and big breasts that look real, not that I'd know the difference. Since there's no question I'm not allowed to ask, I pose that one to Flynn.

"Yep, they're real."

"How can you tell?"

"Please, sweetheart. I grew up in LA. I could tell the difference between real boobs and fake ones by the time I was eight."

"Why am I not surprised? So what's the difference?"

"Real ones," he says, cupping mine in his big hands, "move the way they're supposed to. They're softer, more pliable. Fake ones are harder, closer together and don't move like real ones do." As he speaks, he manipulates my breasts to make his point.

I release a deep breath that I've been holding. His touch is always electrifying, but here, in public, it's even more so. "Good to know."

Kristian blindfolds his sub and secures her to the cross at the wrists, ankles and waist. We are far enough away from them that I can't hear what he's saying to her, but he's speaking to her constantly as he prepares her for their scene. Her color is high, as if she's nervous or excited or perhaps both. With her legs propped open, I can also see she's totally bare between her legs.

He begins by stimulating her nipples with his hands and mouth, working on her until both nipples are tight and red. Then he affixes something to each nipple that makes her cry out.

"Clamps," Flynn says from behind me. "They're connected by a chain. See the third one, hanging from the chain?"

I nod.

"Watch what he does with that one."

I can't look away as Kristian strokes between her legs before attaching the third clamp to her clit, making her scream and fight the restraints. The thought of what that must feel like goes through me like a bolt of electricity, leaving me tingling.

"Doesn't that hurt like crazy?"

"For a second, but then it feels crazy good, or so I'm told. You want to try that sometime?"

"I don't know. Not sure I'd like it."

"Remember what we said? Everything once, twice if we like it?" He runs his finger down my arm, and I shudder, proving I'm nothing more than a giant nerve ending.

"Do they have penis clamps? Because if we're trying everything once…"

His low rumble of laughter makes me smile. "Brat. There're cock rings. We can try that sometime."

"I'll look forward to that."

He tightens his hold on me. "I love you so much, Nat. That you're here with me and asking questions and willing to explore this world with me... You can't possibly know what it means to be myself, entirely, with you."

I squeeze the arm he has around me. I love that I've made him happy, which is so important to me.

Kristian teases his sub with feathers until she's writhing on the cross, begging for relief with every move of her body. But Kristian is in no apparent rush. He reaches for a large pink vibrator from the table that holds his supplies, and after applying lubricant, he teases her with it and then pushes it into her. He strokes the vibrator in and out of her and then releases the clamps one at a time. She comes with screams that echo through the club, and I hear them clear as anything, despite the voices and loud music.

Watching the scene unfold has me right back on the edge again, my entire body tingling with the need for release.

"You said something about private rooms?"

"Is my baby feeling hot and bothered?"

"Maybe just a little."

He takes me by the hand to lead me deeper into the club. "We've got one more stop we need to make before we see about something private."

I suppress a moan at the thought of waiting longer for relief. Being here, watching Kristian's scene, allowing Flynn to touch me in public... I'm on fire from the inside. My skin is tight and tingling, the throb between my legs is like a second heartbeat, and I want to grab Flynn and drag him to the nearest dark corner.

He applies his hand to a device on the wall, and a door slides open.

"What is this?"

"It's the dungeon. Only the five of us have access to it."

The word *dungeon* trips my already heightened senses into overdrive as I try to imagine what goes on here. I see right away as we step into the huge room that pulsates with loud music... Cresley is suspended from the ceiling. Natural-colored rope has been wrapped around her body in an intricate pattern that is strangely beautiful. The elaborate scheme is held together by a single knot that falls just above her clit, which is clamped, as are her nipples.

When Hayden swings her around, I notice she is plugged in the front and the back. What that must feel like, to hand over that much control to another human being, to trust him with so much outside a committed relationship… As I have that thought, my own plug begins to vibrate.

Flynn's arm around my waist keeps me from losing my footing. "Talk to me, sweetheart," he whispers gruffly in my ear. "Tell me what you're thinking."

"Why does she like it? She's a successful, powerful woman. What makes her want to be dominated so completely?"

"It's because she's so successful and powerful that she enjoys giving over control to someone else for a few hours. It takes her away from all her responsibilities and gives her a kind of freedom she can't find anywhere else."

"I…"

"I wish I could crawl inside your head right now so I could know your every thought."

Laying my hand on top of his arm, I want to share those thoughts with him. "I wonder what it's like for her to give up that kind of control to someone she doesn't love."

"She does love Hayden. They're old friends, and there's trust in friendship."

"Still, to do that with a man she isn't in love with… That takes…"

"Balls?"

"Yeah," I say with a nervous laugh, "that's for sure."

"It's a form of relaxation for both of them."

"Relaxation… Um, okay." I'd be anything but relaxed in Cresley's position.

"No, really, look at her. Take a good look."

Cresley's eyes are closed, her face is slack, her lips are parted ever so slightly, and she appears to be floating above the room in what I now see, upon closer examination, is a blissful state.

"We call that subspace, when the submissive reaches a place of total trust and absolute submission. She relies upon her Dom for everything in that moment. It's total surrender."

"Would they mind that we're here?"

"No, sweetheart, they love being watched. Most of us do. It's part of the thrill." He leads me to a sofa I hadn't noticed in a dark corner and positions me in front of him, between his spread legs with his arms around me.

"Will they actually have sex?"

"Probably. They usually do. We allow actual intercourse only in the dungeon and private rooms, not in the main room upstairs."

Because he wants to know my every thought, I say, "I'm not sure how I feel about watching Hayden have sex and then seeing him at the party tomorrow."

"Do you want to leave before they do?"

I'm torn between wanting to see this through to completion and not wanting to watch Hayden have sex. Yet I can't look away. "We can stay."

The scene progresses slowly. I have no idea if we're there half an hour or two hours, because I'm so caught up in what's happening between them.

Flynn's erection is pressed tight against my bottom and the vibrating plug, his hand is flat against my belly, and I'm on the verge of begging him to touch me when he tugs on the button to my pants.

I'm immediately filled with panic and excitement and desire that's hotter and more potent than anything I've felt before.

He pulls down my zipper, slowly but insistently, as if he's waiting for me to stop him. But stopping him is the last thing I want to do. I raise my hips against his hand, encouraging him to touch me before I die from wanting him to.

Across the room, I see Hayden remove the dildo from Cresley's vagina. He drops his pants, and I think about diverting my gaze, but I don't. I watch as he swings Cresley's body close to him and impales her. She cries out from the impact.

Flynn's hand slides inside my pants.

Because they suddenly feel about ten sizes too small, I want to pull them off to give him room. I shaved down there earlier, so my skin is ultrasensitive. Every nerve ending in my body seems to have arrived in one place to party for the night. All it will take is one brush of his finger over my clit to detonate an orgasm for the ages. Naturally, he must know that, because he touches me everywhere but where I need him most.

"So wet," he whispers as he slides his fingers into me.

"Flynn… Don't tease me."

"Who am I here?"

"S-sir. Please…" I open my eyes to see Hayden pounding into Cresley. I hadn't intended to watch, but I can't look away.

"Do you like watching them, Nat?"

The whisper of his breath against my ear whips through me on a tidal wave of sensation. I raise my hips, trying to get him to move his fingers, but he won't be rushed.

"Natalie? Answer me."

"Yes, I like it. I like to watch." Saying it out loud, admitting to it, is like gas being thrown on the already out-of-control wildfire that burns within me.

"Mmm, I can tell."

He keeps me impaled on his fingers, pulsing them inside me in time with the insistent throb that beats through me. "Hayden can keep this up for hours. I can, too."

"*No…*" The single word is expelled on a whimper.

"No, who?"

"*Sir.* No, Sir."

"Are you saying no to me, Natalie?"

"I'm begging you, Sir. Please let me come."

He sets the vibration in the plug to the next level, the most intense level, and I cry out before I can remember where I am or that I might disturb the others. But they are so caught up in what they're doing, they don't notice me.

"I can't… I have to…"

Flynn's fingers find a spot deep inside me that triggers the epic release that's been building for a long time now. As wave after wave of nearly unbearable pleasure overtakes me, it occurs to me that he never gave me permission to come. Anticipating the punishment I'll receive triggers a second smaller orgasm.

"Someone is in big, *big* trouble," he whispers as he brings me down slowly, dropping the vibration to a lower level. His fingers are still buried deep inside me, snug against the spot that set me off. If he keeps pressing against me there, it's going to happen again, which I'm sure he already knows.

"Sir…"

"Yes, Natalie?"

"Please take me home now."

"As you wish, my love."

CHAPTER 15

Flynn

I've never experienced anything sexier than Natalie's reactions to the club and the scenes we watched together. The way she positively detonated in my arms has me clinging to sanity as I drive us home as quickly as I possibly can. I can't wait to administer her punishment and then fuck her until I slake this unquenchable need that seems to grow and multiply every day we spend together.

"When we get home," I say after a mostly silent ride, "you have five minutes to go into the bedroom, remove your clothes and present yourself for punishment."

"H-how shall I present myself?"

"I'll leave that up to you." Goddamn, this is fun. To be able to have this sort of relationship with the woman I love more than my own life is my every dream come true. Except even I never could've dreamed the perfection that my life has become since I met Natalie.

I park the Vanquish in the garage and glance at my watch. "Five minutes starts now."

Without another word, she gets out of the car and goes into the house.

As I watch her go, my entire body is tight with desire and anticipation and love. I love her so fucking much, even more than I did before bringing her fully into my world and my kink. That I can have her and this, too…

Fluff's frantic barking gets me out of the car and into the house to deal with her while Natalie prepares herself for me.

I take Fluff into the backyard so she can pee and then give her a few treats, hoping she'll go back to sleep so we can get down to business. I crouch down and hold out my hand to her, a tiny dog biscuit sitting in the middle of my palm. A few weeks ago, she'd have taken part of my hand with the treat. Tonight, she approaches me and gently removes the biscuit from my hand and eats it while gazing at me adoringly.

"Thanks an awful lot for bringing your mom to me." I scratch her ears. "I know we got off to a rough start, but I really am so grateful for what you did that day. I was lost until you girls found me."

She leans into me, wanting more of the scratching that she loves so much.

"I need to go see Mommy. You go back to sleep like a good girl, okay? If you're good, there will be more treats."

At the word "treats," she perks up, but she's smart enough to know she's gotten all she's going to get for now. She trots over to the spot on the sofa that she's claimed for herself and, after repeated circles, plops down. I pour a couple of fingers of Bowmore and down them in one shot before heading to the bedroom to see what my wife has planned for me.

At the doorway, I'm brought up short by the sight of her lounging on the bed in black garters, thigh-high hose, four-inch black heels and nothing else—except the red plug, which stands out in stark relief against her creamy white skin. My hand lands on my chest, perhaps to see if my heart is still where it belongs. "Holy fucking hell, Nat. You ought to warn a guy before you do that to him."

"And miss seeing that expression on your face? Never."

"What're you doing to me?"

"Just what I was told to do."

"You're awfully smug for a girl who has already earned one punishment tonight."

"I've learned to rather appreciate your brand of punishment."

"Perhaps I'm not doing it right, then."

"Oh no, you're doing it right. I'd let you know if you weren't."

I can't help but laugh at her cheekiness. I love her confidence and how far she's come from the first day when she told me she wouldn't sleep with me, or any man, unless she was married. She was hiding then, running from her traumatic past. And now… Now she's quite simply magnificent.

I remove my clothes, leaving them in a pile on the floor to be dealt with later. "Are you the same virtuous girl I met all those weeks ago who gave me such a run for my money?"

"I'm the new and greatly improved version of her."

Laying my hand flat against her belly, I lean in to kiss her. "You were perfect then, and you're perfect now."

"I'm more perfect now that you've helped me to see all that I'm capable of." She gestures to her sexy outfit. "I never would've been able to do this, to *be* this, before you. You gave me wings so I could fly."

"You had them all along. I just helped you spread them."

She raises a brow in a sultry, sexy look that brings me to my knees. "Are we still talking about my wings?"

Smiling, I kiss her again. I love her this way, saucy and fearless and up for anything. "Talk to me about the club."

"I-it was very… Interesting and exciting."

Kissing her neck and jaw, I say, "Exciting how?"

"Watching, having others watch us… All of it."

"I loved having you there, gauging your reactions, knowing you were aroused by what you were seeing."

"Aroused," she says with a laugh. "That's one word for what I was."

"Did it surprise you? To be so turned on by it?"

"A little. I expected to be more nervous and perhaps a bit intimidated. But I wasn't either of those things. I was… Transported. I don't know how else to describe it."

"That's a good word, and I know exactly what you mean. There's something about being there, in a safe, sane environment where such things are encouraged and condoned, that allows you to let go in a totally different way than you can anywhere else."

"Yes, that's it exactly."

"Do you know what it means to me that you get it? That you saw what I see at the club, why it matters so much to me? Why I enjoy it as much as I do?"

"I think I do. I also think I might like to try what Kristian did in our playroom sometime."

I stare at her, wanting to take in every amazing detail of her face. "I wish there was some way for me to properly convey to you what it feels like, for the first time in my life, to be exactly where I'm supposed to be, with the person I'm meant to be with."

"That part I get, because I feel the same way." Her hand, which has been flat upon my chest, begins to slide down, leaving a trail of fire behind.

Though I don't want to stop her, I place my hand on top of hers. "Are you trying to seduce me so I'll forget about your punishment?"

The look she gives me is pure sexy innocence. "I would never do that."

"Yes," I say, laughing, "you would." I sit up against a stack of pillows and pat my lap. "Come to me, my love. Assume the position." I absolutely fucking *love* the way her face flushes and her lips part when she realizes my intentions. "Now."

Moving hesitantly, she crawls to me—which is fucking sexy as hell—and drapes her body over my lap, presenting that delectable ass to do with whatever I like. And there are so many things I'd like to do… I cup her supple cheeks, squeezing and shaping them. "How many do you think you deserve tonight?"

"None?"

I spank her right cheek, and she gasps from the surprise as much as the impact. "Try again."

"That counts as one."

"Are you topping from the bottom again, my love? Do I need to remind you who's in charge here?" She is. We both know it, but what fun is it if I don't try to pull rank on her once in a while?

"N-no."

That little stutter makes me harder than I already am. "So what's a good number for coming without permission at the club?"

"Five?"

"Nowhere near enough."

"Seven."

"Getting closer. I think twelve would do it. A nice even dozen."

She moans, but the way her back arches in anticipation tells the true story. She loves this as much as I do.

I start off easy, giving her three quick spanks intended to get her attention, in case I didn't already have it. After the third one, I switch on the vibration in the plug, and she nearly levitates off my lap. Her entire body flushes with heat that nearly sends me over the edge I've been clinging to since I first saw her in this sexy getup. I run a finger under one of the garters and then down between her cheeks, where I discover she's as wet as she was at the club.

Her hands are gripping the down comforter, her head is lowered, and her rapid breathing mesmerizes me. I love knowing I can do this to her, that I can take her to this place of sharp, intense arousal. Making her count off each stroke of my hand against her bottom, I continue with the "punishment" that has us both so hot and bothered I worry that I won't get through it without embarrassing myself.

She wrecks the control that has been a source of endless pride to me as a Dom. But no other woman has been like this woman.

After the twelfth spank, I stroke and caress her red bottom, making sure the pain becomes pleasure, until she is practically purring in my arms. I grasp the base of the plug and gently begin to withdraw it.

Her head comes up, and her entire body goes tense.

I press it back into place, drawing a low, keening moan from her. I repeat that same move, over and over again, until she's a quivering mess of sensation. "Nat… I want to fuck you here so bad. You have to tell me you want it, too."

"I do," she says without hesitation. "I want you. I want everything with you."

"Turn over, sweetheart." I need to see her face and her eyes, to ensure she's doing this because she wants to and not just for me.

I help her to turn until I'm holding her in my arms, looking down at her face. "Tell me again."

"I want you, Flynn. Every way I can have you." She never blinks or hesitates or shows an ounce of fear.

"Are you sure?"

"Very sure."

My heart gallops in my chest. "I'll make it so good for you, baby."

"I know you will."

Her trust in me is the most powerful aphrodisiac I've ever experienced. Nothing has ever been a greater turn-on than knowing this woman, who has every reason to trust no one, trusts me with her life, her pleasure, her happiness, her well-being. I kiss her softly and sweetly, all the while denying my baser urges to take, take, *take* what she is giving me so freely.

But we're going to work up to it, one step at a time. Step one is kissing—deep, erotic kissing that goes on for what seems like hours. I cup her breast and pinch her nipple between my fingers, planning to draw this out for hours if necessary to ensure it's good for both of us. I want her to love it so much she wants to do it again and again.

Eventually, I move us so she's on her back and I'm above her.

She looks up at me with those big eyes, the color different now from when I first met her, but no less compelling than it was then. I see her every emotion reflected in those eyes that look at me with love and trust and desire. I want to always be worthy of all that she has given me.

I kiss her neck and work my way down to her breasts, feasting on each nipple until they're tight red nubs. Each rib gets my attention, and her belly quivers as I run my lips over the soft skin there.

"Flynn..."

"What, honey?"

"I thought you wanted to... That we were going to..."

"I do, and we will. Eventually."

Sighing, she sags into the mattress, understanding now that nothing about this is going to be fast or immediate.

I lift her legs over my shoulders and hold her open for my tongue. She's so wet and so primed that I could make her come with one stroke of my tongue. But what fun would that be? Setting the plug to the most intense vibration, I set out to drive her mad with my tongue and fingers.

"Don't come until I tell you to."

Her hands fist my hair, and she's pulling so hard it hurts. I couldn't care less. All I can think about is the sweet taste of her pussy, the muscles clamping down on my fingers and how much I love her.

Ready to move things along, I latch on to her clit and suck, drawing the tight nub of flesh into my mouth and running my tongue back and forth. "Come, sweetheart. Let me hear you." I suck harder and drive my fingers into her as deep as they'll go.

She shrieks as she comes, her legs tightening around my head to keep me from getting away.

I bring her down slowly, gently, and then rise to my knees to push into her channel, riding the waves of her orgasm. The plug makes it an especially tight fit as I thrust into her, over and over again, needing to take the edge off this mad, clawing desire so I can give her the tenderness she needs for what's next.

Her legs wrap around my hips, her hands grip my ass, and when she squeezes, I lose it, coming with a roar that's ripped straight from my gut. Christ have mercy… And then I feel her come, too, again.

I collapse on top of her, my head spinning from the wild ride. I open my eyes to see the red tip of her breast calling to me and raise my head to draw it into my mouth. Even after an explosive release, I want more.

She moans and raises her hips, and I come alive all over again, hardening inside her. I begin to move, thrusting until I'm fully hard.

"You're going to kill me," she whispers, her eyes closed.

"Never. I love you too much to kill you." I kiss her lips, which are puffy and soft. "Ready for more?"

"Not sure if I can take any more."

"You want to stop?"

She opens her eyes. "Did I say that?"

I smile down at her. "I want to see your face for this, but it might be more comfortable for you on your belly. What do you prefer?"

"I want to see your face, too."

I kiss her again before withdrawing my extremely hard cock from her very tight pussy, making us both moan. From the bedside table, I grab a condom and a bottle of lubricant.

Natalie watches me closely. "Have you done this before in this bed?"

"Never."

As I roll on the condom, I realize my hands are shaking ever so slightly. "I want you to stop this if you don't like it, Nat. I mean it. You don't have to do anything you don't want to do."

She reaches up to caress my face. "I know how to stop it."

"It'll hurt at first, but the more you try to relax and let me in, the easier it will be."

Swallowing hard, she says, "Okay."

"Ready to remove the plug?"

She bites her bottom lip and nods.

I begin slowly, drawing the plug out before reseating it.

Natalie groans. "Why do you have to torture me?"

"I'm getting you ready."

"Torture."

"Preparation."

I withdraw the plug to the widest point, letting it stretch her and leaving it there as I bend over her to suck on her nipple. "You're doing great, sweetheart."

"Hurts," she says softly.

"I know." I don't remind her that I'm a lot bigger than the plug, and I want her to be as ready as she can be to take me. After long minutes of letting the plug stretch her, I remove it, and she sags in relief that's short-lived. Flipping open the cap on the bottle of lube, I squirt a healthy amount onto my fingers and slide them into her, ensuring she's prepared from the inside out. "Talk to me, honey."

"Can't."

"Try."

"Tight."

"Yes, it is."

Her pussy is so wet, it's running down to where my fingers slide in and out of her ass. I bend my head to lick her, startling her when my tongue connects with her clit. After stroking her a few more times with my tongue and fingers, I withdraw both and apply another handful of lube to my cock.

I've done this many times before—too many to count—but it's never mattered as much as it does now. I want so badly to make it good for her, and my love for her makes it so much more intense than it's ever been.

I press the head of my cock against her tight opening and push, slowly and easily, watching her face carefully.

Her mouth opens, her back arches, and her head falls back.

"Nice and easy, sweetheart. Push against me, let me in."

Reaching under her, I grasp her cheeks and open her as I give her a little more.

Her sharp gasp stops me in place as she spasms around me. The pressure is so tight and so intense that I have to summon every ounce of control I possess to keep from coming.

"Talk to me."

Her low grunt is the only response I get. She's concentrating so deeply and trying so hard to give me what I want that she can't speak.

I give her a little more.

"You're doing so great, baby. I wish you could see what I see, the way you're stretched around my cock and taking me in. It's so fucking hot." I reach down to press my thumb against her clit, which is tight and hard. "You can come any time you want to."

Tears leak from the corners of her eyes, and I kiss them away.

"Are those tears of pain?"

She shakes her head, and I'm filled with relief.

I continue to caress her clit, hoping to give her something else to focus on. Her thighs begin to quiver, and she rocks against me, coming with a scream that allows me to enter her fully. Holy God… It's the most amazing feeling. Her entire body is convulsing around me, so I hold on tight to her, riding wave after wave of incredible sensation.

When she finally begins to calm, I start to move, slowly withdrawing and then pressing back in, over and over again, rocking gently against her.

"God, Nat, you're so fucking hot. You're making me crazy right now."

She raises her hips, and that tiny bit of encouragement is all I need to let loose, giving her deeper thrusts that have me on the brink of release. I hold off, wanting her to come again before I give in.

"I'm staying right here until you come again," I whisper against her ear.

Her deep moan makes me smile.

I press deeper and begin once again to stroke her clit, thrusting into her in small, tight increments. Next time we do this, I'll use a finger vibe so I can keep her coming the whole time. I keep up the dual actions until she's writhing under me, coming again, harder this time than the last, which is all it takes to trip the most intense orgasm of my life.

Though I never take my eyes off her face, I nearly lose all sense of time and place as I hammer into her, taking as much as giving.

She clings to me, crying out as the release overtakes us both.

Gripping the condom, I withdraw from her as slowly as I went in, watching her the entire time. I use a tissue to dispose of the condom so I don't have to leave her for even a second.

"Sweetheart…"

"Hmmm."

"Can you open your eyes?"

It takes a minute, but they flutter open, glassy and moist and full of love that fills me with relief.

"Good?"

"Mmmm."

"I need the words."

She licks her lips. "Good. Different but good."

"Hurt?"

"Yeah, but not as bad as I expected."

"Would you do it again?"

"Now?" she asks, seeming alarmed.

Laughing, I say, "No, not now."

"I'd do it again. You were right about the orgasm… Phew… It was so powerful."

I'm so glad to hear her say that. It's not for everyone, but I love it, so I'm glad to know she wasn't so put off by our first time that she wouldn't be willing to do it again.

"Thank you for trusting me enough to do that with me."

"Thank you for being so gentle with me."

"I'll always be gentle with you." I kiss her and hold her close. "Let me clean you up, and then we'll get some sleep." I release her only long enough to retrieve a warm washcloth from the bathroom that I use to clean us both.

She releases a satisfied-sounding sigh as the rough terrycloth rubs her sensitive flesh.

I look up to find her watching me tend to her, a small smile on her lips.

"What?"

"Just looking at what's mine."

I love that she's possessive of me when that quality has driven me insane with other women. This woman is welcome to be as possessive of me as she'd like to be. "So am I."

She holds out her arms to me.

I toss the washcloth on the floor and go to her, dragging the covers up and over us. We come together, arms and legs wrapped around each other, bodies pressed tightly. It's the only way I can sleep now, with her warm, sweet softness snug against me.

"Are you hurting, sweetheart?"

"No, not really. I'm still throbbing."

"And throbbing is a good thing?"

"In this case, yes."

"I want you to know that I wish I'd told you the truth about myself from the beginning, that I'd had the faith I should've had in you and that core of inner strength that is so much a part of who you are."

"While I wish I'd heard it from you rather than your ex-wife, you were probably wise to hold it back from me. I wouldn't have been able to handle it at the beginning, and I might've done something stupid like run away from you."

"I would've run after you." I stroke my hand over her hair. "Go to sleep, sweetheart. We have a very special day ahead tomorrow."

"Can't wait to marry you all over again."

"Me, too." Long after she's asleep, I remain awake, enjoying the simple pleasure of holding her while she sleeps.

Chapter 16

Natalie

My entire body is sore from what we did last night. I can't seem to move as I force my eyes to open on a new day, one in which we will celebrate our marriage with Flynn's family. I'm disappointed that neither of my sisters could get the time off from school and work, and that Leah couldn't get anyone to cover her shift at the bar. Aileen had another round of chemo on Friday, so she can't come either.

I tell myself I'm okay with none of my people being here, but I can't deny I'm disappointed that none of them could make it work, even after Flynn offered to fly them out for it.

I need to get up. I need to take a shower and wash my hair so I'm ready when the hair and makeup people get here to help me get ready. I told Flynn and Addie I didn't want all that, but he insisted on full pampering today.

"Hey, you're awake," he says when he and Fluff come into the room. Wearing only a pair of basketball shorts, Flynn is carrying a tray, and the scent of coffee has my full attention. "Happy Valentine's Day."

I try to sit up and instantly regret moving.

"Oh God, baby. Is it bad?"

"I'm okay."

"Tell me the truth."

"I'm sore."

“I’ll run you a hot bath after you eat.” He gestures to the plate with eggs and bacon and pancakes.

My stomach growls loudly. “Did you make all this?”

“No, Fluff did. But I supervised.”

I laugh despite my aches and pains.

Fluff barks and jumps up on the bed to “help” with my breakfast.

I struggle to find a comfortable position, and when I’m settled, he places the tray on my lap. “I’ve never had breakfast in bed before I met you.”

“What do you think of it?”

Taking a bite of bacon, I smile at him. “I could get used to it.”

“We’re fine with that.”

“Have you been up long?”

“Couple hours. I took a run and did some work.” He accepts the bite of pancake I offer him. “It’s no fun being awake without you.”

I waggle a finger at him to bring him closer so I can kiss him. “Happy Valentine’s Day to you, too. Sorry I slept so late.”

“Don’t be sorry. You were worn out.”

“Extremely.”

“Are you sorry… Do you wish…”

I lay a finger over his lips. “I loved it. No regrets, no second-guessing.”

He takes a deep breath and releases it slowly. “Ready for that hot bath?”

“Sounds heavenly.”

“You should have plenty of time to soak before the masseuse arrives.”

“*Masseuse?*”

“You heard me right. I want my wife nice and relaxed for her big day.”

“You’re too good to me.”

He leans over to kiss me. “You’re good to me, too.” Then he’s gone to the bathroom to turn on the tub for me, Fluff following close behind him.

I meant what I said about having no regrets. I love happy, satisfied, relaxed Flynn, who isn’t wound so tightly he might burst from trying to deny who and what he is. I said I wanted all of him, and I got that last night. I have absolutely no regrets.

Flynn returns to the room with Fluff once again hot on his heels.

"Have you noticed she follows you around now the way she used to follow me?" I ask.

"Does it bother you that she likes me now?"

"Of course not. I want you guys to be friends."

"I thought you wanted us to be father and daughter."

I giggle at his indignant expression. "That, too."

He comes over to the bed and removes the tray, placing it on a nearby footstool. "My love, your bath awaits you. Put your arms around my neck and allow me."

Because I'm so achy, I do what I'm told and enjoy the way his strong arms scoop me up like I'm weightless. "Hey, what happened to my garters and the rest?"

"I took them off after you conked out last night."

"I'm worried about how much time you spend awake while I'm sleeping."

"I'm always watching over you, sweetheart." He deposits me into the tub, which is full of bubbles and something else.

"What is that? What do I smell?"

"Eucalyptus. It'll fix what ails you."

"This is very decadent." I reach for his hand. "Come in with me."

He drops his shorts and climbs in behind me. The tub is even bigger than the one in his New York apartment, so there's more than enough room for both of us.

With his arms around me, I recline against his chest and sigh with contentment. "Already the best Valentine's Day ever."

"For me, too, sweetheart. Are you excited for the party?"

"Very. I can't wait to see what your mom put together for us. I'm sure it'll be amazing."

"She does love to throw a party. At this very moment, I picture her with a clipboard and a bullhorn, ordering everyone around. My sisters are probably nowhere near there. They know better."

"A *bullhorn*?"

"She does her best work with amplification."

I giggle madly at that image of his classy mother barking orders into a bullhorn.

"Don't worry. With Stella at the helm, it'll be a hell of a party."

"I have no doubt. I just wish my sisters could've come, and Leah and Aileen."

"I know, sweetheart. I feel so bad that they can't make it."

"It's not your fault. Even you can't make other people's bosses give them time off."

"We'll celebrate with them the next time we see them."

After my bath, I stroll out of the bedroom to find the living room has been filled with red roses that perfume the air with their fragrant scent. The blinds are drawn against the bright morning sun, and a massage table has been set up where the coffee table usually sits.

Flynn is in the kitchen with a tall blonde woman he seems to know well. "There's Nat. Sweetheart, come meet Jasmine."

Her name is Jasmine, and the only thought in my head is whether or not he's slept with her.

"Could you come here for a quick second, Flynn?"

"Excuse me for one second, Jas."

Jas… I want to growl with jealous rage.

"I'm going to take this call," Jasmine says, holding up her phone as she heads for the pool deck. "I'll be right out here when you're ready."

He comes over to me. "What's wrong?"

"Is she… Have you… Been with her?"

I see the surprise before the hurt registers, and I immediately regret the question. He speaks softly so only I can hear him. "You think I would bring someone I've fucked before into our *home* to tend to you?"

"I… No. I'm sorry."

He seems stunned. "How can you think…"

"You didn't tell me about Marlowe."

"Oh my God, Nat. That was a hundred years ago and lasted minutes."

"You didn't tell me."

"Do you want a list of all of them? Like a spreadsheet, maybe?"

"It's a fair question, Flynn."

Shaking his head, he looks at me as if he's seeing me for the very first time. "I'm disappointed that you would think that of me."

"I'm sorry you're disappointed."

"Do you still want the massage?"

I don't. I want to walk away from him and be alone, but after he went to the trouble to arrange such a lovely surprise for me, I don't do that. "Yes, please."

"I'll get her."

He walks away, and that's when I realize my heart is beating hard, and I'm light-headed from the unusually contentious exchange. Returning with Jasmine, he introduces us and leaves us to get on with it, never once looking directly at me.

Jasmine is cheerful and professional and tries to make me feel comfortable under the heated blankets, but knowing he's angry with me—fairly or unfairly—makes it impossible for me to truly enjoy the massage.

I'm torn between calling a halt to it and fearing I'll hurt her feelings if I do.

She's turned me from back to front when I hear Flynn's raised voice coming from the pool deck. I try to hear him, but I can't make out what he's saying. "Jasmine, I'm sorry, but I have to stop."

"No problem at all, Mrs. Godfrey. We can do it another time."

"Yes, please. Another time would be great. And call me Natalie."

"I will, thank you, Natalie."

She hands me my robe and turns her back to gather her supplies while I put it on. I leave her to finish cleaning up and head for the deck.

He's pacing, phone pressed to his ear, body rigid with the tension that reminds me of the days that followed David Rogers's decision to sell my story to the highest bidder. Turning, he spots me there and lowers his voice.

I feel left out, excluded from whatever is happening, but I resist the urge to turn my back and go inside. Rather, I wait for him to end the call, which he does a few minutes later.

"Did Jasmine leave?"

"Yes."

"That wasn't an hour."

"I couldn't seem to concentrate or relax. I heard you yelling. What's wrong?"

"Rogers's wife has gone to the media to pressure the FBI into making an arrest in her husband's case."

"Anyone in particular she wants to see arrested?"

"Who do you think?"

"Flynn…"

"Don't worry. They've got nothing on me, or we'd know it by now. I talked to Emmett. He says our guy on the ground in Lincoln is making progress and should have something soon."

"Can you make his wife stop saying you did it?"

"Emmett is handling that, too."

It's a warm day and the sun is beating down on the deck, but I'm chilled to the bone nonetheless. Normally, Flynn would be holding me as he offered comfort, but now he keeps his distance.

"You're angry with me."

"A little, I suppose."

"I may ask that question again in the future."

"For the record, I'm not close to nor do I regularly associate with any woman I've slept with other than Marlowe."

"What about Cresley?"

"We're friendly. We don't hang out except for once in a while at the clubs. I don't talk to her between visits or hit her up when I'm in New York. I like her. We've partied together, I've met her son a few times, we had sex a few times with Hayden. That's all it's ever been or will ever be. She's not going to suddenly drop by here out of the blue to hang with us."

"Will she be at the party?"

"No."

"Are there other women coming to the party that you've slept with?"

He doesn't like the question, but I don't care if he likes it. "Other than Marlowe, no."

"Do you think I'm out of line to ask these things?"

"No."

"Then why do you look so pissed off?"

"Because! You think I'd hire someone I've fucked to come in here and run their hands all over you. You actually thought I'd do that."

"I didn't know if you would do that because your attitudes toward sex are very different than mine were until I met you. I'm still learning the rules of how it's done in your world."

He seems to lose some of his rigidity as that point strikes home. "Okay, that's fair enough, and I wasn't seeing it from your point of view. But you have to know I'd never disrespect you that way."

"I do now."

He takes a step toward me and then another.

I do the same, meeting him halfway. "Did *that* count as a fight?"

When he smiles down at me, I'm thrilled—and relieved—to see the tenderness is back in his sexy brown eyes. "Maybe. You kinda got me right here asking me that." He rubs his hand over his breastbone.

"I didn't mean to hurt you, but I have questions. I'll probably have others as we go forward. I need to know I'm allowed to ask them."

His hands encircle my hips, and he gazes down at me in that intense, all-consuming way of his. "You're allowed to ask, just as I'm allowed not to like it."

"But you'll always answer me truthfully?"

"Yes, I promise."

I go up on tiptoes to kiss him. "She rubbed oil all over me. Seems a shame to let that go to waste, doesn't it?"

"Mmm," he says, biting my earlobe. "That would be a damned shame."

CHAPTER 17

Flynn

On our way to Beverly Hills in the chauffeured Bentley my dad sent for us, Natalie sits close to me, holding my hand. She's wearing the same dress she wore for our wedding in Vegas. I'm in my favorite Armani tux. From what I've been told, the celebrity news programs are ablaze with the accusations Rogers's wife is making against me, but I'm comforted by the FBI's public statements that I'm not a suspect.

I hope they mean that. They haven't actually told me that—yet. Emmett has spent the day on the phone trying to get more information out of them, but other than what we've seen on TV, they're letting me continue to twist in the wind.

I didn't kill David Rogers. I never met the guy. Am I sorry that someone else killed him? Not at all. After selling Natalie out to the press for money, he got what was coming to him.

Today, I need to put all that aside to focus on my gorgeous wife and the many surprises I have in store for her this afternoon and evening. In cahoots with my parents, I've ensured this will be a day she never forgets. Our argument earlier today has left me feeling unsettled, despite the spectacular makeup sex that followed.

I hate that she thought for one second I'd bring a woman I'd fucked into our home and pass her off as hired help. Not that I think of Jas that way. She's done massages for the Quantum team for years now and is actually a close friend of

Marlowe's. It never occurred to me that Natalie might think I'd slept with her. But, with hindsight, I can see why she'd ask even if I'd hated that she asked.

My lifestyle is still very new to her, and I've encouraged her to ask questions. I have to be willing to answer them, even the ones that make me uncomfortable. I've never been ashamed of the way I've approached sex and women, and I'm not going to start now with second-guessing myself or the choices I've made.

However, now that I've found the woman I want to spend forever with, I do wish there were fewer situations and people for her to ask about.

We arrive in Beverly Hills, and my parents' street has been shut down by event security. They wave my dad's car in.

"Wow," Natalie says. "They closed off the street. Do the neighbors mind?"

"No, they understand, and they have full access to their homes. If the word got out about this, we'd be overrun with paparazzi. The neighbors would rather have the security than the photographers."

My parents come out to greet us when we arrive. Wearing a champagne-colored gown, Mom is fairly sparkling with excitement. She's waited a long time for this day, and it makes me happy to give her something she has wanted for me. Dad loves any and all time he gets to spend with his family, so he's also beaming as he welcomes us with hugs and kisses. He's decked out in a sharp black tux that makes him look twenty years younger than he is.

"Your mom has gone all out," he tells me.

"I have no doubt. I warned Natalie."

Dad's booming laugh echoes through the foyer as they escort us upstairs to the second floor.

"Come see." Mom throws open the doors to the small ballroom that has hosted many of the most important Godfrey family events over the years. Inside, tuxedoed workers are scurrying about, applying finishing touches.

"Oh my God," Natalie says, her eyes glittering as she takes in the elegant, intimate scene before her.

I try to see it through her eyes, as if I'm seeing the room for the first time with its high ceilings and elaborate crown moldings. The centerpiece is a huge crystal chandelier that bathes the room in soft, romantic light. Mom has put a tasteful emphasis on Valentine's Day through red accents but thankfully hasn't gone overboard with the hearts. Round tables are laden with china, crystal, candles and red roses.

"It's absolutely beautiful, Stella," Natalie says, her eyes shimmering with tears.

"I'm so glad you're happy with it, honey. We're thrilled to officially welcome you into our family." As Mom hugs Nat, I contend with a huge lump in my throat. It's at moments like this when all the crazy shit that surrounds me fades away, and I'm reminded of what's truly important in this life. "Come," Mom says, taking Natalie by the hand. "You two can relax in Flynn's old room until the guests begin to arrive. We don't want them to see the gorgeous bride and groom before we're ready."

She deposits us in my old room, which is exactly as I left it, right down to the vintage poster of Farrah Fawcett on the wall, the Dodgers pennant, the surfing posters, the trophies from my short-lived career as a lacrosse star and posters of the metal bands I'd worshiped in high school.

While I flop down on the bed and wish for more time alone with my wife in my old room, Natalie looks at everything. "Metallica? Seriously?"

"It was a phase."

"Tell me you didn't have a mullet."

"Okay, I didn't have a mullet."

"*Did you?*"

"I dare you to find a picture of me in this room where I have a mullet."

"I'll ask your sisters. They won't lie to me."

"Come over here, Mrs. Godfrey, and make all my teenage boy fantasies come true."

"No way am I coming near you when I'm all ready. You like to mess me up too much."

"You're wearing the panties, right?"

"Yes, Flynn," she says with a long-suffering sigh that makes me smile. "If you turn them on when I'm talking to friends of your parents, I'll kill you. Do you understand me?"

"Yes, ma'am."

A knock on the door makes my heart beat faster with excitement because I know who it is, and I can't wait to see her reaction. I pretend to check my phone. "Can you get that, hon?"

"Sure."

Natalie heads for the door, and I keep my phone out to take pictures. I want to capture every second of this to show her later. She opens the door to Candace and Olivia, who are wearing matching red silk dresses.

"We heard you needed bridesmaids today," Candace says.

Natalie lets out a shriek that reminds me a little too much of other times she's made that particular noise, but I quash those thoughts to fully wallow in her joy at seeing her sisters. It's the first time she's seen Olivia in person in more than eight years, and the three of them cling to each other, all of them talking at once.

I told Addie to tell Nat's makeup artist to use only waterproof mascara. I'm glad now we thought of that.

The girls are still carrying on when Leah and Aileen appear in the doorway.

"Is this a private party, or can anyone join the fun?" Leah asks.

Natalie lets out another scream and launches herself at her friends, who wrap her up in hugs. "Oh my God! *I'm surrounded by liars!*"

"It was so hard," Aileen says. "We all felt *terrible* telling you we couldn't come."

I'm pleased to see her looking a thousand times better than she did the last time we saw her. My father's doctor friend set her up with the top breast cancer doctor in New York, and he has made some changes to her treatment that have her feeling much better. She and Leah are also dressed in the red gowns the four of them chose to wear as Natalie's attendants.

Natalie turns to me, shaking her head. "And you… *You* did this."

I go to her, put my arm around her and kiss her forehead. "You couldn't get married—again—without your people here."

"Thank you so much." She looks up at me with those eyes that have held me in their thrall from the first time I ever saw them. "Thank you."

"Anything for you, my love." I release her to hug my sisters-in-law, who are pretending not to stare at me. "I'm Flynn. So nice to finally meet you both."

"Doncha love how he says that?" Leah asks with a giddy grin. "'I'm Flynn.' Like the whole freaking world doesn't already know that."

"He's got *manners*, Leah," my wife says dryly. "You might want to get some."

"Manners are so overrated."

Laughing, I hug her and then Aileen. "Did you have a good trip?"

"The private plane totally sucked," Leah says. "We all hated it."

"I worried that you might." She cracks me up. To Aileen, I say, "Where are the kids?"

"Oh my God," Nat says. "Logan and Maddie are here, too?"

"Yep." Aileen glances over her shoulder. "They're downstairs with your nephews, raising hell out by the pool. I just hope they don't fall in."

"Is Ian with them?" I ask of my eldest nephew.

"He's the one who looks like you, right?"

"So I'm told. He'll keep an eye on things. My dad says he was born a thirty-year-old."

Speaking of the devil, my dad appears at the door carrying a huge box of flowers for the girls, red for the attendants and white for Nat. Mom has truly thought of everything.

"We're ready whenever you are, kids."

Natalie clears her throat. "Max… I wondered if you might be willing…" She takes a deep breath, seeming to fortify herself. "I could use an escort downstairs."

"It would be my honor, honey," he says softly.

Okay, I'm done. You can stick a fork right in me. She's so fucking sweet, and she just totally unmanned my dad *and* me with one adorably hesitant request.

I hold out my hand, palm up. "I need to borrow your ring, Mrs. G, so we can do this all over again."

She's as hesitant about removing her wedding ring from her finger as I am about removing mine.

"Just for a short time, and then they'll never come off again," I whisper to her as I kiss her. "See you downstairs?"

"I'll be there."

"You'd better be."

As I go down the stairs in the home where I grew up and head out to the yard where my wife and I will exchange our vows in front of our family and friends, everything is right in my world.

Natalie

I can't believe he flew in the girls, although I probably should've expected something like this. He thinks of everything. I have to give them credit—they were all very convincing telling me they couldn't come and sounding appropriately heartbroken to miss out on a chance to attend a big Hollywood party.

"Are you mad that we lied?" Livvy asks in a small voice that tugs at my heart.

I hug her again because I can. "I'm thrilled that you lied and gave me the best surprise of my life. I was so sad that you couldn't be here, but I didn't want to admit it even to myself."

"It was all Flynn's idea," Leah says. "He thought it would be fun to surprise you, and it was! You should've seen your face when we walked in here."

"I thought I was seeing things."

A yip from the hallway has me running to the door again, where I see Addie leading Fluff on a leash. I bend to scoop up my baby, who runs to me when she sees me. "What's she doing here?" She's wearing a special new red collar and a red bow on the top of her head. I can't believe she allowed that.

"Flynn made sure the security guys brought her over. He knew you'd want her here."

"After he told me she'd be happier at home. He's too much. Thank you, Addie, for anything and everything you did to make this day so special for us."

She hugs me. "My pleasure. Ladies, let's get you downstairs." Addie lines up the girls so Leah and Aileen go first, followed by my sisters.

Max extends his arm to me. "Shall we, my dear?"

"Yes, please." I tuck my hand into his elbow, struck by how sad it is that my parents' choices make it so they can't be part of my life. Although, looking back on it all now, I wouldn't change a thing because everything that happened in my past led me to Flynn.

Though nothing about this house is familiar to me, it already feels like home in a way. For the first time since I left my home so many years ago, I feel like I'm exactly where I belong. Who knew the home of my heart would be in Beverly Hills among superstars known the world over by their first names?

Accompanied by the sounds of a string quartet, Max escorts me down the winding stairs and out to the yard, where a gazebo and chairs have been set up for the ceremony.

We emerge from the house into warm, soft late-afternoon Southern California sunshine. The yard is full of people, but the only one I see is Flynn. He is standing with Hayden, Jasper, Kristian and Emmett, the brothers of his heart, by his side, and he is zeroed in on me as I come toward him on the arm of his father.

Max delivers me with a hug, a kiss and wishes for a long, happy life together.

Flynn receives a hug from his father and takes my hand, smiling widely at me. His joy is mine, his happiness essential to me. And I've never seen him look happier than he does right now.

I hand my flowers to Candace so I can hold both his hands while the judge, who is a close friend of Max's, leads us through the recitation of our vows. It is no less emotional the second time I pledge my life and my love to this extraordinary man who has changed my life so profoundly.

"Flynn and Natalie have pledged their lives and their love to each other, and now they wish to share some personal thoughts. Natalie?"

Since Flynn and I agreed to do this, I've thought a lot about what I want to say to him, but now that the moment is upon me and people are watching, my brain is frozen until he squeezes my hands, smiles and gazes into my eyes in that intense way of his. I forget about everyone else and focus only on him.

"If someone had told me six weeks ago today that I'd be standing in this lovely yard in Beverly Hills, gazing into the eyes of Flynn Godfrey and pledging to love him forever, I'd have had that person committed. Things like this don't happen to people like me. Or so I thought until I met you and found out that dreams really do come true, that true love exists, that fairy tales aren't just for the movies. I never could've imagined being loved by anyone the way you love me, and I'll be thankful for and protective of that love for the rest of our lives. I can't wait for what's ahead for us, and I look forward to every minute of our lives together. I love you so much. You'll never know how much."

His eyes brighten with unshed tears as he listens to me, and when I finish, he kisses me, sending a soft wave of laughter through the rows of guests looking on.

"I'll never forget that life-changing moment in Bleecker Park," he begins, gazing down at me as he speaks, "the first time I ever laid eyes on you and I knew,

I just *knew* you were the one I never expected to find. I love that you couldn't care less about my job or any of the baggage that comes with it. I love that you see me, just me, the way no one else ever has. I love that I can be fully myself with you and that you accept every part of me."

A flush of heat travels from my breasts to my face at his reference to the parts of him that I've fully accepted. I have to tamp down the urge to laugh at his outrageousness, which only I and a few others will recognize as such.

"I'll spend the rest of my life making sure I'm worthy of all the priceless gifts you've given me, Natalie. I love you now and forever."

We kiss again, and the judge clears his throat, reminding us we're not done.

Laughing, we exchange rings—again—and kiss more intently after the judge declares us husband and wife. Again.

Though it felt as real as it could get in Vegas, this time it feels official because those we love best witnessed it. Fluff circles our feet, barking and yipping.

Flynn bends to pick her up and places her in my arms before leading me down the aisle between the rows of chairs where his sisters, their families and others I haven't met yet cheer for us as we go by.

We take hundreds of pictures in the Godfreys' beautiful garden, some by ourselves and others with family and friends. We drink champagne and kiss as often as we can before we're ushered inside and upstairs to the ballroom for the party. The wedding party I didn't know I had until today is announced, until only Flynn and I remain outside the doors, holding hands and kissing with Fluff dashing between our feet.

"I would've have said we didn't needed this," I tell him, "but I'm so glad we did it."

"I am, too. It feels somehow more official now that we have all these witnesses."

"I thought the same thing earlier. No getting out of it now, Mr. Godfrey."

He kisses me again, lingering longer than he probably should have with a room full of people waiting for us to make our appearance. "No desire to get out of anything, Mrs. G."

From inside the room, we hear, "Please join us in welcoming Mr. and Mrs. Flynn Godfrey."

"That's our cue, sweetheart." He extends his arm to me.

I slip my hand into the crook of his elbow.

The room erupts into applause when we enter, Fluff trailing along beside us like the star of the day that she is. Without her, none of this would be happening. Candace picks up Fluff, and I send my sister a thankful smile. I still can't believe she and Livvy and Leah and Aileen are here. I blow kisses to Logan, who is beaming, and his sister, Maddie.

I'm absolutely stunned to see a ten-piece orchestra, a stage and Jason Mraz.

Jason Mraz?

"Surprise," Flynn whispers as he leads me to the dance floor as Jason sings "I Won't Give Up," the song we chose as our wedding song that night in Vegas.

"Oh my God, I can't believe this!" I'm overwhelmed by the incredible surprise as we dance to the song that will always bring back such beautiful memories of the first time we said "I do." And now this, too… "Amazing surprise. Thank you so much."

"You'll have to thank my mom. She called in a few favors with the record company." He draws me in closer to him, close enough that I can feel his arousal hard and heavy against my belly. "I won't give up, Nat. No matter what, I'll never give up on us."

I rub against him as shamelessly as I'm able to without making a scene. "I won't either. I promise." I gasp when the vibrating bullet in the panties he made me wear comes to life between my legs. I experience the same thrill I got at the club when people were watching us.

"Save some of those moves for the honeymoon."

Raising my head off his shoulder so I can see his face, I say, "What honeymoon? We've been on our honeymoon for weeks."

He scoffs. "Please. Give me a break. Hanging out at home is *not* a honeymoon."

"Flynn…"

"Shhh." He kisses the words off my lips. "Enjoy your wedding."

When the song ends to resounding applause, Jason calls Estelle Flynn to the stage and hands the microphone off to her. Thankfully, Flynn turns off the vibrator, and I sag against him in relief. My entire body is humming from the drumbeat of desire. I'm beginning to accept that as a permanent part of my new life with Flynn.

"Thank you so much, Jason," Stella says. "Wasn't that amazing?" She leads another round of applause for the singer, who takes a courtly bow and blows a kiss to us before he exits the stage.

I try not to swoon in the arms of my new husband.

"Max and I are so pleased and honored to welcome Natalie to our family. We have hoped and prayed that our wonderful son would someday find someone who brings him the kind of joy he's experienced with Natalie. We love you both, and we're so happy for you today." After some more applause, Stella continues. "I understand my new daughter-in-law and I have something in common, so I'd like to dedicate this to her and to my beloved son." She nods to the orchestra, which plays a familiar tune that immediately brings tears to my eyes.

"Oh, Flynn…"

Stella sings "Something Good" from *The Sound of Music*, and I absolutely melt into the arms of the man I love as his mother serenades us. It is, without a doubt, one of the most incredible moments of my life.

The entire evening is something out of a dream. I meet extended family—Max's sister, Stella's brother—Flynn's cousins, family friends, a few of them celebrities, but nothing about this day is about celebrity. It's about celebration and love and family and all the things that matter most in life. We enjoy a delicious meal, cut our cake and drink more champagne—headaches be damned.

After dinner, I tell Flynn I'll be right back and get up to speak to Leah. "Come with me for a second."

"Um, okay. What's up?"

"You'll see."

I lead her over to the table where Marlowe is chatting with Flynn's sisters. I introduce them all. "Marlowe, I want you to meet my roommate from New York, Leah. Leah, Marlowe."

Though she is totally starstruck, Leah manages to shake hands with Marlowe.

"Great to meet you," Marlowe says.

"Yes," Leah says, trying not to stare. "Same here. Heard a lot about you from Nat."

"All good, I hope."

"All good."

"So Marlowe desperately needs an Addie, and Leah needs a job. I thought you two might be able to help each other out."

Leah stares at me, her mouth agape. "You… I…"

"She's normally much more articulate," I say to Marlowe, who is smiling broadly.

"How soon can you be here, Leah?"

"W-what? You can't be serious. I'm a teacher, or I was a teacher. I don't want to be a teacher, and oh my God, I'm babbling."

"The job is yours if you want it. Natalie is right—I desperately need an Addie, and Addie could teach you everything you need to know about being an Addie. Will you consider it?"

"You don't even know me."

"I know Natalie, and if she says you'd be great, that's all I need to hear. I'd want you to relocate out here, though, since most of my life happens here."

"Move here. Work for Marlowe Sloane. Someone pinch me."

I gently pinch her arm, making them both laugh.

"So that's a yes?" Marlowe asks.

"Yes!" Leah's eyes are dancing with delight. "A million times yes."

"Excellent!" I'm pleased with my matchmaking and to know my best friend from New York will soon be living close by in Los Angeles.

As I dance with Max much later, Hayden dances with Addie, Marlowe with one of Flynn's younger cousins, and Jasper with Flynn's sister Ellie. Kristian and Emmett are standing by the side of the dance floor, a gaggle of women surrounding them. Flynn sways to the music with his nieces, India and Ivy, who giggle at his antics. He's going to be such a wonderful father.

"His mother and I had nearly given up on hoping this day would ever come," Max says softly, for my ears only. "Look at him with the kids. He's so great with them, and they love him so much. We couldn't bear to think of him missing out on having his own family, but it didn't seem like it would happen. And then he met you, and well… We're so happy for both of you."

"Thank you, Max, and thank you for this unforgettable day. I told Flynn earlier that I wouldn't have said we needed a big party, but I'm so glad we'll have these memories. And I also want to thank you and Stella for the way you've opened your arms to me. You'll never know how much that has meant to me."

"You've got a great big new family who loves you and your sisters. This is your home now, and you'll always be welcome here."

With tears in my eyes, I hug my new father-in-law until my husband comes to claim me, making jokes about his dad moving in on his girl.

Flynn wraps his arms around me, and I sink into his embrace, overwhelmed by the emotional day and the weeks that preceded it.

"What do you say we get out of here, my love?"

"Ready to go home?"

"I'm ready to be alone with my wife."

"Hopefully this wedding night will go a little better than the last one," I say in a teasing tone.

"I have no complaints whatsoever about the first one." With his hands on my face, he kisses me in that tender way that always disarms me. "Come on, let's go."

CHAPTER 18

Flynn

It's been an outstanding day, full of all the things that matter most to me. We've been surrounded by the love of our family and friends, but now it's about us, and I want my wife all to myself. Her sisters and friends will be spending the night with my parents before heading home tomorrow. My parents are also taking care of Fluff for us for the next week, not that Natalie knows that when she says good-bye to her baby for what she thinks is just tonight.

We hug and kiss Candace, Olivia, Leah, Aileen and her kids, and my family before we take our leave, again in my father's Bentley. The driver knows where we're going, so as we drive away from the place where I grew up, I'm able to give Natalie my full attention.

"I was thinking," she says.

I nuzzle her neck. "About?"

"Your idea for a movie about my story."

I wouldn't have thought anything could interest me more than the sexy column of her neck. "What about it?"

"It would make for a good movie, especially with today as the happy ending."

"You really think so?"

"I really do. Everyone already knows, so it's not like we'd be telling a story that would expose me or my secrets. I don't have any secrets anymore, and I like it that way."

"Still, it would result in a lot of renewed interest in your past."

"Perhaps one of the things I was meant to do with my newfound celebrity is bring attention to the strength and resilience of sexual assault survivors. My story is proof that it doesn't have to ruin a life or define it."

"Nat…" My voice is little more than a whisper. "I've said it before and I'll say it again and again, your courage is awe-inspiring. It would be such an honor for us to tell your story. We'd give it our very best. I promise."

She tugs on my bow tie, untying it. "What part would you play?"

"I'd have to play myself, the dashing hero whose life is saved by the feisty heroine who showed him what really matters."

Her laughter fills my soul. "The *dashing* hero, huh?"

"I did have to dash after you to keep you from getting away."

"That's true." She gives me a sly, sexy look that makes me instantly hard. "Of course, some parts of our story will have to remain private."

"Of course."

"My husband is a very public figure who wouldn't appreciate me selling his secrets to Hollywood."

"No, he wouldn't. Those secrets are only for you." I kiss her then, the way I've been dying to for hours now. Her arms encircle my neck, and she gives herself up to me with the sweet submission that makes me so fucking hot every time. She doesn't even know she's doing it. That's the best part. She gives me everything I need without me having to tell her how.

In deference to my dad's driver, who's worked for my family for decades, I withdraw from the kiss gradually and regretfully. We'll have plenty of time to pick up where we left off.

Natalie glances out the window. "Where're we going?"

"Not home."

"I see that. More surprises?"

"Maybe…"

"You're not going to tell me?"

"What fun would that be?"

"I didn't bring anything with me."

"You don't need anything."

"I need a toothbrush."

Smiling, I kiss her again and then once again because once wasn't enough. "Your every need shall be seen to, my love. Don't worry about a thing."

"As long as I'm able to make my foundation board meeting on Tuesday, I'm all yours."

"Um, yeah, about that…"

"What about it?"

"I moved it to next Tuesday."

"Flynn! You can't just move my meetings around without telling me."

"I can if I want to surprise you with the honeymoon I've been promising for weeks now." Before my eyes, the head of steam that had been building in her seems to dissipate. "Am I forgiven?"

"Depends on where we're going."

"You'll see soon enough."

"I'll let you know if you're forgiven when I see where we're going." She tugs on my tie again. "After this, no more surprises. We've got to get back to a normal life. We've been self-indulgent sloths for weeks now. I need to be productive."

"You've been very productive, sweetheart."

"Flynn! You know what I mean."

"Yes," I say, endlessly amused by her, "I know what you mean, and I need to get back to reality, too. If I weren't self-employed, I would've been fired by now. But we're taking this week for ourselves first. We're newlyweds. We deserve a honeymoon."

"Most people would say that more than a week at a Malibu beach house followed by days and days by a pool in the Hollywood Hills would count as a honeymoon."

"We're not most people, and I can do better."

She lays her head on my shoulder.

"You're not mad, are you?"

"No."

"I like to surprise you."

"I know."

"I won't take liberties with your schedule after this, unless I have a really, really good reason. Okay?"

She curls her hand around mine. "Thank you."

"For what?"

"For all the surprises today, for knowing what I needed to hear just now, and for making sure I get everything I want and need all the time. Having the girls there today… It made an already perfect day so much better than it would've been without them."

"If they honestly couldn't have come, we would've rescheduled it. I hope you know that."

"It was a miracle to get that many of the people who matter to us in one place at one time. I never would've expected you to reschedule it."

"We wouldn't have done it without your sisters and closest friends there, Nat. I told my mother that from the beginning, and she totally agreed."

"I loved the song your mother sang for us."

"She was very excited about that."

"It was all perfect."

"Wait till you see what's next."

"I can't wait."

We arrive at LAX for the two-and-a-half-hour flight to Cabo San Lucas. I can't wait to show Natalie the place I bought there a few years ago after numerous visits to the resort town made it one of my favorite places to get away. I carry a single small duffel bag onto the plane and tuck it between our seats. It contains everything we'll need while we're there.

I've got to be back on Saturday for Oscar rehearsals, but the next six days belong solely and completely to Natalie. My parents and Addie have the number at the house in Cabo in case of an emergency. Otherwise, my cell phone is turned off, and it'll stay that way until we get back to LA.

She's about to find out what a real honeymoon entails when you marry a sexual dominant. My dick gets hard just thinking about the six full days I plan to spend totally naked with my new bride.

After we take off, I can tell she's waiting for something to happen. Something always happens when we're on an airplane together. But this time, I decide to let the anticipation build by pretending to nod off in my seat. When she sees that I'm "asleep," she settles in, too, putting her feet up and pulling a throw blanket over her. I wait until she's all tucked in before turning on the vibe in her panties, drawing a gasp and then a moan from her.

"Very dirty trick."

"Hmm?"

"Don't act like you have no idea what you're doing."

"I thought I was sleeping."

"You're not sleeping. You're torturing me."

I open my eyes and turn toward her, taking in her adorable indignation. "Sweetheart, if I wanted to torture you, I could do much better than that."

"How?"

The single-word question hits me like a Taser, sending a current traveling through my body that gathers in my groin. "How would I torture you?"

She bites her lip and nods.

"In a perfect world where I could do anything I wanted?"

Though slashes of color have appeared on her cheeks, she nods again.

"I'd tie you to the bed, wrists and ankles. I'd blindfold you and clamp your nipples. I'd fill your ass with the biggest plug I have and use a vibe in your pussy that also stimulates your clit. I'd tease you with ice and feathers and everything else I could think of, but I wouldn't let you come, perhaps for hours."

She shudders visibly. "And you would like that? Doing that to me?"

"I'd fucking love it."

"Why?"

"Why would I love it? Because I'd hold your pleasure and your well-being in my hands, because you trust me enough to give me that." I take her hand and run my fingers over the sensitive skin on her inner wrist. "Because by the time I let us both come, it would be so explosive you'd never forget it—and neither would I."

"I want to do that. Everything you said… I want it."

I shake my head. "Blindfolding is a hard limit for you."

"Could we do the rest of it?"

"Like the playroom, that scenario is something we work up to, a little at a time. You are very new to this and I don't want to scare you."

"I was scared before I knew how much I love to turn over my pleasure to you."

I shift in my seat because I'm so hard for her, I ache. "Nat, fuck… You don't know what you do to me when you say things like that."

"What do I do? Tell me."

I drop our joined hands to my lap and flatten her palm against my cock.

Before I have a second to gauge her intentions, she's out of her seat and on her knees before me. "Could I help you with that, Sir?"

It's the first time she has initiated play, and it does something to me to see her on her knees in front of me, wearing the pretty dress she changed into before we left my parents' house and offering to service me. She's like every wet-dream fantasy I've ever had come to life in one perfect woman. How I ever got so lucky to find her is something I will think about every day for the rest of my life.

"Free me from my pants." My voice is nowhere near as firm or as steady as I'd like it to be. But it doesn't have to be with her. She has no expectations, no preconceived notions of what a Dom should sound like. I can be anyone I wish to be with her, and it will never be wrong.

Natalie keeps her head down as she goes to work on the fasteners on my pants. Before she can remove them, I withdraw the vibrator controller from my pocket and curl it into my hand. The drag of the zipper over my cock has me fighting for control, and she hasn't even touched me yet. She reaches around me, grasping my pants and boxers, and gives a tug.

I lift to help her remove them.

She unbuttons my shirt and pushes it aside, hovering over me for a breathless moment. "You are so beautifully put together."

"As are you." I curl my finger around a long lock of her hair. "I wouldn't change a single thing."

"Neither would I."

"I want you naked." Natalie dutifully stands and presents her back to me so I can unzip her dress, which falls into a pool around her feet, leaving her bare except for the crystal panties, a garter belt and thigh-high hose. She picks up the dress and drapes it over the other chair before returning to her position between my legs.

She drops her head to my chest and kisses and licks and nibbles a path down the front of me. By the time she wraps her hand around the base of my cock, I'm leaking copiously. She sticks out her tongue and cleans me up, making me gasp from the aching pleasure. I could tell her to take me in her mouth. I could make her suck me and stroke me, but I wait to see what she'll do on her own.

And she doesn't disappoint. With her hand moving around the wide base, she opens her mouth and takes me in, sucking and licking as she goes. Before she makes me forget, I turn on the vibe while hoping she doesn't lose track of what she's doing and bite me. Thankfully, she doesn't do that, but she does lose her rhythm for a second and look up at me with an arresting expression in her eyes. She's gotten good at this in the weeks we've spent together, learning how to open her throat to allow me to go deep. She knows just where to lick and how to stroke and when to suck, but I've yet to come in her mouth. That's not something I would just do.

"Nat… Sweetheart…" I tug on her hair, hard enough to get her attention but not hard enough to cause pain. "I'm going to come. Sweetheart…"

Rather than release me the way she normally does, she doubles down, practically swallowing me into the tight spasm of her throat. *Fucking hell…* I hold off for as long as I can, giving her time to change her mind, but then she presses her fingers to the back of my balls, and I detonate.

She swallows every drop, bringing me down slowly and gently. It is, without any doubt, the most intense blowjob of my life.

My dick pops out of her mouth, and she leans her forehead against my abdomen, both of us breathing hard.

"Was that okay?"

"Nat, Christ, it was the best I've ever had."

Propping her chin on my belly, she looks up at me. "Yeah?"

"Oh yeah. Come up here."

Straddling my hips, she crawls up my chest and into my arms. I cuddle her in close to me, needing the contact, the scent, the essence of her. The buzz of the vibe in her panties has my cock stirring back to life.

"Are you going to turn this thing off?" she asks after a quiet moment.

"Not until you come."

"How do you want me?"

"Sit up and move against me." I guide her into position, my hands on her hips, her hands flat against my chest. "That's it, sweetheart, now move however you need to. Take what you need." I've never recovered as quickly as I do with her, especially when she's writhing on top of me, her entire body flushed with heat, her nipples high and tight, her lips parted and her eyes closed. She's a fucking goddess, and she's all mine. "Give into it, love. Let it happen."

Her entire body goes rigid in the seconds before she comes, biting her lip to hold back her cries of pleasure. I can't wait to be completely alone with her in Mexico so I can hear those cries over and over again.

She sags into my arms, and I toss a blanket over her back. I hold her for the rest of the flight. I feel myself relaxing in a way I seldom have before. I can't wait to focus on nothing but my beautiful, sexy wife for the next six days. I plan to give her a honeymoon that neither of us will ever forget.

Natalie

Flynn's home in Cabo San Lucas is breathtaking. Situated high on a hill that looks down over crystal-blue water, it's all terracotta tiles with white paint and colorful pottery. I absolutely love it at first sight. The rooms are big and airy, the furniture designed for comfort and relaxation.

"What do you think?" he asks after showing me around.

"It's fabulous. I can see why you love it so much."

He slides his arms around me from behind. "We're completely alone here."

"What about security?"

"None, other than the gates that surround the place. Hardly anyone except my family and closest friends even know I have this place. It's where I go when I truly want to run away from it all." He tugs on the zipper to my dress as he drops hot, openmouthed kisses on my neck. "Since we're completely alone and the house is fully stocked with everything we'll need, it's probably a good time to tell you this will be an entirely naked honeymoon."

I've been so caught up in what he's doing to my neck that his words take a second to register. "Wait. What did you say?"

"You heard me. Six full days. No clothes allowed."

"By no clothes, you mean—"

With the zipper fully open, he runs his finger down my side, over my ribs, stopping at my hip. "No. Clothes. I want to see you and only you the whole time we're here."

The thought of it has my entire body zinging with sensation. My heart is beating faster, and my skin suddenly feels tight and constricted. "We can't loll around in the nude for six full days."

"You don't think so?"

"If that's what you want, why did you pack a bag?"

"I'm glad you asked. Once you remove your dress and everything you're wearing under it, you can unpack our bag and put everything on the bed. I'll be in shortly."

I stand there for a second, feeling frozen in place.

"Natalie?" He tucks my hair behind my ear. "You know how to say no, sweetheart."

His softly spoken words remind me of the rules of our game and the power I have in a single word that can stop everything. I don't want to stop this. I want to have this experience with him, to see what he has planned for us, to enjoy every second of the time we have alone together.

Our lives will be busy and complicated once we return to reality. To have this slice of time completely alone where we're able to explore our every desire is exciting, even if the thought of six full days in the nude is disconcerting. Before him, I didn't like to be naked in the shower, a thought that makes me smile as I pick up the duffel bag and head for the bedroom.

When he showed me the room, he opened the doors to a deck. A warm breeze billows into the room, making the gauzy white curtains flutter. The ceiling fan is made of bamboo and palm fronds, and the bed is a huge four-poster with white linens. I place the bag on the bed, and after I remove the dress that is barely clinging to my shoulders, I unzip the bag.

He hasn't brought a single stitch of clothing for either of us, but he has brought a large selection of toys, which I remove one by one. I find an assortment of dildos in various shapes and sizes, rubber plugs, a flogger, a paddle, progressively larger rubber balls on a string, a curved item with two heads, a thick rubber ring, a large bottle of lubricant, silk scarves, a box of condoms, long pieces of Velcro, a length of red satin ribbon, a chain with clamps at either end of it and another chain with a third clamp, three glass plugs in increasingly larger sizes and several scented candles.

I line up each item on the bed until they stretch from one end of the mattress to the other. My husband has clearly put a lot of thought and planning into this honeymoon I didn't know we'd be taking. Anticipating his arrival and whatever else he has planned, I move quickly to remove my clothes. I hang my dress in the walk-in closet. It's the only item in the huge closet, which makes me giggle. He's made sure there are no other clothes to be found in the house.

When I step back into the bedroom, Flynn is standing in the doorway. He's beautifully, gloriously naked and fully aroused. "What do you think of what I brought?"

"I was afraid we'd be bored with this all-naked-all-the-time business, but I see you thought of that possibility and planned ahead."

His smile stretches across his face. "I did indeed."

I eye the items on the bed with a feeling of trepidation that's countered by overwhelming desire. "So what do you want to do?"

"I don't know about you, but I'm starving. How about we eat and take a swim?"

And he loves to keep me deliciously off balance by revving me up and then making me wait.

"Am I expected to cook in the nude as well?"

"Of course not. There's a lovely local woman who made us enough food to feed an army. All we have to do is heat and eat."

"Mmm, locally made Mexican food?"

"Only the best for my wife." He holds out a hand to me, and I cross the room to him. His arms slide around me, bringing me in tight against his body. "We're going to have the best time. I promise."

"I have no doubt."

Chapter 19

Flynn

Natalie floats on the surface of the pool, her hair spread out like a mermaid's, the tips of her magnificent breasts breaking the surface. I love her like this—uninhibited, relaxed and free of the worries she's carried with her for so long. I'll never forget the shocked look on her face when I informed her that this would be a totally naked honeymoon. Her shock was quickly replaced by stark curiosity and desire that set me on fire for her.

I slide through the water, moving slowly so I can take her by surprise when I bend over to draw the tip of her nipple into my mouth. Her eyes open, and her hand slides languorously through my hair. Cradling her in my arms, I tease her nipple for long moments, as if I don't have another care in the world, which I don't. Then I bite down on it, as hard as I dare, drawing a gasp from her.

"I want you to go inside, choose three items from what I brought, and put them on the bedside table with the bottle of lube and the red ribbon. Put the rest of the toys in the drawer in the table on your side of the bed. Once you've made your choices, I want you on your knees in the middle of the bed, facing the door, head down, hands folded. Any questions?"

"Just one." She looks up at me, her gaze open and trusting. "How long will you make me wait for you?"

"Not long." I put her down, kiss her and send her along with a pat on her gorgeous bottom. I can't wait to see what she chooses for our playtime.

Natalie

Despite the cool, refreshing swim, I'm on fire after receiving his instructions. I dry off from the pool and leave the towel outside to dry. I pad inside, marveling at how he has me walking around naked like it's the most natural thing in the world to me when only a few weeks ago, it would've made me incredibly uncomfortable.

It's one of many things that has changed since we met. The toys lined up on the bed are a reminder of other things that have changed. I study each item carefully. Knowing I don't have much time to decide ramps up the tension and intensifies the throb between my legs that began with Flynn's attention to my nipple in the pool.

Feeling rushed and off balance—exactly what he intended—I choose the chain with two clamps, the balls on a string and one of the candles, figuring to give myself a break with the last selection. With my choices made, I gather up the other items and put them away before arranging myself on the bed per his instructions.

Even knowing I won't have to wait long, the anticipation grows and multiplies with every minute that passes. Before long, my legs are quivering, and I feel like I could hyperventilate as I rethink my choices. He's going to use the clamps on my nipples. I chose them because I've been curious about what that feels like, but now that it's about to happen, I'm not so certain I want to know. And the balls on a string… Where will he put them? My body clenches as if it's already trying to keep them out.

Maybe I still have time to change my mind. I begin to move toward the table, but I'm stopped by a shadow that falls across the floor. I scramble back into the assigned position, hoping I haven't just earned a punishment. Though I've learned to enjoy his form of punishment.

"Everything all right in here?" he asks in the stern voice he uses for these moments.

"Y-yes. Sir."

As he comes into the room, I want to look to see if he's naked, too, but I don't raise my eyes to check. He goes to the bedside table to inspect my choices. The jingle of the chain makes my nipples hard and tight.

"Very nice choices, my love. We'll have a lot of fun tonight."

The bedside drawer opens and then closes, making me wonder if he's adding one of his own choices to mine. That possibility hadn't occurred to me when I made my decisions. The scrape of a match and the pungent scent of sulfur fills the air as he lights a candle and sets it back on the bedside table.

"What would you like to play with first, sweetheart? The clamps, the balls or the hot wax?"

I swallow hard at the mention of hot wax. That possibility never occurred to me when I chose the candle.

"Natalie?"

"Th-the clamps, please, Sir."

"I'll need you on your back, arms over your head and legs spread. Once you're in position, I want you to stay perfectly still."

My limbs feel leaden as I move into position, resting my head on a fluffy pillow. In this position I can see him, and he is naked, too. His cock is big and thick against his belly, the head purple and leaking. I love that he's so incredibly aroused by what we're doing. I love that I'm pleasing him and making him happy with my submission.

"How do you feel about your arms being tied with the ribbon?"

"I'd be willing to try it."

"That's my brave girl." Using the long piece of ribbon, he secures my wrists to each other, but not so tightly that anything hurts. "I love you in red, sweetheart. I'm going to loop the ribbon over this hook on the bed. Is that okay?"

"Yes, Sir."

"Close your eyes and try to relax." I do as I'm told and feel him crawl up the bed until he's between my legs. "I love you like this, Nat."

"Like what, Sir?"

"Open and willing to try anything."

"Anything once, twice if we like it."

"That's right. I want you to like it all so you'll want to do it again." He bends over me, kissing my belly and letting his soft stubble rub against the sensitive skin there. "Are you still sore from the other night?"

"No, Sir."

"So anal is on our twice-if-we-like-it list?"

I lick my lips, which have suddenly gone dry. "Mmm, yes, Sir."

"That's good to know." His mouth is now pressing into me above my pubic bone, making me want to arch into him. "Stay still, sweetheart. Nice and still."

With my eyes closed, I can't see where he's going to kiss me next, which keeps me hovering on the edge of release, wondering if I could come from anticipation alone. I want to rub my legs together to ease the ache, but I'm not allowed to move.

I feel his stubble against the underside of my breast. "What are you thinking about?"

"How I could come, and you've barely touched me, Sir."

"That's all part of it, the waiting, the thinking, the expectation… It's as much about the mental and the emotional as it is about the physical. You're beginning to understand the connections."

"*Yes*," I say, gasping when his lips close around my nipple.

He sucks and tugs the way he did in the pool, focusing all his attention on that one turgid bit of skin until I wish I could pull his hair to make him stop. My hands roll into fists and my fingernails dig into my palms. I'm thinking about the word Fluff when my nipple pops free of his mouth. He soothes it with soft strokes of his tongue, over and over again, until I begin to float on a sea of pleasure that is abruptly interrupted by the fierce, stinging pain of the clamp.

It hurts. Holy shit, it hurts. A scream surges from my belly and gurgles in my throat before busting loose in one long stream of sound.

"Easy, sweetheart." As he speaks, he strokes between my legs, pressing against my clit and giving me something to think about other than the pain. "It only stings for a minute. Take a deep breath. That's it. Now another." He kisses circles around the place where the clamp bites into my flesh. The initial blast of raw pain has subsided into a not-unpleasant thrum of sensation that comes in waves from my nipple and travels straight to my clit. "What's your safe word, Nat?"

"F-Fluff."

"Do you need it?"

Only because I'm determined to try everything once, I shake my head.

He moves to the other side, and because I know what's coming this time, I'm seized with tension. "Keep breathing, sweetheart. Lots of breath." He kisses and teases my other nipple until it too is standing at attention. As if it's not attached to me, I want to warn it about what's coming. I want to tell it to take cover. It pops free of his mouth, and again he provides comfort with soft, caressing strokes of his tongue. But I'm wise to him this time. I don't let down my guard, so I'm better prepared for the searing pain of the second clamp.

However, I'm not able to contain the scream or the thrashing need to move away from the pain.

His hands on my hips keep me in place.

When I feel his lips on my face, I realize tears are spilling down my cheeks, and he's kissing them away. Time seems to stand still. I have no idea if we've been here an hour or a day. My entire world has been reduced to the compressed tips of my breasts. I tremble violently from the painful pleasure that radiates from my clamped nipples, making the rest of me feel tight and liquid and hot, so very, very hot.

He's kissing my neck, his hard cock is pressed tight against my belly, and I'm desperately afraid his chest will brush against my abused nipples. "Ready for more, sweetheart?"

Though I'm not sure I can take any more, I bite my lip and nod.

"Words, Nat. I need the words."

"Yes, Sir," I say, sounding breathless even to my own ears. "I'm ready for more."

"Keep your eyes closed and remain still. I need your promise that you won't move."

"I won't move."

"No matter what?"

"No matter what."

And just that quickly he has brought me back once again to the edge of sanity. I hear him blowing on something, and then smell the candle being extinguished. I'm so aroused and anxious, I can barely get air to my lungs, but I do as he wishes and keep my eyes shut and my body still.

Until the first splash of hot wax connects with my belly.

The sound that comes from me is a combination moan and a groan. It doesn't hurt so much as sting, the heat radiating from the spot where the wax landed. A second splash lands on my left breast, the next one on my right breast. He leaves a trail of wax down the front of me, saving the last heated blast for my bare mound.

"Talk to me, Nat. Tell me how it feels."

"It… I… Hot. I-it's hot."

"Not too hot?"

I shake my head.

"Do you want to come?"

"Yes, please."

"Not yet. We've got one more toy to play with, but first I need to do something about the mess I made with the wax." He kisses the center of my belly. "Stay right there." I feel the bed shift as he gets up. "Keep those eyes closed."

I sag into the mattress, taking advantage of the break to force deep breaths into my lungs. I'm acutely aware of the pinch of the clamps on my nipples. It's no longer a fiery pain but more of a dull ache. The wax has dried on my skin, making it feel tight.

"Those eyes had better be closed," Flynn says as he returns and gets back on the bed. He's loving this. I can hear it in the euphoric tone of his voice, and I can't deny that I love it, too. I love not knowing what's going to happen next. I love anticipating that the end, however we get there, will be spectacular.

An icy chill hits my skin, sliding from my core to my belly and up to my breasts. Ice. Oh God…

"Hold still, sweetheart."

The ice connects with my clamped nipples—both at the same time—and I nearly levitate off the bed. I make noises that barely sound human, but I can't seem to control them.

"God, you're so hot, baby. The way you respond to everything is so amazing."

His words permeate my addled brain. I'm pleasing him. He's happy. I'm floating on a cloud of contentment even as the drumbeat of desire continues its relentless march. "I'm going to turn you over now, sweetheart."

I'm aware of him turning me, the ribbon twisting loosely around my wrists and of the sharp pull of the clamps as my breasts fall forward over a mound of pillows.

He's kissing my back, my bottom, between my cheeks, licking me, making me crazy. He sucks for one, glorious second on my clit before leaving it begging for more. I hear a click, and the liquid sounds of lubricant have me on alert. "Just my fingers, love." He's pressing against my back entrance in that insistent way of his. I know how to stop him, but I don't say the word. Then his fingers are gone and something else is there. Oh God, the balls, the string, he's pushing them into me, one at a time. I try to remember how big the biggest one was and squirm a bit, trying to seek relief from the unrelenting pressure.

The slight movement causes a tug on the chain that connects the clamps, setting off a fiery blast of pain. I don't want that to happen again, so I remain still as he continues to insert the balls. How many of them were there? I wish I had counted.

"Tell me what you're thinking, sweetheart."

"That's enough." The words sound as if they are ripped from me.

"That's only half of them."

I grunt as another one, the largest one yet, presses against my entrance. "It's *enough*," I say on a whimper as I begin to sweat.

"You know how to make it stop." He holds me open for his tongue, swirling it into me, around my clit and back to where the balls are stretching me. Then he reaches under me and gives the chain the slightest of tugs, making me scream. The balls continue to come. If I'd known he was going to put them back there, I never would've chosen them, but it's too late to change my mind now.

"Three more," he says. "The big ones."

"N-no… No more."

He rubs my bottom with his big hand. "You can do it, sweetheart. Here we go."

My safe word is on the tip of my tongue, but I don't say it. I can't say anything as I focus on the overwhelming pressure and intense sensation that burns through me as the final three balls are inserted. He kisses my back. "You did it, honey. You took them all."

I can't speak or breathe or move from the fear of jostling one of the areas on my body that's been taken over by him. Then I feel his hard cock pressing at the entrance to my body, and I begin to tremble all over again. Because of the balls, the fit is exceptionally tight.

"Try to relax and let me in," he says gruffly.

"It's too big."

He laughs. "He gets bigger when you compliment him."

"That wasn't a compliment."

That only makes him laugh harder as he rocks into me a little at a time, gentle but insistent. I'm convinced he's going to split me right in half.

He tugs on the handle connected to the balls, drawing the largest one partially out of me and letting it sit half in and half out until the pressure becomes so intense that I nearly utter the word that would stop everything.

Seeming to sense I'm reaching my limit, Flynn reseats the ball, presses his fingers to my clit and reaches under me with his other hand to remove the clamps. "You can come, Natalie."

As the blood rushes back into my nipples in a flood of excruciating pain, I explode. I come apart so completely, I lose all sense of place and time as everything goes dark.

My eyes flutter open to discover the room itself has gone dark. I glance at the clock on the bedside table, and I'm shocked to discover it's an hour later than it was when I came in here. An hour. My God…

Flynn is snuggled up to me, his front to my back, his arm around me, my arms untied from the ribbon. He kisses my shoulder. "Welcome back, sweetheart."

"What happened?"

"You came so hard, you passed out."

"That's a thing? That can happen?"

"Yeah, baby. It happens."

"How long was I out?"

"Only a few minutes. I was right here with you the whole time, making sure you were okay."

"Wow."

I cover the arm he has around me with my hand. "Did you…"

"Oh yeah. Big-time."

Shifting to find a more comfortable position, I discover the balls are still in place, and I groan.

"What's wrong?"

"The balls…"

"I knew I forgot something."

I elbow his belly because he never forgets anything.

Nuzzling my neck, he says, "I wanted you fully awake and aware when they come out."

"You're just too good to me."

He cups my breast and squeezes my sore nipple gently between his fingers. "You did so great, Nat. You gave yourself over to me. You gave me your trust and your desire. You gave me everything. It means so much to me to receive those things from you and to know you love me."

His words of praise and approval go straight to my heart. "I do. I love you so much."

"I love you more."

"No way."

"You just have to accept it."

"Never."

His low chuckle makes me smile.

"Did we really just have sex for an hour?"

"Yep."

"Damn, you weren't kidding when you said you know how to draw it out and make it last."

"But the ending…"

"The ending was spectacular, as promised."

"Glad you think so. Tell me more about how it was for you. I want to know everything." As he speaks, he runs his fingers through my hair, which calms and soothes me. Gone is the Dom, and in his place is the tender lover who has initiated me into a decadent life of sensual extremes.

"The clamps hurt more than I expected them to."

"I was surprised you chose them when you could've picked anything."

"I was curious about them after seeing them used at the club the other night. I can't imagine the clit clamp, though. That just went on my list of hard limits."

"Fair enough."

"I chose the candle because I thought you'd only use it for atmosphere."

Laughing softly, he says, "A common rookie error—underestimating the imagination of your Dom."

"I'm learning that's a bad idea where you're concerned."

"My imagination knows no limits, especially when I get to play with you. What did you think of the wax?"

"I couldn't believe that it was actually arousing to have hot wax spilled on my body. I wouldn't have thought I'd like that."

"Everything once..."

"...twice if we like it."

"So we liked the wax?"

"We did. The ice was a bit much, though."

"Fastest way to get rid of the wax. Hot and cold play often go hand in hand. The two extremes make for a heady experience."

"If I wanted to do that to you sometime, would you let me?"

"Which part?"

"The hot and cold."

"I might be willing to cede control, but only temporarily."

"Ohhh... In that case, I want the cock ring in the mix, too."

He releases a low groan. "That can be arranged. What did you think of the ribbon and having your arms bound?"

"I liked it and the way it forced me to give over control to you."

"I liked that, too."

There's something else I want to tell him. I just hope I can find the right words. "I was thinking..."

"About what?"

"I love that what we do together is nothing at all like what happened to me so long ago. It's not even remotely similar."

"I'm so glad to hear you say that."

"Feels like an epiphany of sorts to realize one has nothing at all to do with the other."

"No, it doesn't." He nuzzles my shoulder. "You want to get rid of those balls?"

"Any time now."

He begins slowly, tugging on the string with one hand and stroking my bottom with the other as the largest ball pops free, leaving me gasping and sweaty. The others come easier, but he takes his time, drawing out the removal for maximum effect. By the time he drops them on the floor next to the bed, I'm hot and bothered and on the verge of yet another orgasm.

"Flynn…"

"Yeah, baby?"

"I want to come."

His low growl is the only warning I have before he rolls me onto my back and buries his face between my legs. It takes three strokes of his tongue to finish me off.

I open my eyes to him looking down at me with a goofy smile on his face.

"Why are you smiling like that?"

"Because I love you. I love that you just asked me to make you come. I love having you here in this place that I love and knowing we have days and days to spend together with no one and nothing to bother us."

"Don't you mean days to spend *naked* together?"

He drops his head to my chest. "Mmm."

I run my fingers through his hair, loving the silky feel of it. "You've actually brought me here to make me your sex slave, haven't you?"

"You've figured me out."

We stay like that, wrapped up in each other, for a long time, long enough that the moon begins to rise over the water.

"Hey, Nat?"

"Yeah?"

"Despite how it might seem, I'm actually *your* slave. You know that, don't you? I'm completely and utterly at your mercy."

"And I'm at yours."

"You can't ever leave me."

I love when he, who could have any woman he wants, shows me his heart and his vulnerability where I'm concerned. "There's nowhere else I'd rather be than right here with you."

Chapter 20

Natalie

By Thursday night, we've tried everything twice and much of it three times because we liked it so much. My body is vibrating from the hours he spent building me up only to shatter me into a thousand pieces and then put me back together the way only he can.

It has been the most blissfully relaxing and sensually charged week of my life. That I've been able to relax so completely despite the nearly constant hum of desire is amazing to me. I'm sad that we have to go home tomorrow, but I'm ready to get back to some sort of productive routine after the beautiful weeks I've spent with Flynn.

I also miss Fluff. This is the longest we've ever been apart, and I hope she's behaving for Flynn's parents. Other than my weekly appointment with my therapist, Curt, which Flynn insisted I keep, we haven't spoken to anyone but each other in days.

My body feels beautifully used, my bottom cheeks stinging from being spanked, my inner thighs sore and my most tender areas tingling from the burn of his big cock entering me over and over again. I'm officially addicted to that big cock and all the amazing ways he uses it to love me. We're lying in bed, our bodies cooling from another round of vigorous lovemaking, when the house phone rings, startling us both.

"Probably just the pilots confirming departure," he says as he gets up to answer it. "I'll tell them we're not ready to go."

"We are ready. We've got the Oscars this weekend, and we're going. My husband is favored to win."

He growls and makes a playfully sinister face at me. "I can't believe you said that out loud."

Smiling, I watch him leave the room. The sight of his tight buns never gets old, even after nearly a week of looking at his naked form.

Listening to the low hum of his voice in the other room, I begin to doze. I'm as relaxed as I've ever been after the idyllic time with him. We've done nothing but swim, lie in the sun, eat delicious food, drink margaritas and more wine from the Quantum vineyards and make love as often as we possibly could. Every part of me—and every part of him—is tanned from the hours in the sun. We've spent entire days in bed, talked about every possible topic and made more plans for our foundation. While I wish our time here could last forever, Flynn assures me we can come back again soon. In the meantime, I'm looking forward to digging into my new role with the foundation and making a difference for hungry children.

I wake with a start when his arm wraps around me from behind. How long was I asleep? How long was he gone?

"Everything okay?"

"That was Emmett."

Three little words put me immediately on alert. I turn to face him. "What's wrong?"

"They've made an arrest in the Rogers case."

"That's great news! Oh my God, what a relief. Now they'll leave us alone."

"Nat…"

"What? Who did they arrest?"

"Your father."

Flynn

I hate having to tell her this news. I have no idea how she'll take it or what it even means for her or us.

She sits up in bed, tucking the covers around her breasts. It's the first time she's felt the need to cover herself all week. "My father. He killed David Rogers? But why? He didn't even know him."

"Emmett didn't have the details yet, and of course Vickers isn't taking his calls now that I'm no longer a suspect."

"I… I don't understand."

Her confusion and disbelief make me furious. She was so relaxed and free of worries. And now this. I put my arms around her. "You haven't seen your father in a long time. Perhaps he had some dealings with Rogers in the ensuing years. You never know."

"I suppose. But why would he kill him now after he goes public with information about me?"

"Emmett said our investigator was actually the one to tip off the FBI to your father's possible involvement. He said they didn't want to bother us while we were here, so they held off on telling us until he'd been arrested. Apparently, the investigator caught the scent of your father because he decided to look into everyone who was involved in the Stone case from the beginning."

"I need to call Candace and Olivia. I need to tell them…"

"Okay, sweetheart. I'll get your phone." I get up to retrieve the phone that's been stashed in her purse all week. On the way back to the bedroom, I turn it on for her. The phone goes crazy beeping with text messages and voice mails. "It's probably safe to say they already know." I hand it over to her.

She begins to return the text messages from her sisters.

"What're they saying?"

"They're in shock and hiding from reporters."

"I'll set up some security for them." I use my phone to send a message to Gordon Yates, our director of security in LA, asking him to work with Addie to arrange for immediate security for Natalie's sisters.

I'm already on it, Gordon replies right away. I share that news with Natalie.

"Thank you. I hate to think of them being pursued by reporters and their lives upended *again* because of this."

"What about your life, sweetheart?"

"My life is just fine, and it will continue to be fine. This has nothing to do with me."

"Nat…"

"What? It doesn't."

"Is it possible your dad did this because he wants to make things right with you and he saw killing Rogers as a way to do that?"

She shakes her head, and I can see the disbelief has been replaced by anger. "It's not about me. He did it because Rogers resurrected all the shit about Oren. In his mind, he was protecting Oren by killing Rogers. It's always about Oren with him, even now."

"You don't know that for sure."

"Yes, I do. And the only thing that matters to me is that the FBI is no longer looking at you for his murder."

"Emmett said the press is driving Liza crazy wanting a statement from us about the arrest."

"You could have her say that Natalie hasn't seen or spoken to her father in more than eight years. His actions have no reflection on her or her sisters, who are also not in contact with Martin Genovese, and we ask that you respect her privacy and that of her family."

"You're sure that's what you want?"

"Absolutely."

Natalie

I'm awake all night thinking about things I'd much rather forget. My father killed David. With hindsight, it makes a sick sort of sense. He must've been enraged to have the sordid tale resurrected after David went public with my story. Seeing Oren's name once again dragged through the mud and every sick detail of what he'd done to me rebroadcast to a whole new audience probably sent my father into a rage. The audience was much larger this time around thanks to my relationship with Flynn and the insatiable appetite of the Hollywood media machine.

Despite my horror over what my father did, I'm sick with relief to know the spotlight is off Flynn.

"I can feel you spinning, sweetheart," he mutters.

I thought he was asleep.

"Talk to me."

"Nothing much to say."

"What're you thinking about?"

"That the only thing that matters is that the FBI no longer considers you a suspect."

"That's not the only thing that matters. You matter, too."

"This can't touch me if I don't let it, Flynn. What does it matter to me if my father lost his mind and killed David? He hasn't been my father in any way except biologically since the night he dragged my mother out of the ER after his *friend* savagely attacked me. When he left me there, he drew a line in the sand that can never again be crossed."

"I was going to ask if you wanted me to see about getting him a lawyer."

"No. He's on his own. He's made his choices, and now he can live with them. I don't want anything to do with him or what he did."

"Whatever you want, sweetheart. I'm following your lead. What about your mom?"

"What about her?"

"I wondered if you might want to see her now that you're back in touch with your sisters."

"I've thought about that, about her, and I have to admit that it hurt me all over again to hear she'd finally left my dad when she couldn't bring herself to do that when I needed her most. Since I'm back in touch with the girls and I intend to be fully present in their lives, I suppose I'll run into her at some point, but I can't imagine ever having a close relationship with her."

"I can totally see where you're coming from. She had her chance to step up for you and she didn't."

"No, she didn't, and there's no way she can ever truly fix that as far as I'm concerned." I link my fingers with his. "I want you to know… If something like this, my dad killing David, had happened before this, before us, it would've set me back again to day one, but I'm stronger now than I've ever been, and it's because of you."

"No, baby, it's because of *you*. You're the strongest person I've ever known."

"Our love has made me stronger than I was alone. And it's made me happier than I ever could've imagined being."

"Me, too."

"Thank you for chasing after me the day Fluff bit you."

"Thanks for turning around, for giving me a chance."

I smile at him, madly in love and free from the past. "As if I ever had a choice."

"The choice has always been yours, sweetheart."

"I choose you. I choose us."

He wraps his arms around me and kisses me. "I'll always choose you, too."

Safe and secure in his arms, I feel like I can take on the world and win every time.

EPILOGUE

Natalie

It's been a very good night for Quantum Productions. Jasper has just won the Academy Award for cinematography for his work on *Camouflage*, and now we're waiting for the Best Director award to be announced.

Hayden brought Addie as his date, a development Flynn and I have been whispering about all night. Addie told Flynn it was so she could be here for his big night, but we don't think that's the only reason.

My husband leans in to whisper in my ear. "I think she's holding his hand over there."

"I'm more excited about that than I am about the awards."

He smiles at me and drops something into my hand.

I look down to see the red ribbon we played with in Mexico, and my entire body ignites at the memory of it wrapped around my wrists as he had his wicked way with me. I've become more comfortable with being bound and I hope one day to be able to play in the room in the basement. But Flynn says it will be a while before I'm ready for that kind of bondage. That's okay. We've got all the time in the world to get there together.

"It matches your dress."

I've worn a red Givenchy gown for his big night because he loves me in red. "What am I to do with this?" I ask, full of mock innocence.

He winks at me. "Keep it handy for later."

The epiphany I had in Mexico about the kind of sex I have with Flynn being nothing at all like what my attacker did to me has helped to free me from the shackles of the past.

I don't worry anymore about triggers or flashbacks. I've battled through and found my way to the other side. I'm able to separate everything that happens with my beloved husband from what happened long ago to the girl I once was.

I'm a woman now, a woman in love with the most extraordinary man, and he has shown me the limitless possibilities of our love. I want to soar to the heavens with him as my guide and companion. I want to fully experience everything this life has to offer us. I've been to hell and back, and I survived. I'm not afraid anymore.

My father has been formally charged with the murder of David Rogers. After we released our statement to the media, they've mostly left us alone. The fact that my father and I have been out of touch for most of a decade put a damper on the story as far as the Hollywood press is concerned. I'm sure it's a big story in Nebraska. It's not a big story in LA, and I've chosen to keep my distance from it. I've encouraged my sisters, who are here with us tonight, to do the same.

They are sitting somewhere toward the back of the huge ballroom with Flynn's family. I had the time of my life getting ready with them earlier, sharing my excitement and pride in my husband with the two people I love most—after Flynn and Fluff, of course.

When Hayden's name is called for the directing award, we rise to our feet to cheer for him. He kisses Addie square on the lips in front of everyone before heading to the stage to accept his award.

Tears stream down Addie's face as she watches him. Her stunned expression upon receiving that kiss is priceless.

Flynn and I exchange a smile. He's so happy tonight, and I love to see him sharing in this special moment with his closest friends.

"Thank you so much to the Academy," Hayden says once the roar of the crowd dies down. "*Camouflage* was a very special project for all of us, and to see it recognized with these awards tonight is the greatest thrill of my life. I have so many people to thank, including the entire team at Quantum, all of my friends and family who supported me during the making of this film, and our amazing cast, headlined by the one and only Flynn Godfrey, who gave the gutsiest performance of his career as Jeremy. To the movie-going public that fully embraced Jeremy's story and, by extension, the stories of all our injured servicemen and women… Thank you for letting them know you care, that you remember, that you appreciate the many sacrifices military members and their families make for all of us." He holds up the gold statue. "Thank you again for this incredible honor."

By the time Hayden leaves the stage, I'm mopping up tears from his heartfelt acceptance speech. Addie, Marlowe and I are all a hot mess, which makes the guys laugh.

After an endless commercial break, the show continues with the Best Actress award, which goes to an old friend of Flynn's. He's delighted for her, but he's grasping my hand because it's finally time for his category.

Last year's actress winner takes the stage to announce the nominees for Best Actor in a Leading Role. Clips from each actor's performance are played as their names are read. Flynn appears in a scene from the hospital, half his face burned as he talks another injured warrior out of giving up on his recovery. It is among the most powerful moments in the film, and the crowd in the Dolby Theater gives the scene a huge round of applause.

"And the Oscar goes to… Flynn Godfrey."

For a brief second, it's just him and me, caught together in this moment in time, disbelief and amazement reflected in his gorgeous eyes. Then he leans in to kiss me before standing to accept hugs and congratulations from his producing partners and closest friends.

Everyone around us is in tears as we stand and cheer for Flynn.

He goes up the stairs to the stage and accepts the award, hugging the actress who presented it before turning to face the crowd. It takes another full minute for the applause to die down. In that time, Max and Stella appear on one of the screens, both of them smiling and crying and on their feet, applauding for their son.

I hope he's able to see them from his vantage point on the stage.

"Thank you so much. Thank you." He glances down at the gold statue in his hand. "Wow. I thought I knew what this might feel like, but apparently, I had no clue. Thank you to the Academy and to everyone involved in the making of

Camouflage. We knew from the first time we read the script that this would be a special project. We had no idea how special it would become to all of us, and I'm deeply thankful to the Academy for this award as well as the others you've bestowed upon the film tonight. You all know it's been a wild couple of months for me professionally and personally. I want to thank my friends and colleagues in this room for your unwavering support during the tough times. I've seen the heart of this community more in the last few weeks than I have in my entire career before now, and I'm deeply appreciative. To my beautiful, courageous, *incredible* wife, Natalie, I thank you for showing me what's really important in this life. I love you so much, sweetheart." He raises his award over his head. "Thank you again."

I love that he used the word *incredible*. Our word. I love that he called me sweetheart for the whole world to hear. He dodges the ushers who want him to head backstage and comes down the stairs to sweep me up into his arms. He's still holding me when *Camouflage* wins the award for best picture. Flynn and most of our friends take the stage to receive their awards for producing the film.

As executive producer, Kristian speaks for all of them. "Like Hayden said earlier, it's been a once-in-a-career honor to bring this special story to life. I know I speak for everyone at Quantum and everyone involved with the film when I say none of us will ever forget this moment. Thank you to the Academy for your recognition of *Camouflage*, and to our servicemen and women, past, present and future. You have our undying respect and admiration. Thank you again."

There are photos to be taken, interviews to be given and parties to attend. But after the show ends, Flynn comes down from the stage, an Oscar in each hand, and heads right to me. I wrap my arms around him and hold on tight. We are indeed victorious.

Keep reading for a sneak peak at Rapturous, Book 4 in the Quantum Series, featuring Hayden and Addie.

Rapturous
Chapter 1

Addie

Camouflage cleaned up at the Oscars, and Hayden Roth kissed me. I'm not sure which is a bigger deal. We're surrounded by Oscar gold. Hayden won for Best Director, Flynn for Best Actor, Jasper for cinematography and all the Quantum principals for producing the year's Best Picture. They're euphoric as they celebrate at one party after another. But all I can think about is that when Hayden won, he kissed me—and he kissed me like he meant it.

He kissed me the way I've wanted him to for almost as long as I've known him, which is going on ten years now. That's how long I've wanted him. At times, and never more so than when he kissed me earlier, I've suspected he wants me, too, but neither of us has ever given in to the attraction that simmers between us.

It could be because I work for Flynn, Hayden's best friend and business partner, as well as Hayden and the other Quantum principals. Or maybe he thinks I'm too young for him, although six years isn't that big of a deal. It's not like I'm seventeen. I'm twenty-seven and fully grown, but I fear he thinks of me as the little girl I once was and not the woman I've become.

Flynn's wife, Natalie, puts her arm around my shoulders and gives me a squeeze. "Having fun?"

"Absolutely. You?"

"Best night ever. They're so happy."

"Flynn is flying high because you're here, not because of the Oscars." The two of them are wildly in love, and though I'm thrilled for my friend and boss, I'm envious, too. I want that. I want the connection they have, and I want it with a man who is perpetually unavailable to me.

"I'm so glad he won," Natalie says. "He deserves it."

"Yes, he does." Flynn's fearless, gutsy performance as a severely injured veteran has been the talk of the award season this year, with a clean sweep at the Golden Globes, SAGs, BAFTAs and now the Oscars.

Hayden deserves a big chunk of the credit as the director who'd coaxed that gutsy performance from his best friend. The two of them are gold together, as evidenced tonight and over the last couple of months.

We're crammed into a booth at the Vanity Fair party. Hayden is on one side of me, Natalie on the other. The heat of his leg pressed against mine has my full attention, whereas Natalie's leg on the other side doesn't do a thing for me, as much as I adore her.

No, Hayden is the one I want, in all his complicated, maddening, sexy, frustrating glory. It has occurred to me often during the years I've nursed this impossible crush that I could've chosen a far simpler man to worship from afar. I could've chosen a man who isn't my boss's best friend and business partner, two things that put me more or less off-limits to him. I could've chosen a man with fewer sharp angles and rough edges.

I'm a smart woman, and I'm well aware this fixation I have on such a difficult man isn't healthy for me. Tell that to the heart that does backflips and handsprings any time he's in the room, let alone wedged up against me, radiating the kind of heat that has me fantasizing about being naked in a bed with him.

I don't care if it's not in my best interest to want him. I don't care that Flynn probably wouldn't approve or that Hayden is more secretive than the CIA when it comes to his private life. I don't care that my dad can't stand him or that many of the people who work for him live in fear of his unpredictable rages. I don't care that his family is one of Hollywood's most dysfunctional—and that's saying something in this town.

None of that matters. I want him, and after the way he kissed me tonight, I'm on fire with desire and determination. Tonight is the night. When he takes me home later, I'm going to make my move and to hell with the fallout. I'm sick and tired of wishing for something and not doing a damned thing to get what I want. It's time to put up or shut up.

I groan at my own cliché-ridden thoughts, but this situation has become one giant, ridiculous cliché. If he doesn't want me the way I want him, then why would he kiss me like a lover when he won the Oscar?

As if he can read my thoughts, Hayden turns away from the conversation he's been having with Jasper to smile at me. Although, to call the subtle movement of his lips a smile is giving it far too much credit. It's more like a cocky smirk than an actual smile.

"You okay?" he asks, his usually cold blue eyes gone warm with what might be affection.

I have to resist the urge to sigh with the pleasure of having his undivided attention. "I am. You?"

"Never better," he says with an honest, genuine smile, so rare and so fleeting that I wish I could get a photo of it before it disappears.

"I'm so thrilled for you guys. I know how hard you worked on *Camouflage*. You deserve all the awards and accolades."

"Thank you. I'm rather thrilled myself."

Hayden is a complicated mix of brilliant and moody, driven and ambitious, ruthless and loyal. To see euphoria creep into that mix of intense qualities fills me with an unreasonable amount of happiness on his behalf. He works so hard and rarely takes the time to enjoy his success.

In the tight confines of the booth, he somehow manages to raise his arm and lay it across the back of the banquette. One small move, and that arm could be around me.

I squirm slightly, enough to press against him, jarring his arm. It falls to my shoulders, and I venture a glance at him, surprised to see heat and desire in his eyes that only add to my determination.

The poor bastard has no idea what he's in for.

Hayden

I'm dying a slow, miserable, painful death jammed into this fucking booth with Addie's sweet body squeezed against me, my cock as hard as a freaking rock for her and not a goddamned thing I can do about it. I can't believe I kissed her when my name was called earlier. I didn't plan to do that. In fact, I actively planned *not* to do anything inappropriate where she's concerned tonight.

Flynn asked me to bring her as my date so she could share in the celebration we expected for *Camouflage.* I agreed because he's right—she deserves to be here after the way she supported our entire team during the grueling shoot.

If I'm being honest, I wanted her here for me, too. I like to look at her. I love to breathe in her sexy, alluring scent and fantasize about burying my face in her thick blond hair while I fuck her. I want to lose myself in her and never come up for air.

But I won't. I won't lay a finger on her, as much as it kills me to resist an urge that seems to multiply exponentially every time I'm around her.

I avoid complications the way some people avoid germs. Everything about my obsession with Addison York is complicated. Other than the fact that Flynn would fucking kill me if I so much as look at her cross-eyed—and that's not an insignificant *other than*—she deserves much better than me.

She should be cherished, not tied in my web of ropes and fucked to within an inch of her life, which is exactly what would happen if I ever let my inner beast run free with her. That's *not* going to happen.

Now if only my fucking cock would get the message and stand the hell down, I might actually be able to enjoy this incredible night. It's not happening with her, no matter how badly I might wish otherwise. I repeat this refrain to myself over and over again, but when she snuggles into my embrace, laying her head on my chest, my cock tells me to fuck off.

I look to my left to find Flynn eyeing me with an astute look that tells me I'm not fooling him by trying to act like I don't care that Addie is lying all over me. I care. I fucking care way more than I should, and Flynn knows it, even if I've never fully owned up to his suspicions about my feelings for her.

He called me out on it recently, going so far as to insinuate that I'm in love with her. I did what I always do when my name and Addie's are mentioned in the same sentence—I denied it. What else can I do? Everyone loves Addie, and the last thing I need is my closest friends and business partners turning against me when I fuck things up and hurt her.

Because I would fuck it up—and I would hurt her. I have no doubt at all about that, which is one of the many reasons I keep my distance. Or I usually keep my distance. With her body pressed against mine, I allow my hand to curl around her shoulder, enjoying the rare lack of distance.

I instantly realize I've made a huge mistake by touching her.

Holy fuck. Her skin is like silk, soft and smooth. One touch will never be enough. And was that… Fucking hell, she *moaned.* I have to get out of here. I have to get away from her and the wicked temptation she represents. Except I can't move a fucking muscle with our whole crew crammed into this goddamned booth.

Not to mention, I'm so hard there's no way to escape without giving myself away to Addie and everyone else in the room. FUCK! I break out in a cold sweat. Then her hand lands on my abdomen, and I nearly lose my shit.

"Move," I growl to Jasper, who's next to me.

"What?" he yells over the loud music and voices.

"I need to take a leak."

"Oh, okay. Let Hayden out, you guys," he says to Kristian and Marlowe.

"Be right back," I mutter to Addie. Jarred by my sudden movement, she sits up, a stunned expression on her face—as if she just realized she was lying on me. Not that I minded. I didn't mind. In fact, I loved it a little too much. As I slide out of the booth, I remove my tuxedo jacket and fold it over my arm, hoping it will hide my raging "problem."

I'm reminded of eighth-grade science class, when I popped a boner for my lab partner, Jamie, when we were presenting our findings in front of the class. She had the best rack of any girl in our grade, and I was hard for her for a solid year. I thought everyone must've noticed, but no one ever said anything—and they would have if they'd seen it. I've never forgotten how humiliating it was to discover that I had absolutely no control over what—or who—my dick chose to get hard over.

As an adult, I've devoted a lot of time and energy to the concept of control. So it's galling, to say the least, to lose control the way I have twice tonight.

I can't remember the last time any woman made me sweat just by sitting next to me. I'm a fucking Dom, for Christ's sake. My control is legendary. Except, apparently, when Addison York is pressed against me.

With my jacket still strategically positioned, I make my way through the crowded room, accepting handshakes and congratulations from colleagues on the way to the men's room. Once there, I lock myself in a stall, hang the jacket from the hook on the back of the door and lean my head against the cool tile on the wall.

Get it together, will you?

I want to pound the shit out of something. Anything to rid myself of the frustration and desire that possess me like a demon I can't shake no matter how hard I try. What the *fuck* was I thinking when I kissed her? I wasn't thinking. I just acted. In the biggest moment of my career, I took what I've wanted for as long as I can remember. I took *her*. I took Addie.

I fumble with my belt and the irritating buttons and hooks on my tuxedo pants, nearly swearing out loud at how cumbersome the process is. Then my cock springs free, hot and hard. I take myself in hand, looking for relief from the most painful desire I've ever experienced.

I *cannot* have her. I *will not* have her. I *cannot* have her. I *will not* have her.

The thoughts parade through my mind as I relive that kiss, that one fleeting, magical moment in which I had absolutely everything I ever wanted—the ultimate career success and the woman I love. *Fuck.*

Hearing voices outside the stall, I bite back a moan. I've never admitted to anyone—even myself—that I love her. Motherfucking hell, I *can't love her.* I *cannot.* I *will not.* I grip my cock so hard that it hurts. Part of me can't believe I'm actually doing this here, a heartbeat away from colleagues and paparazzi, but I can't stop what she started in that booth.

I can't control that which cannot be controlled. I love her. I want her. I need her. *I can't have her.* From deep within my sex-addled brain, I have the foresight to reach for my handkerchief in the seconds before I come. Every muscle in my body participates in the soul-cleansing release. The relief is immediate and overwhelming.

Breathing hard, I close my eyes and stay perfectly still, letting the oxygen feed my starving muscles. I stand there until my cock begins to finally retreat, satisfied for now. With shaking hands, I clean myself up and knot the soiled cloth into a tight wad that I store in the pocket of my jacket.

I know better than to dispose of a cloth full of my DNA that also bears my initials in a public restroom at a Hollywood event. Such is the life of a celebrity. "Leave nothing behind" is one of our mottos.

I give myself another five minutes to calm down before I take the leak I came in here for. I restore my clothes and inhale a series of deep breaths, determined to get through the rest of this night, to get her home and then head for Club Quantum, where I'll find someone who can help slake the need she stirs in me.

I emerge from the stall to a room that's empty except for an attendant. Thank God for small favors. I wash my hands and splash cold water on my face, mopping it up with the towel the attendant hands me. I suspect he knows exactly what I just did.

Whatever. With the evidence tucked away in my pocket, let him try to prove it.

I'm heading for the door when Flynn comes in, placing a hand on my chest to move me backward into the room.

"We need to talk."

"No, we don't."

"Yes, we do!" Thankfully, he keeps his voice down. "So this thing with Addie… It's happening?"

"No, it's not happening."

"We all saw you kiss her. We saw her eyes light up with surprise and joy that you finally did *something*."

"It was just a kiss." I keep my tone intentionally nonchalant, even though I feel anything but. "Nothing to go crazy over."

"Except *she* is going crazy because you gave her hope! I swear to God, Hayden, if you hurt her, I'll kill you."

Flynn is one of the few people in this world who I genuinely love. But right now, I want to pummel his movie-star face. "Thanks for the warning. Can I go now?"

"Hayden... If you aren't in this, really *in* it, you can't. You absolutely *cannot.*"

I keep my voice down, lest Flynn and I be all over the tabloids tomorrow for "fighting" at the Vanity Fair party. "Do you think I need you to tell me that?"

"Either go all in or hands off," he says through gritted teeth. "I mean it."

"You're a fucking hypocrite, you know that?"

"What the hell is that supposed to mean?"

"Remember when I told you that you had no business getting involved with Natalie?"

"That's not the same thing."

"Isn't it? Isn't it exactly the same thing? A nice girl who deserves better than us?"

With industry people and press in and out of the room, we can't afford to let this get out of hand. So as much as we might like to let loose and go at it, we know better.

"It's not the same. Addie is—"

I raise a brow in inquiry. "*Special?* Is that what you were going to say? And Natalie isn't?" It's never a good idea to drag a man's wife into an argument, but I need Flynn to acknowledge his own double standard. Before he can pounce, I do. "Leave me alone, Flynn. I'm not going to touch her—and I'm certainly not going to hurt her. Why do you think I've kept my distance all this time? I don't *want* to hurt her."

I start to walk away, but he grabs my arm, spinning me around to face him. "Give me your word."

I look into the eyes of my oldest and closest friend, my business partner, one of those few people I truly love. "Fuck you." I rip my arm free of his hold and leave the room before I make the huge mistake of punching him.

Thank you for reading Victorious and the initial Quantum Trilogy! I hope you enjoyed reading Flynn and Natalie's story as much as I enjoyed writing it. If you wish to talk about Victorious with other readers—with spoilers allowed and encouraged—join the Victorious Reader at GroupFacebook.com/groups/VictoriousQuantum3. And remember to join the Quantum Reader Group at Facebook.com/groups/QuantumReaders.

And now for the thank-yous! To my HTJB team: Julie Cupp, Lisa Cafferty, Holly Sullivan, Isabel Sullivan, Nikki Colquhoun and Cheryl Serra, thank you for all you do to make it possible for me to do almost nothing but write. And to my husband, Dan, who runs our lives so I am free to write as much as possible. To my kids, Emily and Jake, who are so endlessly supportive of my career—you guys are the light of my life, and I love you to the moon and back. Thank you to my son Jake, who was my car consultant for the first three Quantum books and chose all of Flynn's cars for the various occasions—without reading the books.

Thank you to my beta readers Anne Woodall, Ronlyn Howe and Kara Conrad. To my copy editor, Linda Ingmanson: thank you for always making time for me when I need you. And to my proofreader, Joyce Lamb, you're the best, and I love having your eagle eyes on my books before they go live. Joyce did an amazing job helping me to keep all the details straight, and I appreciate her so much! To Sarah Spate Morrison, family nurse practitioner, thank you for your assistance with medical details.

And to my lovely, wonderful, amazing readers who have changed my life so completely, thank you so much for taking this wild ride with me. I'd be nowhere without each and every one of you, and I appreciate you more than you'll ever know. Thank you from the bottom of my heart!

xoxo

Marie

Other Titles by Marie Force

Other Titles by M.S. Force

The Quantum Series

Book 1: Virtuous

Book 2: Valorous

Book 3: Victorious

Book 4: Rapturous

Book 5: Ravenous

Book 6: Delirious

Other Contemporary Romances Available from Marie Force:

The Gansett Island Series

Book 1: Maid for Love

Book 2: Fool for Love

Book 3: Ready for Love

Book 4: Falling for Love

Book 5: Hoping for Love

Book 6: Season for Love

Book 7: Longing for Love

Book 8: Waiting for Love

Book 9: Time for Love

Book 10: Meant for Love

Book 10.5: Chance for Love, *A Gansett Island Novella*

Book 11: Gansett After Dark

Book 12: Kisses After Dark

Book 13: Love After Dark

Book 14: Celebration After Dark

Book 15: Desire After Dark

Book 16: Light After Dark

Gansett Island Episodes, Episode 1: Victoria & Shannon

The Green Mountain Series

Book 1: All You Need Is Love

Book 2: I Want to Hold Your Hand

Book 4: And I Love Her

Novella: You'll Be Mine

Book 5: It's Only Love

Book 6: Ain't She Sweet

The Butler Vermont Series

(Continuation of the Green Mountain Series)

Book 1: Every Little Thing

The Treading Water Series

Book 1: Treading Water

Book 2: Marking Time

Book 3: Starting Over

Book 4: Coming Home

Single Titles

Sex Machine

Sex God

Georgia on My Mind

True North

The Fall

Everyone Loves a Hero

Love at First Flight

Line of Scrimmage

Romantic Suspense Novels Available from Marie Force:

The Fatal Series

One Night With You, *A Fatal Series Prequel Novella*

Book 1: Fatal Affair

Book 2: Fatal Justice

Book 3: Fatal Consequences

Book 3.5: Fatal Destiny, *the Wedding Novella*

Book 4: Fatal Flaw

Book 5: Fatal Deception

Book 6: Fatal Mistake

Book 7: Fatal Jeopardy

Book 8: Fatal Scandal

Book 9: Fatal Frenzy

Book 10: Fatal Identity

Book 11: Fatal Threat

Single Title

The Wreck

About the Author

M.S. Force is the erotic alter-ego of *New York Times* bestselling author Marie Force. All three books in her initial Quantum Trilogy were *New York Times* bestsellers in 2015, and the Quantum Trilogy became the Quantum Series with Rapturous and Ravenous, with more to come!

Marie Force is the *New York Times* bestselling author of more than 50 contemporary romances, including the Gansett Island Series, which has sold nearly 3 million books, and the Fatal Series from Harlequin Books, which has sold 1.5 million books. In addition, she is the author of the Butler, Vermont Series, the Green Mountain Series and the erotic romance Quantum Series, written under the slightly modified name of M.S. Force. All together, her books have sold more than 5.5 million copies worldwide!

Her goals in life are simple—to finish raising two happy, healthy, productive young adults, to keep writing books for as long as she possibly can and to never be on a flight that makes the news.

Join Marie's mailing list on her website at marieforce.com for news about new books and upcoming appearances in your area. Follow her on Facebook at www.

Facebook.com/MarieForceAuthor, on Twitter @marieforce and on Instagram at www.instagram.com/marieforceauthor/. Contact Marie at marie@marieforce.com.

CPSIA information can be obtained
at www.ICGtesting.com
Printed in the USA
LVHW03s2331020718
582586LV00009B/159/P

9 781942 295136